Cookin

"A high-speed ride through the joys and vicissitudes of relationships, the trials of attending a cookery class when you are the world's worst cook, and of trying to solve a murder when the police think you probably did it . . . A good series debut that leaves the reader wondering what is going to happen next." —MyShelf.com

"Charming . . . a blissful who-done-it that is filled with some very funny scenes and characters who care about each other." —*Midwest Book Review*

"The writing is spellbinding. The blend of mystery, humor, and romance keeps the reader hooked to the pages. The characters are entertaining, and it is not surprising that I find myself eager to read more about this duo. The addition of recipes in the back of the book only adds to its charm. Culinary-mystery fans will need to add this book to their reading piles." —*Roundtable Reviews*

"A fun, quick read. A new twist on the favorite culinary mysteries." —*The Mystery Reader*

"Light and breezy, touched with humor and a bit of romance. The protagonists are spunky and adventurous, and readers will be cheering for this delectable duo to crack the case." —*Romantic Times*

Cooking Class Mysteries by Miranda Bliss

COOKING UP MURDER
MURDER ON THE MENU
DEAD MEN DON'T GET THE MUNCHIES

Dead Men Don't Get the Munchies

MIRANDA BLISS

BERKLEY PRIME CRIME, NEW YORK

THE BERKLEY PUBLISHING GROUP
Published by the Penguin Group
Penguin Group (USA) Inc.
375 Hudson Street, New York, New York 10014, USA
Penguin Group (Canada), 90 Eglinton Avenue East, Suite 700, Toronto, Ontario M4P 2Y3, Canada
(a division of Pearson Penguin Canada Inc.)
Penguin Books Ltd., 80 Strand, London WC2R 0RL, England
Penguin Group Ireland, 25 St. Stephen's Green, Dublin 2, Ireland (a division of Penguin Books Ltd.)
Penguin Group (Australia), 250 Camberwell Road, Camberwell, Victoria 3124, Australia
(a division of Pearson Australia Group Pty. Ltd.)
Penguin Books India Pvt. Ltd., 11 Community Centre, Panchsheel Park, New Delhi—110 017, India
Penguin Group (NZ), 67 Apollo Drive, Rosedale, North Shore 0632, New Zealand
(a division of Pearson New Zealand Ltd.)
Penguin Books (South Africa) (Pty.) Ltd., 24 Sturdee Avenue, Rosebank, Johannesburg 2196,
South Africa

Penguin Books Ltd., Registered Offices: 80 Strand, London WC2R 0RL, England

This is a work of fiction. Names, characters, places, and incidents either are the product of the author's imagination or are used fictitiously, and any resemblance to actual persons, living or dead, business establishments, events, or locales is entirely coincidental. The publisher does not have any control over and does not assume any responsibility for author or third-party websites or their content.

PUBLISHER'S NOTE: The recipes contained in this book are to be followed exactly as written. The publisher is not responsible for your specific health or allergy needs that may require medical supervision. The publisher is not responsible for any adverse reactions to the recipes contained in this book.

DEAD MEN DON'T GET THE MUNCHIES

A Berkley Prime Crime Book / published by arrangement with the author

PRINTING HISTORY
Berkley Prime Crime mass-market edition / December 2007

Copyright © 2007 by The Berkley Publishing Group.
Cover art by Stephanie Power.
Cover design by Rita Frangie.
Interior text design by Kristin del Rosario.

ISBN: 978-0-425-21839-6

BERKLEY® PRIME CRIME
Berkley Prime Crime Books are published by The Berkley Publishing Group,
a division of Penguin Group (USA) Inc.,
375 Hudson Street, New York, New York 10014.
The name BERKLEY PRIME CRIME and the BERKLEY PRIME CRIME design
are trademarks belonging to Penguin Group (USA) Inc.

PRINTED IN THE UNITED STATES OF AMERICA

10 9 8 7 6 5 4 3 2 1

One

✄

I, ANNIE CAPSHAW, AM THE WORLD'S WORST COOK.

There, I admitted it, and I'm not even ashamed.

Don't get me wrong, I'm not completely without scruples when it comes to the culinary arts. I know enough to be embarrassed every time I set off the smoke alarm in my kitchen. I'm appalled at the thought that I've burned water. I'm sorry—truly—about all the roasts I've seared beyond recognition, the many cakes that have flopped, and the fried foods that in my not-so-able hands give a whole new meaning to the word *crispy*.

But I'm not ashamed. Why should I be? Some people are born to be artists, right? And some are born to sing. Some people have a natural talent for things like trading stocks, or doing brain surgery, or (as weird as it seems) for cooking.

I am simply not one of them. And that, as the saying goes, is that.

Or at least it should be.

It would be, if not for the fact that in addition to my day job as a teller at Pioneer Savings and Loan, I'm also the business manager of Bellywasher's, a pub and restaurant in Alexandria, Virginia.

Yeah, I know, it's pretty ironic. And on days when simply considering it doesn't scare me to death, I think it's pretty funny, too.

Me, working in a restaurant.

Lucky thing, the cooking gods don't seem to be holding any of this against us. We've been successful, thanks to the talents and genius of our owner, Jim MacDonald, a staff that's as good as any, a warm and welcoming atmosphere, and prices that are reasonable (and could be just a little higher, I think, but then, I'm the one who watches the bottom line). In the six months since it's opened, Bellywasher's has become a favorite of the locals and a real destination for people from all over the D.C. Metro area who are looking for interesting menu choices and fresh ingredients. Starting tonight, with our Best Bar Foods, Bar None class, we are also the official home of Bellywasher's Academy, where every Monday, folks who are interested in learning more about cooking can kick back, create, and eat some really good food.

With a little luck and a lot of hard work, Jim and I and the rest of the staff are planning on keeping things going great guns, too.

And we will. Provided I don't go anywhere near the grill, the oven, the prep area, or the dessert table.

Oh, and as long as no more dead bodies show up.

The very idea made me jump on the barstool where I was seated. Or maybe that was because I was so lost in thought, I hadn't realized Margaret Whitemore, the cooking student who was just checking in, was tearing a check out of her checkbook.

"That will be $120," I said, and when I did, my throat was tight and my mouth was dry. Thinking about murder will do that to a person. "You can go right back," I added, and because Margaret was a white-haired granny who wore thick glasses and moved with all the speed of Beltway traffic in rush hour, I raised my voice so she was sure to hear me and pointed in case she couldn't see. "You're assigned to . . ." I checked the list on the bar in front of me. "Desserts. Jim's in the kitchen. He'll show you to your workstation."

Margaret gathered her tote bag, her umbrella (it wasn't raining, but there was talk of it for later in the evening), her coat, and her purse. While she did, I had a little time to kill.

Poor choice of words, and as if she could read my mind, Eve leaned over from the barstool next to mine. In an uncharacteristic show of restraint, she kept her voice down.

"This is perfect!" Eve's blue eyes sparkled with excitement. She didn't have to tell me; I knew she'd taken advantage of Bellywasher's being closed that afternoon. She'd been to the spa; her blonde hair was sleek, shiny, and newly trimmed. "Now we finally have a chance to talk. So what do you say, Annie? You're the detective. What would you do? Do you think I should wear a disguise?"

I had hoped that Eve was long past remembering what we'd been discussing before our students started to arrive. No such luck.

I slid her a look. Though after thirty-some years of friendship, I was long past the stage of comparing my cuteness to her astonishing beauty, I self-consciously combed my fingers through my brown, uncontrollably curly hair. "I told you, Eve, this isn't the time, and besides—"

"You think I'm crazy."

"I didn't say that." I hadn't, but let's face it, when your best friend breezes in and asks about the most effective way to follow somebody and not be noticed, the *you're crazy* part doesn't need to be spoken out loud. Still, I cut Eve some slack. Mostly because she *was* my best friend, and I didn't want to hurt her feelings. Partly because after what happened last fall (I mean, the whole thing about her fiancé trying to kill us), I had made a vow to be as gentle and understanding as possible with Eve.

It wasn't always easy.

I drew in a breath and watched as Margaret Whitemore dropped her tote bag and bent in slow motion to retrieve it.

I was saved from jumping off the barstool to help when the next student in line came to Margaret's aid.

"It takes a lot more than a couple murders to make someone a real detective," I reminded Eve, even though I knew she'd dispute this and tell me what she had told me so many times: because I'd investigated and solved murders, I was a detective. Of sorts. In an unofficial kind of way, of course. I didn't want to hear it; that's why I went right on. "Besides, detective or no detective, I can't offer an opinion. You haven't told me what's going on."

Eve looked up the way people do when they're nervous or uncomfortable and slid her gaze to behind the bar, where we'd stenciled a border of greenery and thistles to go with the Scottish theme of the place. "It's not that I don't want to," she said. "It's just that it's sort of . . . I dunno . . . I guess you could say it was a secret."

Coming from anyone else, this would not have been a shocking statement. But the words *Eve* and *secret* in the same sentence were as incongruous as thinking that the Democrats and the Republicans who ran this town would ever get along. Eve is, in a word, open and sometimes bluntly direct. About everything. (OK, so that's more than one word, but it pretty much explains Eve in a nutshell.) She doesn't keep secrets. Not from me, and usually not from anyone else, either. Which should have made me really curious about all this talk of disguises and following people.

Instead, it made me really nervous.

I was all set to grill Eve further when Jorge Macillon, the next student in line, finished helping Margaret and stepped forward, credit card in hand. Jorge was young and eager to get started, so I simply reminded him that he was assigned to drinks for this first class, asked if he had all the ingredients he'd need for the margaritas he'd be making (he did), and told him to head on back.

"I don't believe it," I said, and though Eve can sometimes be dense when it comes to things like current events, money, and men, she knew exactly what I was talking about. That's why she blushed.

She put a hand on my arm. "It's not that I don't want to tell you, Annie. You know I do. The last secret I ever kept from you was the one about how David Lang back in high school had a crush on you."

"He did?" I remembered David. I had a crush on him, too. "Why didn't you say anything? I mean—"

I listened to my own words and gave myself a mental slap. "That was nearly twenty years ago," I grumbled, just so I didn't forget how much it didn't matter. "I don't care anymore, and I'll bet David Lang—wherever he is— doesn't, either. What I do care about is you talking about disguises. And following people. You've got me worried."

Eve laughed. "Oh, don't be. It's nothing at all, surely nothing dangerous." Her smile settled. "You know I'd tell you if I could, Annie. It's just that . . . Well, if it was just me, I wouldn't hesitate. But there are other people in- volved."

"Will they be wearing disguises, too?"

"So you *do* think that's the best way to handle this! I told them that's what you'd say." So much for sarcasm— Eve took my comment at face value and sailed right on. "I thought you'd agree with me, so I stopped this afternoon and bought a long, dark wig. Very Penelope Cruz. Oh, and I was thinking maybe I'd wear a miniskirt. And knee-high boots with tall heels. That and sunglasses ought to do it. Don't you think?"

I glanced down at the outfit Eve was wearing that night. It was March, and though everyone who lived in the area knew that spring wasn't far away, it had yet to make an ap- pearance. The weather was gray and raw, and in deference to it, Eve was wearing tall boots with high heels. She was wearing a miniskirt, too, along with a white cashmere sweater that I knew for a fact cost more than she could af- ford on her salary as Bellywasher's hostess.

"This would be different, how?" I asked her. "Aside

from the wig, I mean. If you're going to wear a disguise, wear a disguise! Go for it. Come rummage through my closet. You can dress as one of the homeless."

"Really, Annie, it's not that I don't admire your taste, but I really don't think that will work." Eve might be a little slow on the uptake at times, but what she lacked in brains, she made up for in heart. She wasn't being as critical as she was being simply honest. Eve is a fashionista. I'm an also-ran. But hey, I don't have nearly six feet of gorgeous body to work with like she does. If I pull back my shoulders and stand really straight, I'm five foot two. I'm too curvy to be fashionable, and ages ago I learned not to even try. Unlike Eve who's into high style (whatever that high style happens to be on any given day), I stick with the basics: dark pants, blazers, understated blouses. OK, I take it back. Eve wouldn't look homeless if she dressed in my clothes. She'd look like a nun.

Who could blame her for passing on my offer?

Fortunately, we didn't have a chance to get into it. Our next student stepped forward at the same time Eve's cell phone rang.

"Got to take this." She slid off the stool and headed into my office, which was directly across from the bar. "If you need help once class starts, you just give me a holler."

I promised I would and got down to business, checking in the rest of the students who were waiting. All told, there were six stations set up in the kitchen: grill, salad table, drinks, prep and side dishes, desserts, and presentation (that is, flowers, dishes, and table settings). There were two students assigned to each station. That meant twelve students total, and by six fifty, ten minutes before they were set to get started, nine of them had arrived. When the front door swung open, I knew for a fact it was student number ten.

I glanced down at the list near my elbow. The three MIAs were Brad Peterson, Genevieve Landers, and Kegan O'Rourke. Since this was a man, I ruled out Genevieve.

"Brad," the man said. He was a good-looking guy with sandy hair, rough-hewn features, and a way of carrying himself that said he was comfortable with the world and his place in it—though the tilt of his chin made it clear that he thought that place was definitely up at the top of the food chain. "They haven't started without me, have they?"

Was it my imagination? I got the distinct impression there was a challenge in his voice, one that said, *They wouldn't dare start without me,* without him actually speaking the words.

I gave myself the paying-customer speech—the one I used to remind myself that I wasn't going to do anything, ever, to hurt Bellywasher's reputation—and smiled. Brad didn't smile back. "You've still got a few minutes." I accepted the paperwork he'd downloaded from the Bellywasher's site and tucked it in the folder appropriately labeled with his name. "You're on—"

"Prep and side dishes. Yeah, I know." Brad was carrying a shopping bag from a nearby grocery store, and he set it down long enough to write a check. "I was counting on doing something a little more interesting than chopping vegetables. Grilling and drinks, that's the stuff men do in the kitchen. The rest is just women's work."

I bristled. But, big points for me, I kept my mouth shut.

At least until I was ready to speak without telling Brad to hit the road.

I wondered if Brad realized my words were stiff because they came from behind gritted teeth. "I'm sure Jim has plenty of good reasons for designing the class the way he did. Jim's the expert, and he's determined to give all of you a complete cooking experience. That's why you'll be taking turns at each of the stations. This week, you're on prep. Next week—"

"Yeah, whatever. I'm sure I'll find out." Brad headed toward the kitchen even before I told him he could. "Hope I'm not doing flower arrangements for the tables anytime soon. Talk about women's work!"

I was still smiling when I crossed Brad's name off drinks for the next week's class and slotted him into presentation.

Genevieve had arrived hot on Brad's heels, and I took care of her. I hadn't so much as had a second to sit back and relax when the door popped open one more time.

"I'm so sorry."

Kegan O'Rourke may have had a romance hero's name, but he looked like anything but. He was a tall, lanky kid (I use the word liberally. Since I'm thirty-five, in my book, it applies to anyone under thirty.) His hair was dark and cut short enough for me to see his scalp, and he was dressed in crumpled khakis and a heavy fisherman knit sweater that hung from his scrawny shoulders. The creamy color of the wool did nothing to help his pale complexion.

"Am I late?" Kegan's question floated at me along with a note of desperation. "I'm sorry. I didn't mean to be. I was stuck in traffic. I hope they didn't wait. Not for me. I wouldn't want to think that anyone—"

"Not a problem." Rude of me to interrupt, I knew, but it was that or watch the poor kid self-destruct. I didn't have the heart for that! "You've still got a couple minutes, so don't worry. Besides, it always takes longer to get going on the first night of class. You know, with everyone finding their places and storing their things. I'd bet money Jim hasn't started yet."

I glanced away only long enough to check Kegan off the list. When I turned again, he was holding out a fistful of ten dollar bills toward me.

"You're taking me up on my bet?"

His expression was blank for a fraction of a second. Then he caught on. He gave me a grin that was a little lop-sided and as bright as the sunshine that had been so noticeably absent in Virginia these past months. Kegan's laugh was clear and honest. "You mean about Jim not starting yet. I get it. That's a good one. But this money isn't for the bet. This is to pay for class."

"Of course!" I took the money and wrote out a receipt. "You're on prep and side dishes tonight," I told Kegan. "You've got your supplies?"

He held up one of those cotton market bags. "Everything's in here. I can't wait." He shifted from foot to foot and darted a glance toward the kitchen, but it was clear he was too polite to run off before I gave him permission to go. "I really like to cook, and I read in a review in the *Washington Times* that your chef here doesn't believe in hydrogenated oils and lots of fats. That's exactly the kind of cooking I want to learn."

"Then you've come to the right place." I hopped off the barstool and walked at Kegan's side. "I'll show you the way. I have to tell Jim that I'm all done and heading home."

A swinging door separated the restaurant from the kitchen. Kegan pushed it open, held it, then stepped aside to let me walk through first.

We were just in time to see that had our bet been for real, I would have lost. Jim was standing near the big walk-in cooler. He was a couple sentences into the short welcoming speech I'd helped him prepare.

"Just because it's bar food," he was saying, "doesn't mean it can't be fresh, delicious, and healthy."

I knew he was about to go on to talk about things like shopping for the freshest ingredients, and how good, healthy, and fresh didn't always have to be expensive.

I didn't mind. I stepped back and listened. After all, looking at and listening to Jim . . . well, those just happened to be two of my favorite things in the whole, wide world.

Time for me to come clean. Again. Just like I admitted that on a scale of one to ten, I'm a zero when it comes to cooking, on a scale of one to ten, I'm somewhere up around a thousand when the subject is Jim.

Aside from being tall, athletic, and having mahogany hair and the most amazing hazel eyes (green in some lights, brown or gray in others), Jim is the owner of a knee-melting

Scottish accent and a motorcycle that I've learned to be (mostly) at peace with. It goes without saying that he's a fabulous cook, but he's also got a great sense of humor, an unshakable faith in himself and in his dreams, and enough confidence in my mathematic and business abilities to leave the everyday details of the restaurant to me.

Sure, he can be a little overprotective, especially when it comes to me and one of my murder investigations, but have I mentioned that Jim is also the best kisser this side of the Atlantic?

Lest I get carried away on that subject, let me also make it clear that when it comes to romance, Jim and I are taking things slow. My idea, not his. After all, I'm the one with an ex-husband on my hands. Once burned, as the saying goes, and though these days the sting isn't nearly as bad as it used to be, I'm not taking any chances. Jim and I date. We share meals and the ins and outs of running Bellywasher's, a love of visiting the museums in the area, and long walks when weather permits. Just for the record, we have yet to share a bed.

Like I said, we're taking it slow.

None of which means I don't know Jim is a honey of a hunk. Just like when I consider cooking, my pulse pounds when I think about Jim. The big difference is that when it's Jim I'm thinking about, the wild pitter-patter is for all the right reasons.

"And then there's Annie, of course."

The sound of my name spoken in Jim's broad, rolling accent shook me out of my reverie. As far as I remembered, mentioning me wasn't part of the speech we'd prepared. Startled, I paid more attention. And I realized that everyone in class had their eyes on me.

"Annie's our business manager here at Bellywasher's." The kitchen wasn't big. It didn't take Jim more than a couple steps to come and stand at my side. "She's the best and the brightest, and throughout the class, you'll have a chance to get to know her better."

"But not tonight." I waved to the class and smiled before I turned to Jim. "I'm all done, and I'm heading home."

"Not yet you're not." Jim latched on to my hand. He backed away, but he didn't let go. "Ladies and gentlemen . . . You've met Marc and Damien who will be helping you when you need it. They'll also be in charge of cleanup." He glanced toward our two young and talented cooks. "And you've met Monsieur Lavoie as well." Jacques Lavoie beamed a smile at the class from over near the pastry table. "He'll be talking to you later about choosing the right wines to go with your meals. Not that most people think about wine with bar food." He laughed. "But it's a chance for you to learn a wee bit more about which wines complement which foods. And think how you'll impress your friends! Anyway . . ." He got back on track. "You may have met Annie out front. I've got a surprise for you—and for her— tonight." Another tug, and I found myself way too close to the grill for comfort. "For the next eight weeks, Annie's going to be my cooking assistant."

Two

❖

NO, NO, NO!
For what probably wasn't more than a couple seconds but felt like forever, I stood frozen to the spot, my body as numb as my brain. The stark horror of the truth pressed in on me.

Jim had surely lost his mind. He'd forgotten who I was. *What* I was.

Bad cook, remember?

Dangerous in the kitchen. Sure to wreak havoc, not to mention death and destruction, to any food I was so bold as to try to prepare.

I assumed the pleading look in my eyes was enough to remind Jim of all this. But when I turned up the intensity from simple appeal to prayerful petition, all he did was smile.

"You'll be brilliant," he said, and though I had, until that very moment, believed that Jim didn't have an underhanded bone in his body, I suddenly saw the whole truth and nothing but. He was a clever one. That was for sure. He'd chosen his words carefully. There's no way a born-and-bred Scotsman can say the word *brilliant* and not make it sound like sheer poetry.

He knew he had me, damn it. He gave me a wink.

One more little tug, and there I was, right where Jim had set up his own workstation on a table near the grill.

"You're completely out of your mind. You know that, don't you?" Just because I'd folded like an origami stork doesn't mean I was going to go down without a fight. I hissed the words at Jim from the corner of my mouth. "Do you know what you're getting yourself into? I'm going to burn down the restaurant. I'm going to poison your students. I'm going to—"

"Hand out tonight's menu and recipes." His grin still in place, he held out a stack of papers toward me.

But remember, I wasn't folding. At least not completely.

I eyed the papers carefully before I accepted them—just in case Jim had some other trick up his sleeve. It wasn't until I'd determined he was on the up-and-up that I took them out of his hands and started around the room with them.

I got to the dessert table just in time to head off a turf war. Margaret Whitemore had been paired with a thin, mousy woman named Agatha. They were standing shoulder to shoulder and were apparently in the process of determining whose half of the table was whose. From what I could see, the negotiations were not going well.

Margaret, on the right, used the back of one hand to nudge Agatha's grocery bag to the left and give herself a little more room. Agatha retaliated. She stepped to her right and bumped Margaret out of the way with one bony hip.

"Menus," I chirped, stepping between them. I tried for a smile that might diffuse the spark of annoyance in Margaret's rheumy eyes and the look of I-dare-you-to-take-me-on-old-lady that made Agatha throw back her shoulders and stick out her chin. "And you know, now that I look at this table . . ." I pretended to give the logistics careful consideration, even though I'd seen the dessert table a thousand times. "This just isn't going to work. I know." I latched on to Agatha's stick-thin arm and marched her around to the short end of the table, then did the same with Margaret.

It wasn't the perfect solution, but at least with the two of them standing face-to-face instead of slap up against each other, I wouldn't have to worry about bodily harm.

One crisis taken care of, I breathed a sigh of relief and made a mental note not to pair Agatha and Margaret again. Then I continued on. The last station I stopped at was prep and side dishes. Thankfully, Brad Peterson and Kegan O'Rourke looked like they were getting along just fine.

"Here you go!" I slid one packet of papers toward Brad (who, I should note, did not thank me for it) and another in front of Kegan, whose cheeks got pink when he smiled at me.

"You guys all set to go?" I asked them.

"Just about." Ever the eager beaver, Kegan lifted his organic cotton market bag onto the table. But Brad was quicker. He'd already reached for his plastic shopping bag, and he unloaded the contents.

"Vinegar, sugar, salt, carrots, cabbage." One by one, Brad set the items out on the table. "I sure hope we're not making some kind of dip out of this stuff. Sounds awful."

"It's not dip, it's coleslaw." Kegan had been busy ruffling through the recipes. He found the one for the side dish Jim planned to serve with the burgers the duo at the grill would be making and pointed it out to Brad. "It looks delicious! And healthy. See, it's even got celery seed in it, and—"

I knew exactly when Kegan's gaze slid from the printed recipe to the vegetables Brad had taken out. His words ended as abruptly as if they'd been snipped with kitchen shears. His cheeks got pale, and when he swallowed hard, Kegan's Adam's apple jumped.

"You're not planning on using *that* in our coleslaw, are you?"

I think the question popped out of Kegan's mouth even before he knew it. He was instantly apologetic.

"I'm sorry, I didn't mean to be critical." A smile came

and went across the young man's expression. "It's just that—"

"What?" His choice of vegetables apparently in question, Brad aimed a laser look at Kegan before he looked down at the table and the plastic bag full of carrots that sat next to an anemic-looking cabbage. "The instructions Jim e-mailed said cabbage and carrots. That's what I got here. Cabbage and carrots. You got a problem with that?"

Kegan blinked rapidly. He hemmed and hawed and hesitated before he cleared his throat and found his voice. "It's just that . . ." He touched a hand to his own shopping bag. "I just don't think . . . That is . . . I think it might be better if we . . . I mean . . ." He decided showing was better than telling. Or maybe it was just less painful for a kid who was obviously so shy.

Kegan reached inside his bag. The carrots he pulled out weren't wrapped in plastic. They were vivid orange and had a plume of feathery greenery at the top. His cabbage made Brad's look like a reject. It was crisp and round and a beautiful bright shade of green.

"Organic is better," Kegan said. His gaze was on his veggies. His voice was so soft, I had to lean nearer to hear. "It's fresher and better tasting. It's better for you, too."

"Bull!" Brad waved off the comment. Of course, Kegan never saw that. He was still looking at the table. "All that talk about organic food, that's for suckers. Who else would believe that crap about how organic foods are grown under better conditions? I'll tell you what, buddy, my money's on the fact that your carrots come from the same farm my carrots come from. Only they sold you a bill of goods. I'll bet you paid way too much for those vegetables."

"Price is really no object. Not when it comes to a healthy body. And sustainable agriculture." Kegan slid me a look. I guess the fact that I didn't jump on Brad's bandwagon automatically made me an ally. Maybe he figured there was strength in numbers. He drew in a breath and lifted his chin.

"Sales of organic fruits and vegetables increased from $181 million back in 1990 to $2.2 billion just a couple years ago," Kegan told Brad, and when he did, his voice was a little louder, his words a little more confident.

"Proves my point." Brad crossed his arms over his chest. "There are lots of suckers in the world."

"Or lots of people who are worried about their own health and the health of our planet."

"Or maybe they just have too much money to throw around." To emphasize his point, Brad slapped a hand on the table.

It was enough to attract everyone's attention.

When I realized it, I glanced toward where Jim was setting up his demonstration. At the first sign of trouble, he'd already taken a step toward the prep table, but I signaled him to stay put. This wasn't serious, and nothing I couldn't handle. Besides, there was something about Kegan that made me think of him like the younger brother I'd never had. How long could a kid as shy as Kegan put up with Brad's bullying?

My guess was not very long, and something told me that when Kegan was finally forced to back down, he'd need a friendly word and a smile.

Little did I know, there were unplumbed depths to his personality.

When he saw that everyone was watching us, color shot up Kegan's neck and into his chin. From there, it spread to his cheeks. He was clearly uncomfortable, and as red as an organic beet, but surprise, surprise . . . He refused to surrender.

"Here's the thing . . ." Kegan dared a look around the room. As long as everyone was watching, I guess he figured they should all hear what he had to say. He raised his voice. "The pesticides and fertilizers we use on our gardens and farms . . . well, it makes sense, doesn't it? They soak into groundwater and wash into streams and lakes and even into the oceans. The chemicals can kill whole lakes and ponds, not to mention the wildlife and fish that depend on them as water sources. Chemicals and pesticides are responsible for nearly ten percent of our common water pollution, you know. Then there's bioaccumulation." Kegan drew in a breath, but there was no stopping him now. He was on a roll, and we all just stepped back to watch and listen.

"Bioaccumulation, that means that pesticides build up across the food chain. Bugs eat the pesticides, birds eat the bugs, predators eat the birds. It's a circle, you see, and we're all part of it, too." I didn't think it was possible for anyone to get redder than Kegan already was, but by this time, even the tips of his ears were on fire. "Those pesticides end up in our food, too. And in our bodies. Pesticides are designed to poison living things, and we're living things, aren't we? There's even research that links pesticide use to things like mental impairment and cancer and hormonal imbalances and . . ." Something told me that in spite of appearances, Kegan was a keen judge of character. He'd already sized up Brad, that was for sure. That would explain why, as he finished up, he looked his cooking partner in the eye for the first time. "Research proves that pesticides are responsible for lowered sperm counts."

Brad slid his cabbage and his carrots back into his grocery bag.

Another disaster averted, and relief swept through me. If this kept up, maybe there was hope for me in the kitchen tonight. Maybe I wouldn't burn down the building!

I was smiling at the thought and already heading back to where Jim was waiting for me when the kitchen door swung open, and Eve sauntered in.

"Hi, y'all!" Like the beauty queen she used to be, she grinned and waved at the crowd. "I just thought I'd pop in and see if you needed any help. I thought maybe—"

Halfway between the grill and our big walk-in cooler, Eve stopped in her tracks. Her eyes went wide, and her mouth dropped open.

I looked where she was looking.

At the prep table.

"I thought maybe . . ." Eve tried to choke out the words, but it was clear from the start she wasn't going to get anywhere. Her eyes were as round as saucers. Even as I watched, they filled with tears. She snapped her mouth shut, spun around, and ran as fast as anybody who's wearing boots with four-inch heels can.

The kitchen door swished closed behind her.

Always logical, I scrambled to find some sort of explanation for what had just happened. What had spooked Eve? Or maybe it would be more accurate to ask *who*.

I looked from where the door still swung to the prep table. Was it Kegan who'd caused the reaction? Or Brad?

Neither one of them looked like the guilty party. In fact, Brad was in the process of putting his grocery bag onto the shelf below the workstation. He never even looked up. And Kegan . . . well, he had retreated back into his shell. After his speech about the environment, he looked a little winded, and the brilliant color had drained from his face.

Maybe I'd gotten it all wrong? Maybe Eve hadn't been looking at either Brad or Kegan? I scanned the classroom and the blank expressions on each student's face. It was clear that Eve had recognized someone, and whoever it was, it wasn't someone she was happy to see.

It was just as clear that now that she was gone, nobody was going to take responsibility.

"Well, we've started off with a wee bit of a stir!" Of course, Jim was the one who got everything under control. It was one of the things he did best. He tapped his worktable with a wooden spoon and raised his voice. "Now let's get to the real excitement, shall we? Come on, people, it's time to start cooking!"

 IT'S THE WAY JIM SAYS THE WORD, OF COURSE, THAT throws me for a loop. Every single time. *Cooking.*

He draws out those two *O*s and pronounces them like Americans would in the word *kook*.

Cooking.

I should know better, but try as I might, I can't resist.

Which explains why I didn't drop everything and run after Eve to find out what was going on. Don't get me wrong, Jim's not heartless; I don't want to give that impression. I saw the look he darted at the door, and I knew he was as worried about her as I was. But I also knew he was thinking exactly what I was thinking: that we'd both check on Eve later. Right now, we had work to do, and a class that had already been disrupted by the Brad vs Kegan showdown. We'd have the rest of the night to track down Eve and figure out what was going on inside that very blonde head of hers, but right now we had to make a good impression on the people who would tell other people about their Bellywasher's Cooking Academy experience.

So while Jim gave an overview of the night's menu— burgers, coleslaw, old-fashioned potato salad, fudge brownies, and margaritas—I stood back and waited to do what I was told. And when the time came, he taught his students the right way to proceed through each recipe. I demonstrated. We did the burgers, and I dutifully cracked eggs (I needed a couple extra because of the ones that landed on the floor), added garlic, and crumbled the feta cheese that Jim tucked between two meat patties before he placed them one top of each other on the grill. We talked about potato salad, and I ladled mayonnaise into a bowl (too little to begin with and way too much after that), added the chopped pickle, the mustard, and the bit of dill that was Jim's secret ingredient. The cooked potatoes, as it turned out, were already diced. I didn't hold it against him that Jim wasn't willing to take a chance with me and a chopping knife.

Except for the salt and sugar that I mixed up the first time through, the coleslaw went without incident. The brownies . . . well, it's best not to even mention those. Let's just say that before any real damage could be done, Marc and Damien claimed they were tired of standing around doing nothing and took over the mixing and baking duties.

By the time it was all over, I needed one of those margaritas!

No such luck. Because each pair of students had to make enough of their own dish for everyone to share, there was plenty of work to be done, even when we were finished demonstrating. While Jim handled the grill (who knew there was an art to flipping burgers), Damien ran interference between Margaret and Agatha. Marc had bartended at his last job, so he took care of the drinks, and I flitted between the potato salad and where Brad and Kegan were working on the coleslaw.

Just for the record, yes, they were using the organic vegetables.

"How's it going?" I thought this a better way to start my conversation with them than by asking if Eve knew either one of them, and if she did, what she had against that person. But don't worry, I intended to get around to Eve. If I'd learned nothing else in the course of two murder investigations, it was the right way to handle an interrogation. "You two have any questions?"

"Anybody who has questions about how to chop cabbage, bell peppers, and carrots is a moron."

Do I have to point out that this comment came from Brad?

"Maybe some people just aren't as talented as you are when it comes to cooking. Did you ever think of that?" Kegan came to the rescue, and I don't think it was just because Brad was being pigheaded. Kegan had seen the way I struggled up there at the front of the room, and bless him, he took pity on me!

He gave me an uncertain smile. "We're doing fine, Annie," he said. "Look. I've got the cabbage, the peppers, and the onion chopped. Only need to do the carrots." With the tip of his knife, he pointed at the bowl in the center of the table. "Brad's already cooking the stuff for the dressing; it's nearly done. It only takes . . ." He consulted his recipe. "Five to seven minutes. Sound about right?"

"Sounds perfect." It did. I ignored the disgusted look Brad shot Kegan's way, the one that pretty much said he knew Kegan was trying to be teacher's pet. Since I wasn't technically the teacher, it didn't technically apply. Besides, I had other things to think about. As soon as Brad headed over to check the dressing, I decided to do a little snooping.

"Sorry about your cooking partner," I said. "I'll make sure I pair you up with somebody a little more pleasant next week."

"Not to worry." Kegan reached for a grater and got to work on the carrots. "Most people are pretty resistant when they first hear about the theory of sustainable agriculture," he said. "Brad will come around. Someday, everybody will. They'll have to. We're decimating our forests. And destroying whole species of plants and animals. It's a global problem, and it's everyone's concern. There are just some people who don't realize it yet."

"And your job is to make sure they do."

Kegan's cheeks got pink. "I work for Balanced Planet, you know, the ecological think tank group in D.C. I'm afraid sometimes I forget that I'm not at the office. I get carried away. I'm sorry."

"No need to apologize. Hey, if you guys can ignore the way I botched every recipe and Jim had to jump in and show you the right way to do things . . ."

Kegan returned my smile. He glanced toward the front of the kitchen, where Jim was showing one of the grillers the proper way to put out a small grease fire that had erupted. Call me shallow; I was glad to see I wasn't the only one who had to deal with culinary adversity.

"He's the owner, right?" Kegan asked, and when I said Jim was, he went on. "Is he the one I'd talk to . . . you know . . . about making the place greener?"

I looked around at the butter-colored walls and was about to say something about how repainting wasn't in our budget when I realized what Kegan was talking about.

"Greener! You mean the restaurant using more ecologically friendly products. Jim makes the final decisions, of course, but you'll need to come through me for that."

"Then maybe . . ." Kegan's gaze was on the table again. The knife trembled in his hand. "Maybe I could talk to you about it sometime?"

"Sure, if I can talk to you about—"

I was going to mention Eve, but I never had the chance. The first tray of brownies came out of the oven, and a gasp of appreciation went up from around the room.

"That's dessert," Jim called out. "Each of you, get your food in order, and let the folks in charge of presentation get them plated up. Looks like it's time to eat!"

By that time, there was no use even trying to bring up the subject of Eve. I got out of the way, and I stayed out of the way, at least until everyone was out of the kitchen and out in the restaurant.

"You eating with us, Annie?" Jim whizzed by with a tray filled with water glasses. "We've got plenty."

"In a minute," I told him, and he didn't have to ask why. He knew this was the first chance I had to go searching for Eve.

I found her right where I expected: in my office.

She was sitting at my desk, her head in her hands. I knew from the way her shoulders were heaving that she was sniffling.

"Eve!" I put a hand on her shoulder. "What's going on? What's wrong?"

"It's that man!" Eve spun around in my desk chair. Her eyes were red. So was her nose. She was breathing hard, and her shoulders shook. But remember, I know Eve well. I knew she wasn't as upset as she was just downright mad.

She proved it when she popped out of my chair. The

office door was open, and from where she stood, she could see into the restaurant. And our students, just sitting down to eat, could see her, too.

"It's him," Eve shouted. "It's Brad. I'd like to kill that man!"

Three

✖

WHAT WAS THAT I SAID ABOUT DISASTERS?
Even before Eve's words faded, I saw the mother of all PR catastrophes looming in front of me, as chilling and awful and every bit as undeniable as the looks of shock on the faces of the students who stopped what they were doing and turned to stare. Their mouths gaped. Their eyes bulged. I don't think I need to point out that along with his share of the gaping and the bulging, Brad's expression included a whole lot of outrage.

Now remember, I've investigated—and solved—a few murders. I've been cool and calm in the face of a nasty poisoner. And an arms smuggler. I've withstood an attack by a humongous vase of flowers (it's a long story), and I even kept my head when a member of the U.S. Congress tried to off me. Did I panic?

Of course I did!

We were talking Bellywasher's here. Bellywasher's reputation. Bellywasher's standard of customer service. Even as I stood there, furiously scrambling to come up with the magic words that would fend off the nasty publicity and the bad-mouthing we were sure to get from students who weren't used to having one of their number threatened with bodily harm, I pictured Bellywasher's good name circling the drain.

And Bellywasher's, don't forget, is Jim's dream.

In a moment of pristine clarity, I knew there was no way I could let disaster befall the place. Not just because Eve had decided . . .

Well, whatever it was Eve had decided.

I gulped down my mortification and grabbed the proverbial bull by the horns.

"Oh, Eve, you are just too emotional!" I laughed when I said this and hoped it didn't sound as hollow to the folks out in the restaurant as it did to me. A smile firmly in place, I strolled to the door. Right before I pulled it closed, I pretended to notice the stunned faces of our students out in the restaurant. I rolled my eyes and shook my head when I addressed them. "That Eve! Just when she's finally starting to get over it, she reads another tabloid story and she gets worked up all over again. You know what I'm talking about, that whole thing about how Brad chose Angelina over her."

And before anyone could see that I was lying, insincere, or just plain nuts (maybe not in that order), I closed the door.

With that barrier firmly between me and our audience, I stood with my back to the door and took a deep, unsteady breath.

Eve didn't notice. She was too busy sniffling and sobbing and staring at the door as if she could see beyond it and out to the restaurant where Brad was seated. "You want to tell me what that was all about?" I asked her.

"It's him. Brad." Eve's words teetered on the brink of tears. "Don't you remember him, Annie? Brad? Brad the Impaler?"

The fog cleared. Or at least some of it did. The way I remembered it, it all happened just about the same time Peter, my soon-to-be-ex-but-I-didn't-know-it-yet, decided that he never really knew what love was all about until he met the girl who worked at the dry cleaner's. That would explain why I'd forgotten about Eve's troubles. A best friend is important, sure, but divorce trumps just about anything.

Now that Eve mentioned it, I did remember the job she once had at the cosmetic counter of a department store, and a boss who was known as the Impaler because of the not-so-nice way he treated his employees. He had made Eve's life a living hell. His name was—

I let go a shaky breath and dropped into my guest chair.

"Brad Peterson is that Brad? The guy who—"

"Came on to me like gangbusters. That's the one."

"And when you told him you weren't interested, he's the one—"

"Who had me fired. You bet he is."

"And when you applied for another job, he—"

"Well, he never came right out and said it." Eve *harrumphed* to emphasize her point. "But he just about told the woman who called for the reference that I'd been stealing from the cash register and that's why he had to get rid of me. He's the reason I didn't get the job at that designer clothing boutique in Georgetown. You remember that, Annie. I really, really wanted that job."

"I do remember," I said, and because I also remembered how mortified Eve was when she found out Brad was talking trash about her—and how angry she was, too—I leaned forward and patted her arm. "But look on the bright side, if you'd gotten that job you really, really wanted in Georgetown, you wouldn't have been available to take the job here at Bellywasher's. This place wouldn't be the same without you."

Just as I hoped, the compliment made a smile blossom across Eve's face. Unfortunately, even the fact that I was 100 percent sincere wasn't enough to make her smile last. Though the incident with Brad had happened nearly eighteen months before, some hurts were too painful to be forgiven—or forgotten—so quickly.

The waterworks started again, and Eve plucked a tissue out of the box that sat on one corner of my desk. Her words bubbled with tears. "I'm glad I work here, too. But that doesn't make what Brad did any easier to live with. He lied about me. There's no excuse for that. And you know, I could never prove it, but I think that whole story about me stealing . . . I think he said that to cover up some shady dealings of his own. If there was money missing from the cash register, I bet it went right into Brad's pocket." Eve's cheeks, usually a delicate shade of pink, got dusky. Her eyes hardened. "There's no reason a guy like Brad Peterson should even walk the earth," she said.

It was a surprisingly severe statement, even for Eve, who never bothers to hide her feelings. Uncomfortable with her anger, I did my best to soothe her.

"I'm sorry," I said. "If I knew this Brad was the same Brad you worked with, I never would have let him sign up for the cooking class. I can give him a refund and ask him to leave. I know Jim wouldn't mind. Would that make you feel better?"

"Oh, don't worry about me." Eve touched the tissue to her eyes. "I'm over my own personal hurt, Annie. Honest, I am. I mean, I'd still like to see the guy boiled in oil. Or burnt to a crisp on our grill. Or eaten by sharks. But, honest, it isn't me I'm thinking about. Not anymore."

I sat up, interested. "You mean—"

"He's done it to other women. Sure." Eve blew her nose. "It happened to Valerie Conover not two months ago, and she's been down in the dumps ever since. And before that it was Gretchen Malovich. It's not fair, Annie. None of it. Brad Peterson runs over people. He ruins their lives. He's a real Weasel."

"I have no doubt of that." I nodded in sympathy. "Any guy who treats women like that is a scumbag."

"Not just a scumbag." Eve looked me in the eye and pronounced the words slowly and carefully. "Brad Peterson is a Weasel."

There was something about the way she emphasized that last word. We weren't talking lower case. Brad Peterson was a Weasel with a capital *W*. As for the other women Eve had mentioned . . .

"Valerie and Gretchen . . ." I looked at her carefully. "I don't know them, and you've never mentioned them before. Who are they, Eve? And how do you know them?"

It wasn't my imagination—Eve's cheeks got even redder. She looked up at the ceiling. She looked down at the floor. She folded her hands in her lap.

"I'm not supposed to betray confidences," she said.

"And I'd never expect you to. But—"

"Well, I have been dying to tell you." Eve scooted forward in her chair, her eyes suddenly shining not with tears but with excitement. "I wouldn't have said a word," she made sure she added, "if you hadn't talked me into it."

I didn't argue the point. What good would it have done, anyway? And besides, by this time, I was more than just curious. I gave Eve my full attention.

"It's what I couldn't tell you about before. You know, earlier this evening when you were checking students in for class," she said. Now that she was divulging everything she'd been holding back, the words tumbled out of her in a rush, along with a hiccup of excitement. "I mean, not the part about seeing Brad here because, of course, I hadn't seen Brad here yet. I didn't even know he would be here. But Brad and Valerie and Gretchen . . . Yeah, that's exactly what I was talking about."

I remembered our conversation from earlier in the evening, and suddenly, it all started to make sense. Don't ask me why I thought it was important to double-check, but I looked at the door, just to make sure it was closed good and tight. I lowered my voice. "You mean that whole thing about wearing disguises? About following somebody? That all has something to do with Brad?"

"It all has something to do with Weasels. And Brad is a—"

"Weasel. Yeah, I know. But how does all that figure in with—"

"Women Opposed to Weasels." Eve sat up straight, her shoulders back and rock steady. "It's a group I belong to, Annie. Women Opposed to Weasels. We're women who have taken control of our own lives. 'A Weasel-Free World.' That's our motto. We're tough, and we're strong, and we're tired of having our lives manipulated and turned upside down by men who don't care about anybody but themselves. Hey!" This was, apparently, a new thought. Her eyes lit. "You should join. Peter qualifies. He's a weasel, too."

I had no doubt of this, but I wasn't about to commit. Not yet, anyway. "And this Women Opposed to Weasels—"

"WOW, that's what we call ourselves. We get together once a month," Eve explained. "You know, at a coffee place or a martini bar. And we talk about different ways to cope with the men in our lives and how to handle what they've done to us. I heard about the group and joined last winter. You know, after . . ."

I did know, and I wasn't about to make Eve talk about it. It's one thing breaking up with a guy like she had done a dozen or more times. It's another going through an ugly divorce like I had. But it's something else altogether to have the man who says he loves you try to kill you and your best friend.

I guess I understood why Eve was a woman opposed to Weasels.

She didn't want to talk about it, either. She shrugged off the memories. "I heard about WOW and joined. Then at one of our meetings, I realized that I wasn't the only Brad survivor there. Gretchen had the same thing happen to her. And then Valerie showed up at last month's meeting with the same story. Thanks to Brad, she lost a chance for a job at the Department of Labor. All because she wouldn't sleep with the creep, and he gave her a bad reference."

"So you joined forces, you and Gretchen and Valerie." This made sense to me. The disguises did not. Until I thought about it for another minute. "You're not going to follow Brad, are you?" I asked her, even though I knew Eve well enough to know this was exactly what she was planning to do. "I hardly know the guy, but I'm pretty sure he isn't someone I'd want mad at me."

Eve lifted her chin. "We're willing to take our chances. We have to. For the good of women everywhere. And the downfall of all Weasels. Before tonight, I thought following Brad was the only way we could finally get some proof about what he's up to. But this is great, really. Now I know where he'll be every Monday night and I can really keep an eye on him. Nobody believes us when we tell our side of the story. We need some concrete evidence. You know, photos of Brad's hand in the till. Something like that."

It was exactly the sort of thing that had nearly gotten us killed last winter, but I didn't bother to bring that up. Eve was long past listening. I could tell by the way her eyes gleamed. It wasn't her passion that worried me. Like I've said, Eve is never shy about her emotions. But there was a ring of militance in her voice, and this was very un-Eve-like.

As if she knew what I was thinking and was eager to prove me right, Eve's voice hardened with conviction. "We've got to put this Weasel in his place," she said. "We owe it to the sisterhood of women everywhere. Especially since we've found out that even giving in to Brad's demands doesn't get a woman anywhere. Those of us who told him we weren't interested . . . well, he trashed our reputations. But we found out that he's done the same thing to the women who caved. You know, the ones who slept with him. He keeps them around until he gets bored, then he dumps them and tells lies about them and ruins their lives, too. I'm telling you, Annie, this guy deserves an ugly, painful death. He's—"

"A Weasel. I know. What are you going to do?"

"Poison his brownies?"

The way Eve said it, it wasn't funny. I shifted uncomfortably in my chair and carefully rephrased my question.

"What are you going to do about Brad?"

"Wear disguises. Follow him. Teach him a lesson."

I'd leave the discussion of the whole cloak-and-dagger thing for another day, ideally when Eve's emotions weren't running so high. Maybe then she'd listen when I explained that, in my opinion, the best way to deal with a man as arrogant and belligerent as Brad wasn't to antagonize him, it was to simply ignore him.

I cleared my throat. "I mean about Brad and Bellywasher's. About Monday nights. Maybe you should stay home on the nights Brad comes here for class."

"Or maybe I should come after class starts and wait for him outside." As if a bolt of lightning had zapped her, Eve sat up. "I could follow him home from Bellywasher's. You know, see where he goes, what he does, who he talks to. I could slip in and out of the shadows and wear one of my disguises and—"

"Or not." Enough was enough. If Eve wouldn't listen to reason, it was time to put my foot down. I stood. "If the guy's that much of a creep, you don't want to mess with him, Eve. He could be dangerous."

"But that's just it, don't you see? The whole thing about the danger, that's why I told the WOW ladies that I should be the one to keep an eye on Brad. Valerie mentioned that she thought Brad was the type who might resort to violence, but I told her it didn't matter. That's when I explained about how we're detectives and we're not afraid of anything. I told the ladies we'd followed bad guys dozens of times, and we've never gotten hurt. It's all just a part of a private investigator's job."

I wasn't so sure. About the dozens part, for sure, or about the part about not getting hurt.

There was the time I fell off a pile of wooden crates in a dark alley and cracked my head. And the time Eve was drugged and dumped on the floor of an art gallery. There was that time the flower arrangement came down on us, and I ended up with a broken arm. I stayed in the hospital that night, and if Jim hadn't decided to sleep in the chair in my room, I would be deader than a doornail, thanks to the attacker who snuck in and tried to kill me by shooting air into my IV tube.

Call me persnickety; I don't think any of this qualifies as never getting hurt.

And I knew that pointing that out would get me nowhere. Instead, I decided to appeal to Eve's sensitive nature.

"Maybe you're not afraid of anything, but I am," I told her. "I'm afraid of lots of things. Like you promising WOW more than we can deliver. It's not like we're real private investigators."

Eve didn't say a word. She just fixed me with a stare, and I knew what she was saying even though she wasn't saying anything. Being Annie Capshaw—careful, dependable, predictable Annie Capshaw—I refused to acknowledge it.

"I'm a bank teller," I told her and reminded myself. "In the evenings, I show up here to pay the bills. You seat people at their tables and make sure everyone is satisfied and happy with their meals. We're not detectives."

"We detect, don't we?"

I saw the slippery slope rising up before me and pictured myself sliding down into the mud if I wasn't careful.

"We *have* detected," I pointed out. "That's different from being detectives. It sure doesn't mean that we can follow Brad around for no reason."

"Then *we* don't have to." Eve stood, too. Have I mentioned that she's nearly a foot taller than me? In her high boots, she looked plenty commanding. The effect was lost due to the fact that her bottom lip trembled. "I never committed you to anything. I told the ladies I'd follow Brad, and I will. By myself if I have to."

What's that old saying about damned if you do and damned if you don't? Something told me that no matter what argument I came up with, it wasn't going to satisfy Eve. Rather than even try, I got down to the heart of the matter.

"I don't want something happening to my best friend," I told her.

"Oh, Annie, don't be silly." She reached down for her purse, which she kept in the bottom drawer of my desk while she was here at the restaurant. She took it out, and fished for her compact. She peered at herself in the lighted mirror, made a face, and powdered her nose. When she was done, she found a tube of lipstick and added a fresh coat to her lips. "You have nothing to worry about," she said, and she clicked her compact shut for emphasis. "Nothing's going to happen to me. Nothing's going to happen to anyone in WOW. We're tough, strong women, and we're not going to buckle under oppression. Not anymore. Besides, what could possibly happen to me just from following Brad? You're such a worrywart!"

I was. I am. I had long ago made peace with that aspect of my personality, and I opened the door and stepped back into the restaurant, worrying as I did that I'd find everyone had gone, but not until after they demanded their money back and, while they were at it, promised they'd report our unprofessional behavior to the media, the health department, and anyone else who would listen.

When I heard the sounds of conversation and laughter, I breathed a sigh of relief. The class had apparently just finished dinner, and Jim should have been ready to wrap things up for the night.

Instead, he was standing behind the bar, talking on the phone.

He signaled me he'd be right there.

"Everything OK?" I asked when he was done.

He nodded and smiled in a way that said he was fine, and we'd talk about it later. Then he reminded everyone about their assignments for the next week.

When they gathered their things, promised they'd see us

next week, and started filing out, our students were still smiling.

Except for Brad, of course.

Since he'd just had a death threat leveled against him, I guess I could excuse his cranky mood. Still, when Brad looked my way, I pretended not to notice. After learning everything I'd heard from Eve, I wasn't willing to cut him any slack. I headed into the kitchen to avoid him, but Brad stepped into my path.

"If I knew she worked here, I never would have signed up for this class."

Thanks to years of hanging around with Eve, I knew how to play dumb. I gave him my blankest look.

Brad snorted. "You know what I'm talking about." When he looked at my office door (closed, thankfully), his top lip curled. "If you folks checked up on your employees more thoroughly, you never would have let Eve DeCateur through the front door."

"If we checked up on our students more thoroughly, we'd know you were the one who refused to give Eve a good recommendation for that job she applied for in Georgetown. Which is it, Mr. Peterson, slander or libel when you say things that aren't true?"

It was a rhetorical question, but Brad apparently felt obligated to provide the answer. "Slander in person. Libel in print." The smile he aimed at me told me he admired my backbone.

It also made me uneasy. I backed up a step.

Brad's smile inched up. "You stand up for your employees. Even when they don't deserve it. I like that in a woman."

Was Brad coming on to me?

I backed up another step. I didn't like the idea of walking on eggshells for the next seven weeks, wondering if Eve would pop out from behind a potted palm in her Penelope Cruz wig just as class was starting. Being designated Jim's assistant had given me enough to worry about; I didn't need intrigue thrown into the mix. I didn't need a creep (or should I say Weasel?) like Brad, either. Just so there was no mistake about that, I looked him in the eye.

"I stand up for my friends," I said. "If you don't like that—and if you can't show respect for the people who work here—maybe you should think about quitting the class. I'll tell you what, I won't even prorate the cost or wait for your check to clear. One hundred and twenty dollars, cold, hard cash. I'll refund it right here and now."

The way Brad grinned, I thought he was going to take me up on my offer. Honestly, I would have been glad if he did. But before he could say a thing, Kegan O'Rourke walked over.

"Just wanted to say good night, Annie." Kegan had a glob of ketchup on his fisherman knit sweater. I pulled a bev nap (that's restaurant talk for those small, square napkins that every bar in the world hands out along with its drinks), and blotted the ketchup away. Kegan's cheeks got red.

"I wanted to say good night to you, too, Brad." Kegan looked at the man at my side. He stuck out his right hand. "I hope you don't hold it against me, all that stuff I said about the benefits of organic foods. Remember, don't panic, eat organic!"

For a couple seconds, Brad didn't say anything, and I could only imagine it was because he thought Kegan's joke was too lame to deserve a reply. But then Brad's eyes lit and he smiled.

"No problem, buddy," Brad said. He pumped Kegan's hand. "I'll see you next week."

When Kegan walked away, Brad turned to me. "I'll see you next week, too," he said.

And I couldn't help but wonder if that was a promise or a threat.

I was still thinking about it when Jim showed up. "Good news." He looped an arm around my shoulders. "That was my cousin, Fiona, on the phone. She's going to be in town next week, and I've invited her to stay with me a few days."

"Fiona, huh? Is she nice?"

"Haven't seen her in years, but she used to be. We'll find out. She's arriving next Monday evening." Jim slipped his arm from my shoulders and started into the kitchen. "I've promised to pick her up at the airport."

"Monday?" Before he could get away, I grabbed his hand. "How are you going to pick her up at the airport when you've got to be here to teach the class?"

Jim's smile was shaky around the edges. He didn't meet my eyes. "All taken care of."

I held on tighter. Just so he didn't get any ideas about scampering away. "All taken care of, how? Are you going to have Marc teach the class? Damien? I love them both dearly, but I'm not sure either of them is ready for that kind responsibility. And Monsieur Lavoie . . ." I looked over to where Jacques Lavoie was finishing the last of a bottle of wine. "If you leave him to teach the class, he'll take the opportunity to use it as a platform to advertise his own cookware shop and push that Vavoom! seasoning he packages and sells."

"Which is why I'm not leaving him to teach."

"But if isn't Marc and it isn't Damien and it isn't Monsieur Lavoie, who's going to teach?"

Jim grinned and kissed my cheek. "Don't worry, Annie. It's only a cooking class. What can possibly go wrong?"

Four

 THE GOOD NEWS IS THAT I HAD A WEEK TO PLAN FOR the next cooking class.

The bad news?

I had a week to plan for the next cooking class, and every time I sat down to do it, my brain went numb, my stomach tied in knots, and my heart did a cha-cha inside my chest. Call me crazy, but I couldn't get past the oh-no-I'm-going-to-burn-something-down phase. That is, when I wasn't stuck in the oh-no-I'm-going-to-poison-someone stage. Or the oh-no-I'm-going-to-embarrass-myself-to-death part of the equation.

I think it's only fair to point out here that I didn't hold any of this against Jim. Not too much, anyway. He is not, by nature, a cruel man. As a matter of fact, he's a regular honey bunch. Which is the one thing that made this whole Annie-will-teach-the-class scenario so impossible to deal with.

Jim thought he was doing me a favor.

No, honestly, he really did. Because Jim loves planning a menu and shopping for food and cooking so much, he figures everyone else does, too. Terrified? He just doesn't get it when I tell him I am. There's something about the cooking oil in his veins that makes it impossible for him to understand the connection between a close encounter with a stove and deep-down panic. In Jim's soul of souls, he's convinced that one of these fine days, I'll wake up and realize that cooking really is as wonderful and as creative and as satisfying for me as it is for him.

Until then, he knows he needs to push me—just a little harder each time—to get me out of my comfort zone.

Looks like he'd finally succeeded. I was about as comfortable as an ice cube on a hot sidewalk, and as I finished up at Pioneer Savings and Loan and drove to Alexandria on the evening of the next class, I thought about getting on the nearest highway and heading out of town as fast as I could.

But remember, if nothing else, Annie Capshaw is dependable.

The last thing I'd ever do is let Jim down.

Even if I did have static.

I guess I need to explain.

I'd had my yearly review at the bank that day (and I got the highest ratings and—hallelujah—a bit of a raise!). Since I knew the meeting was scheduled, I'd dressed for it in a skirt and sweater. As I parked my car a few blocks from Bellywasher's (the only space I could find), I saw to my horror that my skirt was stuck to my legs.

Not an attractive look, and the last thing I wanted to worry about when I was standing in front of our cooking students. Especially when I had so much else to worry about.

I ducked into the nearest drugstore for a can of antistatic spray and, with the bag tucked under my arm, did my best to talk myself down from the brink of hysteria.

"Chicken wings with teriyaki, hot or lemon pepper sauce. Grilled ratatouille. Corn on the cob. Ice cream sundaes with peach sauce. Chicken wings, grilled ratatouille, corn, ice cream sundaes." There was at least some comfort in the by-now familiar litany I repeated to myself as I waited for a light to change so I could cross King Street. I might not know *how* to cook everything we were cooking that night, but at least I knew *what* we were cooking. It wasn't much, but it was something, and while I was at it, I went over all I could remember of the careful directions Jim had given me about each recipe.

"Chicken wings in the oven. Not too long or they'll dry out. But not for too short a time, either, or they'll be soft and mushy. Light on the sauces. It's easy to add more, impossible to save the dish if your wings are drowning. Don't forget to drain the eggplant before it goes in the ratatouille. Remember to drizzle lemon juice on the peaches."

Or was it drain the peaches and drizzle lemon juice on the eggplant?

I groaned, and yes, the lady waiting to cross the street next to me slid away. But not until after she gave me a weird look.

At that point, I was beyond caring. In less than one hour, I would be front and center with the collective results of the night's dinner in my trembling hands.

It was a formidable responsibility. Nothing could make me forget that. Not even—

Brad Peterson?

I was just about to step off the curb, and I stopped in my tracks and looked across the street to where Brad the Impaler stood between an antique shop and a place that sold wigs and what they charitably called "urban gear" (as far as I could tell, that meant too-wide pants, too-expensive sneakers, and lots of baseball caps). Since it was class night and Bellywasher's was right down the street, I wouldn't have paid any attention to Brad at all—if he wasn't with a tall, gorgeous woman whose blonde hair cascaded in a tumble of curls halfway down her back.

And if they weren't having a knock-down, drag-out argument.

How did I know?

Well, I admit, it *was* six o'clock in the evening, and as usual, Alexandria traffic was bumper to bumper. A horn blared. One of the drivers gunned his engine. I couldn't hear a thing Brad and the woman said to each other. But I didn't need to.

I could see Brad's mouth pull into a sneer. I watched as the woman pointed a finger right at his nose. He snorted. She stepped back, a hand on her hip.

His cheeks were an unbecoming shade of maroon. His mouth opened and closed furiously, and even over the noises of traffic, I clearly heard the words "none of your business." When Brad whirled around to walk away, the woman followed.

So did another woman, one who'd been standing in the shadows of the doorway of the urban gear store. She had a tiny brown, white, and black dog on the end of a leash studded with rhinestones. The dog was wearing a rhinestone collar that matched the rhinestone choker around the woman's neck. Their sweaters matched, too: black angora with white trim.

I'd recognize the dog anywhere.

It was Doctor Masakazu.

The woman holding on to his leash looked a whole lot like Penelope Cruz.

I doubled my pace and caught up to Eve and Doc in no time flat, and I guess the fact that I was out of breath by the time I did explains why I didn't ease into the conversation. My words bumped over the breaths I took to try to slow my heart rate.

"I thought you said you were going to be careful. That you knew Brad could be dangerous. That you weren't going to follow him." None of this was true, of course. Eve had never promised anything of the sort. But I blurted it out, anyway, hoping that the distance of a week would have made our conversation on the subject a little hazy in Eve's mind.

No such luck.

I'd grabbed her arm to hold her back, and she shrugged me off and looked past me to where Brad and the blonde were still going at it.

"I didn't say that, Annie. You did. I said I owe it to the sisterhood of women to do what I can to eliminate the Weasel plague of the Brads of this world."

I don't know where she found the time, but something told me Eve had attended a recent WOW meeting.

I knew with a fresh dose of ideology coursing through her veins, there was no way I was going to change her mind, so I didn't even try. At the same time I stooped to scratch Doc's ears, I looked over at Brad and the woman. "Who is she?" I asked Eve.

"That's Valerie. You remember, Valerie Conover. The woman who didn't get the job at the Department of Labor because of Brad." Eve made a face. "She promised she'd leave the following up to the experts."

I almost asked who she was talking about. I bit my tongue.

"So you're following Brad, and you didn't know Valerie was, too?"

"That's right. She said she wouldn't, but I guess she couldn't resist. But of course, she's not as good at it as I am." I finished patting Doc, and Eve lifted him into her arms. "I followed Brad all the way from the Metro station, and he never caught on. Then Valerie muscled in on my territory. Of course, he noticed her right away. That's when they started fighting. I was going to come to her aid, you know, the way they teach us to at WOW. Every sister helping every other sister. But . . ." When she'd stooped, Eve's wig had tilted to the left, and she straightened it. "I didn't want to blow my cover."

"It looks like Valerie's holding her own, anyway." Even as I looked down the street to make sure Valerie was still OK, she turned her back on Brad and walked away. He watched her for a minute, and I could just about see the steam coming out of his ears. When she turned a corner, Brad spun in the opposite direction and marched on toward Bellywasher's.

"There. It's over." I looked back at Eve. "You can go home now. It's dinnertime. I'll bet Doc's hungry."

"Doc ate before we left the house. And I brought along some snacky-wackies for him." Eve and the dog rubbed noses. "Besides . . ." She looked at me over Doc's head, "you're trying to change the subject."

"The subject is that there is no subject. You're not going to find out anything about Brad by following him around. Nothing useful, anyway."

Eve's lips thinned. "Well, I found out Valerie is following Brad when she promised she wouldn't. That might be useful."

"Or not." The clock was ticking and, Weasel hunt or no Weasel hunt, I needed to get to the restaurant. Aside from setting up my workstation, I needed to take care of my skirt. I plucked it away from my legs, and it immediately settled back into place.

I had to move, and I had to move quickly. I could think of only one way to placate Eve and send her home.

"I'll tell you what . . ." I heaved a sigh. Even before I did, I think Eve knew I was about to surrender. She smiled.

I pretended not to notice.

"I'll do some digging," I promised. "But not tonight. To-morrow. On my lunch hour. I'll get on the computer at work and see what I can find out about Brad. Until then, promise me you'll steer clear."

"Cross my heart." Eve did, and she crossed Doc's, too, just for good measure. "And if you find out anything we can use to nail that sucker to the wall—"

"You'll be the first to know. Really. But right now . . ." I gulped down my misgivings and started walking. When Eve fell into step at my side, I held her back with one hand. "Not you. You're not coming anywhere near Bellywasher's tonight."

"I just want to get a bottle of Pellegrino for Doc. I swear I won't confront Brad. I'll duck into the kitchen, take the water into your office, and—"

"It's not Brad I'm worried about." We were near the restaurant now, and I stopped so that Eve would have to, too.

"It's you," I told her. "I don't want you anywhere near the place when it goes up in smoke."

WHAT'S THAT SAYING ABOUT THE BEST LAID PLANS?
My plan was to get into the kitchen as quickly as I could and try and get myself organized. Right after I was done saying a whole bunch of prayers.

No such luck.

No sooner had the front door of Bellywasher's closed behind me than I found out I wasn't alone.

"Hi, Annie. I'm glad you're here. I've been waiting for you." Kegan popped out from behind the sandalwood screen that separated the entry area of the restaurant from the spot where we had our tables. He gave me that shy smile of his, the one that made him look like a kid. The weather was a tad warmer this week than it had been the first night of class, and he'd topped off his rumpled khakis with a raggy and well-worn T-shirt.

Don't Panic, Eat Organic.

I recognized the phrase as something he'd said to Brad the week before.

Kegan's cheeks were as red as the tomato on his shirt must once have been. "I was hoping we could talk," he said. "You know, before class starts."

I gulped down the spurt of mortification that brought back the ugly scene of the week before. I had hoped the incident was behind us and wondered how many others of our students would show up tonight and demand a refund. Didn't it figure, on the one night Jim wasn't there to charm them into changing their minds.

My shoulders drooped. "You're quitting. I can't blame you. What Eve said about Brad, that was really out of line. But if you give us another chance—"

His chuckle cut me off. "Gosh, Annie, you're so considerate. Always thinking about other people and how they feel. That's really nice, but trust me, it's not what I want to talk to you about. I want to talk to you . . . you know . . . about greening up the restaurant."

I breathed a sigh of relief. Right before my breath stuck in my throat. That was because I glanced at the clock that hung above the bar. Since I'd taken the job at Belly-washer's, I'd learned there was something in the industry called *bar time*. That meant our clock was set twenty minutes later than the actual time so that customers could be cleared out by closing. Even though I knew that, I also knew the clock was ticking away. And every tick brought me closer to the inevitable start of the night's class.

"I'd like to talk. Really," I told Kegan. I wasn't sure that was true, but he was right, I did always think about how other people felt. If I was going to disappoint him, I wanted to let him down easy. "But I don't have a lot of time right now. I've got to set up my workstation in the kitchen, and this skirt of mine!" I groaned and plucked my skirt away from my thighs. "I need static spray, and I need it bad."

With any other guy, I might have been embarrassed, but hey, this was Kegan. When he checked out my skirt, I didn't flinch. He was so sweet and so understanding, I guess I was beginning to think of him as a friend.

"Aerosols are bad for the ozone," he said. "Try washing your clothes with wild soapwort. That will help with the static. Soapwort is a perennial plant, and you can get some of it over at an herb shop in Fredericksburg. I'll get you the phone number. You stir it into water until it lathers and then—"

"Thanks. Really, Kegan, I appreciate the advice, and I'll give it a try. It's just that right now—"

"I know. You're busy. This is a bad time. But really, Annie, you'll be happy with what you can do around here. There are plenty of ways that greener means saving money."

He had me there. "I need to get ready for class," I said. "And I don't have a lot of time to chat. How about if we schedule some time to sit down and talk about it?"

How nice of a guy was Kegan? Instead of taking my

brush-off personally, he fell into step beside me and offered to help. Together we went into the kitchen, and because it looked as if I wasn't going to get to use it anytime soon, I tucked the bag that contained the antistatic spray on a shelf to the left of the stove. I slipped an apron over my head, got one of the trays of chicken wings that Damien had prepared for me out of the cooler, and turned on the oven to preheat.

With that under control, I checked the night's menus and the list of supplies that Jim had tacked up on a bulletin board. "We're going to need the big wok for the ratatouille," I told Kegan. "It isn't something we use very often. I think it's in the supply closet." I pointed the way and hoped for the best. Though I was the world's most organized person, I had long ago vowed to keep my nose out of Jim's kitchen. For his sake and for mine. The office is my bailiwick, the kitchen is Jim's, and my office, needless to say, is a picture of neatness and order.

The kitchen supply closet . . .

When Kegan opened the door, I squeezed my eyes shut, held my breath, and hoped nothing fell out and clunked him on the head.

Between Jim, Marc, and Damien (each with their own ideas of how things should be done and where things should be kept), a hectic kitchen schedule that didn't include much downtime for sorting and organizing, and the whole cooks-as-creative-people-with-artistic-temperaments thing, the closet was Bellywasher's own version of a black hole. I knew that even to start looking for the wok, Kegan would have to pick his way through a minefield of stockpots, chafing dishes, and plastic containers that contained the serving pieces we used for private parties and luncheons. When he disappeared into the closet, I whispered a heartfelt, *"Via con Dios,"* and when he came out again holding the wok, I have to say, I was glad to see he'd sustained no permanent injuries.

I was grateful that he'd put himself in mortal danger for

the sake of my cooking class. And he had mentioned saving money. As I found and arranged the ingredients I'd need to make the wing sauces, I got back to what we'd been talking about earlier.

"You really stand up for what you believe in when it comes to the environment, don't you?" I asked him. Right after I showed him where to put the wok, of course.

The tips of Kegan's ears got red. "I try," he said. "I know some people think it's corny—"

"No, not at all! I mean, think of what the world would be like without people like you. Our lakes and rivers are cleaner than they used to be. And there isn't as much litter along the sides of the roads, and—"

"There's still such a long way to go." Disappointed, he shook his head. "And still so much work to do. Sure, there are lakes and rivers that have made a comeback. But there are plenty more that still won't support life, thanks to the chemicals and other pollutants we pour into them. We do things like say we're protecting whole species of birds, but at the same time, we chop down the forests that are their habitats. It's crazy, Annie, but I'm glad you're at least thinking about it. That's where it all starts, you know. With people thinking about the problem. As soon as they do, they see that we're right. The only way to see a difference is to make a difference."

It sounded like one of the mottos Eve had learned from her sisters at WOW, but I didn't hold that against Kegan. He was an intelligent advocate. I admired that, and I told him so.

Color raced up his neck and into his cheeks. "I'm no hero," he said, and even though I hadn't used that word, I guess that's how I made it sound. "I actually came to appreciate the problem only a short time ago. It was my grandpa Holtz, you see." Kegan looked down at the floor, and for a couple minutes, he didn't say anything at all. When he looked back my way, his eyes shone with tears.

"For forty years, Grandpa worked at a chemical company

in a little place called Crayswing, Pennsylvania. His plant made pesticides. I'm not exactly sure what he did, but he wasn't an executive or anything. He worked in the factory. Of course, back when he got the job, they said they didn't suspect that the stuff those guys were breathing in every day was slowly killing them."

"You mean . . ." I had to clear away the lump in my throat before I continued. "What happened to him?"

Kegan chewed his lower lip. He blinked rapidly before he found his voice. "He died a few years ago. Liver cancer. As it turns out, a lot of the other guys who worked at the factory died of it, too. That's what really opened my eyes. It changed my life. So I came here and got the job with Balanced Planet. I have to work to make a difference, Annie. I have to do it for Grandpa Holtz."

I wasn't sure what I could say to make Kegan feel better, so maybe it's a good thing that Margaret Whitemore trundled into the kitchen with Agatha and a couple other students close behind.

I quickly waved to them all, then turned my back so they couldn't see that I had tears on my cheeks.

The crying . . . well, for once, I couldn't blame it on the cooking.

Five

◼◼

I WAS DIPPING CHICKEN WINGS IN HOT SAUCE WHEN Brad sauntered into the kitchen. We were just about to start class, and I didn't want to upset the applecart, but I couldn't help myself. After the tiff I'd seen outside between Brad and Valerie, it was only natural to be curious. Of course, I couldn't let him know that, so I stifled my curiosity and tried to sound concerned.

"Are you OK?"

Brad was already past me and on his way to the table where he and Agatha would be in charge of the night's flowers and plate presentations. When he realized I was talking to him, he stopped and looked over his shoulder.

"Me? OK? Why wouldn't I be?"

I shrugged. I was wearing latex gloves, and hot sauce dripped off my fingers. "I just thought . . . You know . . . after what happened outside . . ."

As if it would bring his thoughts into line, Brad looked at the kitchen door and out to the front of Bellywasher's. "Outside? I don't know what you're talking about."

"Sure you do." I'd already stepped toward him when I realized I was leaving a trail of hot sauce polka dots on the floor. Fortunately, Marc and Damien were there, and out of the corner of my eye, I saw Damien dart forward, cleaning rag in hand. "You and Valerie Conover. You were fighting. I don't mean to pry, but—"

Like he was sloughing off my comments, Brad twitched his shoulders. "I don't know anyone named Valerie Conover, and even if I did, I sure wouldn't be fighting with her in public. You've got me mixed up with someone else."

I remembered that out on the street, the man I'd seen with Valerie had been carrying a paper shopping bag with a bouquet of spring flowers poking out of the top of it. I looked from the bag in Brad's hands—the one with the bouquet of spring flowers poking out of the top of it—up to his eyes. They gleamed, and hey, he didn't have to say a word. His look challenged me to press my point.

I knew I could, and believe me, I wanted to. I may not always admit to being a detective, but after everything that had happened to me since the first time I stepped inside a cooking class, I had finally come to grips with the fact that I have a healthy what's-really-going-on-here streak in me. I was pretty sure the Valerie/Brad smack down had something to do with WOW and that lost job at the Labor Department, but ask anyone, and they'll say I'm the type who likes all my i's dotted and my t's crossed. It's just one of the reasons I got that raise at the bank that day, not to mention why I'm the perfect business manager for Bellywasher's. As always, I was itching to find out the truth.

Then again, I'm also the type who likes to keep her job.

I reminded myself that whatever the argument was about, it wasn't worth alienating a paying student. Brad was not a man who would keep his comments to himself if anyone ever asked what he thought of our little establishment, its cooking school, or its employees.

"You're right. Of course!" I made sure I smiled in an embarrassed sort of way. That wasn't hard, considering that (detective or not) I wasn't comfortable poking my nose in other people's business. I wasn't happy about lying, either, but if I'd learned nothing else in the course of two murder investigations, it was the value of a well-placed fib. "Now that I think about it, that guy didn't have a shopping bag. And he was wearing a raincoat. You've got a leather jacket on. Boy, isn't it funny how when you see someone out of context, even someone you think you know, you can get the details all mixed up."

Brad's smile was icy. "Told you it was someone else. Someone who looks like me. Whoever he is, I hope he taught that Valerie Conover a thing or two. Any woman who would follow a man, then confront him in public, is obviously a vindictive bitch."

I had not been indoctrinated by the sisters of WOW, so I wasn't sure how I was going to respond to this. It was a good thing Kegan walked by. Bless him, he'd been helping me get everything set up, and he was just headed over to his station. Along with Jorge, he'd be working on the ice cream sundaes, and he had a basket of peaches in his hand.

"Speaking of people who look like people . . ." Brad put a hand on Kegan's arm to buttonhole him. "Couldn't help myself. Kept thinking about you all week. There's something really familiar about you, and I can't put my finger on it. Have we met before?"

Kegan ran his tongue over his lips. "I don't think so."

"You sure?" Brad stepped back and pointed a finger at the faded tomato on Kegan's T-shirt. "That's what did it. Don't Panic, Eat Organic. When you said that goofy thing last week, that's when I knew I must have met you before. That sounds so familiar."

The tips of Kegan's ears looked as if they were on fire. He swallowed hard. "It's not a goofy saying," he said, and because he knew Brad would dispute this and possibly cause a scene, he added quickly, "And you could have heard it anywhere. I didn't think of it. I'm not that clever."

"I guess you're right." I knew it wasn't easy for Brad to admit even that much of a shortcoming, so I shouldn't have been surprised that he didn't let it go. "But that doesn't explain why you look so familiar. Where are you from?"

"Crayswing, Pennsylvania." Kegan looked down to where Brad still had a hand on his sleeve. He looked up again, but even though he smiled, he never quite met Brad's eyes. "How about you?"

"Colorado." Brad paused a moment to let the information sink in. "Ever been to Boulder?"

"Oh, wow." When Kegan lifted the basket of peaches to put both his hands under it, Brad had no choice but to let go of his arm. "Colorado! That's a dream of mine. I've always wanted to visit Colorado. I'll bet the mountains are beautiful. Unfortunately, I've never been west of the Mississippi."

Still thinking, Brad tipped his head. "School?"

"Penn State." We were standing in the front of the kitchen, and much to Kegan's chagrin, he saw that once again, he had become the center of attention. While our students waited for class to start, they listened in on the conversation.

Kegan shifted from foot to foot. "How about . . . how about you. Brad?"

"CU-Boulder. But that must have been years before you were in school. I mean, I know I don't look it, but I'm going to be forty this summer. I'll bet I'm a good ten years older than you."

"Eleven." Kegan's cheeks flushed. His fingers tapped out a nervous rhythm against the peach basket. I could practically see the wheels turning inside his head. He was struggling to find a way to put Brad at ease, and it was no mystery why. Kegan knew that in the same position, he'd be mortified at mistaking Brad for someone else. Being the nice guy he was, Kegan figured Brad felt the same way.

Of course, he didn't know that Brad was a Weasel.

Or that weasels don't have feelings.

When I stepped in, it sure wasn't to help out Brad.

"Hey, it didn't have to be Colorado, did it? You two could

have run into each other right here in the area somewhere."
I turned to Brad. "Kegan works for Balanced Planet. You
know, that environmental group that's got offices in D.C.
You could have bumped into each other there. Or at a
Metro station. Or even on the street."

"Oh, I don't know." Kegan cleared his throat. "Even if
we did, I don't think Brad would have noticed. I'm not all
that memorable."

"Well, you must be!" I laughed and patted Kegan's arm,
hoping that would signal an end to their talk. I was all for
our students getting to know each other, but if I was going
to get through all the recipes Jim expected me to teach that
night, we had to get moving. "You must be plenty memorable if Brad knows he's seen you somewhere."

"That would be something, wouldn't it?" Kegan
laughed, too. I was glad. He was a sweet kid, and I hated to
see him ill at ease. He was still smiling when he took the
peaches over to Jorge.

Brad got settled, too. And me?

With a sinking feeling, I realized how much I'd appreci-
ated the diversion. I gulped down the realization that it was
time to get down to business.

Ready or not, I had to cook.

IN THE INTEREST OF FULL DISCLOSURE, I HAVE TO
admit that there were a couple glitches.

Like the chicken wings that went from plump and juicy
to dry and dusty in no time flat. (I used this as a precaution-
ary lesson and reminded Margaret Whitemore and the man
named Grant who would be her partner preparing the wings
for the class meal to follow the recipe, not my example.)

There was the ratatouille, too. I was pretty sure it was
supposed to be fresh and chunky and not look like ketchup.
Big points for me. I did not do as I was tempted and throw
my hands in the air, sob, and admit my shortcomings. Instead, if I do say so myself, I recovered pretty well. I used

the opportunity to ask Damien to give us a demonstration of the proper way to chop.

All things considered, the class went pretty well. By the time I was ready to demonstrate how to make the peach sauce for our ice cream sundaes, I was feeling content and pretty pleased with myself. From where they stood off in a corner watching and no doubt critiquing the proceedings, I could tell Marc, Damien, and Monsieur Lavoie (who had just joined us and was already sampling a glass of the dessert wine we'd be serving tonight) were, too. No doubt, Jim would be getting a positive report. Three recipes down and one to go (I didn't count the rum punch, since there was no fire involved), and I hadn't set off the smoke alarm even once.

For me, this was a record.

"OK, we already put our peaches in boiling water for a minute or two, we peeled them, and we chopped them." I held up the bowl of peaches for my students to see and hoped they weren't too picky. Some of my peach chunks were big, others were so small, even I had to squint to see them. Some looked more like peach jam than peach pieces. No matter, I told myself. I was on a roll. My confidence boosted, I breezed on as expertly as if I was one of those celebrity chefs on the Food Channel.

"Now we're going to get the sauce going. You know, you could cook this entire dessert on your grill. You'd need heavy aluminum foil, and you'd put everything on it, wrap it up good and tight, and throw it on the grill for . . ." I'd re-membered this much of Jim's instructions, but had to consult his recipe for the rest. "For about twenty or twenty-five minutes. Tonight, since we don't have a charcoal grill, we're going to do the whole thing on the stove." I waved the students closer to the industrial stove that took up most of one wall of the kitchen, and they gathered around.

"I've got my chopped peaches . . ." I scooped them into a pot. "And I'm going to add the lemon juice, the honey, the ginger, and the allspice." This part was easy, since

Marc had already measured out everything and had it waiting for me.

Margaret Whitemore raised a hand. "But what if you don't like all the ingredients?" she asked. "Ginger's too spicy for me. Why, I remember once, I had dinner at an Indian restaurant and I spent the next three days burping."

"And allspice . . ." Agatha rolled her eyes. "Who has that kind of stuff in their cupboards?"

I hadn't expected a mini rebellion. I scrambled, wondering all the while how Jim would handle this.

I could just about hear his voice in my ear. "Cooking is all about being creative," I said just like he would (though I left out the long *ooo* in *cooking*, because I figured that would be too much). "If you don't like the spices, don't use them. You could substitute something like . . ."

I didn't have a clue. I looked to Marc and Damien for deliverance.

"Cinnamon." Marc stepped forward. "It's a spice, too, of course, but it's also a flavor more of us are used to and like. And it goes really well with peaches. The smell is great, too. Think about those cinnamon roll places at the mall. That same aroma . . . it will waft through your whole house."

Listening to a kid with purple hair use a word like *waft* struck me as funny, but our students didn't seem to mind. They nodded in unison.

"Or you could even add a little bit of balsamic vinegar," Damien added. Since the combination seemed odd to me, I wasn't surprised the suggestion came from him. Of all our employees, he was the most like Jim. I don't mean Jim has a prison record like Damien does. Not a chance! But Damien is just as daring and creative as Jim. When it comes to taking chances with flavor combinations ordinary mortals would never dream of, Damien was the guy for the job.

"So, it's whatever you like," I added, along with a smile of thanks to our two cooks. I had the pot with the peaches and the other ingredients in it in one hand and with my other, I turned on the stove. "And remember, Jim would be the first to tell you that if you look at a recipe and don't like everything that's in it, you can change it. Only he'd say *adapt*. He always says that's how new recipes are developed. You leave out the stuff you don't like, you add the stuff you do, and voilà!"

I guess the celebrity chef thing went to my head. To add a little oomph to that last word, I gestured wildly. Too bad I did it with the hand that was holding the pot of peach sauce.

As if it was all happening in slow motion, I saw the sauce slosh and I knew when it splashed over the sides, it was going to rain down on our students in a sticky mess. I tried to compensate, stepping back, but my butt slammed into the stove. The fire was on, and though I knew in my head that I wasn't in danger of getting scorched, I flinched. I darted forward and tripped over my own feet. I would have gone down like a rock if I didn't put a hand out to stop myself.

When I did, I knocked into the shelf next to the stove. It was where I'd stashed the brown paper bag with the can of antistatic spray in it. The sleeve of my sweater caught on the bag.

I knew better. Honest. I knew not to yank my arm away, but remember, it might have felt like it was happening in slow motion, but all this occurred in the blink of an eye.

I was so anxious to at least look like I had the situation under control that I didn't think.

I tugged my arm back, and the bag came with it.

The aerosol can slipped out of the bag and tumbled. It clattered against the tile floor.

The noise of it was still echoing when I breathed a sigh of relief. The excitement was over, and I hadn't fallen flat on my face in front of our students. Or dropped the pot of peach sauce.

Life was good.

I guess that must have been what I was thinking about. That's why I wasn't paying attention until I heard a collective gasp and saw a blur as someone pushed from the back of the crowd of students around me to the front of the group. Before I could register what was happening, that same someone took hold of my shoulders and pushed me—hard—away from the stove.

I must have been hallucinating.

That blur looked an awful lot like a tomato.

HAD KEGAN JUST ATTACKED ME?

The words rang through my head along with the sounds of the voices raised in surprise.

"What happened?"

"Are you hurt?"

"What on earth are you doing?"

Those first two questions were directed toward me, one by Margaret who was fanning her face with one hand and leaning against Jorge, and the other from Damien who'd raced over the second the commotion started.

The last question was mine, and I'll admit I did not sound as cool, calm, and collected as I would have liked. My words were directed at Kegan, who was sitting on the floor beside where I lay. He had his hands on his knees and he was breathing hard.

"I'm so sorry, Annie." Kegan put a hand on my shoulder. Since I was facedown on the floor and struggling to sit up, this was not the best strategy. I pushed his hand away, sat up, and scooped the hair out of my eyes. While I was at it, I picked pieces of peach sauce out of my hair.

Kegan's face was pale. His lower lip trembled. "I'm so, so sorry. But there wasn't time to explain. I had to do something. Before you got hurt."

Since I was already covered with peach sauce, both my knees were scraped and one of my elbows was bleeding, this seemed like a moot point.

"I wasn't going to get hurt," I said. "At least not until you pushed me. I had everything under control."

"But you didn't." Kegan stood on shaky legs. He stooped down to help me to my feet, and once I was up, he kept an arm around my shoulders. "It was the antistatic spray, Annie. I couldn't take any chances."

Huh? would have been the appropriate response, but I had yet to arrive at *huh* stage. Along with everyone else in the kitchen, I simply stood there with my mouth open, staring at Kegan.

He wasn't much calmer than I was. He had that deer-in-the-headlights look, but he managed to glance at the students gathered in a tight circle around us. "It's possible for aerosol cans to puncture when they're dropped," he explained. "And if that happens too near an open flame, the flammable solvents and propane propellant can be ignited. And then . . ." When he looked at me, I swear his face was a little green. "Kaboom!"

Even under its coating of peach sauce, I think my face was green, too. I swallowed hard. "Kaboom?"

Kegan nodded. "That's right. And it can happen fast. There wasn't time to explain. I had to get you out of the way. And the can, too." He looked all the way across the kitchen to where the can was still spinning on the tile floor near the walk-in cooler. "I kicked it as far away as fast as I could, but I couldn't take any chances that the gases might have already escaped and heated. You know, because of the—"

"Kaboom." I filled in the blank. When Monsieur Lavoie showed up out of nowhere with one of the stools from out at the bar, I plonked down on it. "Wow, Kegan, you saved my life!"

Some of the color rushed back into Kegan's face. "Not really. I mean, as it turns out, I don't think the can punctured."

"But if it had . . ." I didn't want to think of the *Kaboom!* scenario, so I didn't finish the sentence. Marc handed me a wet cloth, and I wiped the sticky sauce off my face. "We're grateful," I told Kegan. "All of us. That was really quick thinking."

"It was nothing. Really." Kegan blushed like a teenage girl at her first mixer. "Anybody would have done the same thing."

"But that's not true, is it?"

The question came from Brad, who stepped to the front of the group and clapped Kegan on the shoulder. "Not everybody would have known that stuff about the flammable propellent. You know what I mean, buddy?"

I guess Kegan did, and I guess he was embarrassed by all the attention and about being thought of as a hero by his fellow classmates.

He got pale all over again.

Six

❖

THANK GOODNESS FOR MARC, DAMIEN, AND MON-
sieur Lavoie.

While I hightailed it into the ladies' room to get the sticky peach sauce out of my hair and off my face, they took over like the pros they are. After I blotted the gluey mixture off my clothes with wet paper towels that were a little too wet, they made sure everything was under control while I retreated into my office until my skirt and sweater dried.

I sat at my desk for a while and wallowed in my embarrassment, not to mention my incompetence. But hey, it wasn't the end of the world. If I'd learned nothing else in the course of two murder investigations, it was that there are far more important things in this world than saving face (or peach sauce). I got over it, and when I did, I did the only thing I could think of to make myself feel better: I updated our QuickBooks program and caught up on paying Bellywasher's bills.

Unlike cooking, numbers are dispassionate, predictable, and without pitfalls. The familiar process of checking invoices against orders and packing slips was comforting, and while I was at it and my heartbeat had calmed down at last, I practiced every single excuse I could come up with to explain this latest cooking catastrophe to Jim.

"The peach sauce made me do it."

"I tripped, see, and after that . . ."

Just thinking about everything that had happened—and the messy results—made me shift uncomfortably in my chair. My hair had dried into stiff spikes. My sweater was stained beyond saving. I'd missed some spots of peach sauce on my cheeks and my nose. I knew this for a fact because as I sat there, the honey in the sauce hardened.

"Look on the bright side!" Since I was doing a one-sided role-playing of sorts, I smiled when I said this, just the way I planned on smiling at Jim when I delivered the news of the botched cooking demonstration. I hoped by that time, the skin on my cheeks and nose wouldn't feel as if it was being pulled tight. "None of our students got hurt. Or even splashed with the peach sauce. And I didn't get hurt, either. At least too not much, anyway."

I glanced down at the bandages stuck to my knees and fingered the thick wad of gauze and tape that Monsieur had insisted on wrapping around my elbow. Thanks to his ministrations, I wasn't bleeding anymore, but I wasn't sure I had any blood flow to my arm, either.

"I guess it could have been a real disaster," I said. Since Jim was a practical guy, I knew he'd appreciate seeing the incident from this perspective. "If it wasn't for Kegan . . ."

I stopped to consider this, and when I did, my stomach went cold. The next second, I smiled. When it came to Kegan, there really was more there than met the eye. For all his bashfulness, he really came through in a pinch.

If Kegan hadn't jumped into action . . .

If that can of antistatic spray really had been punctured . . .

If the fumes had ignited in the heat from the stove . . .

I shivered and thanked my lucky stars. Scraped knees

were a small price to pay. Looked like Kegan was living up to that romance hero name of his, after all.

As for Jim . . .

I was finished with the bills, so I clicked out of the program and turned off my computer for the night.

I would explain this incident to Jim the way I explained everything else to him: with the whole truth and nothing but. One of the reasons I was so crazy about him was that he never seemed to hold it against me.

Feeling better, and better able to face our students, I pushed back my chair and headed out into the restaurant.

I was just in time to see that dinner was over and some of our students were heading out the door. Not all of them, though. Kegan was still seated at the table where he'd had dinner. He looked worried and miserable. Until he saw me. Then a look of relief swept over his face. He was seated with Monsieur, who raised his wineglass in salute to me. Marc and Damien each gave me a brief once-over. Satisfied that I'd sustained no permanent damage, they went about their business of cleaning up.

Big surprise—Brad was helping collect plates and carry them into the kitchen.

I watched the kitchen door swing closed behind him. "What's that all about?" I asked Kegan when he hurried over. "Call me crazy, but Brad doesn't seem like the type who would help swab the decks."

"You're OK, aren't you?"

So much for my attempt at avoiding the subject of my most recent culinary debacle. I sighed and turned away from the kitchen door, toward him.

"I'm fine. Honestly. It's nothing that won't heal in a couple days. I might not be fine, though, if it wasn't for you."

Of course, he blushed. By now I'd come to expect it.

I knew if I said anything else about what a hero he was, he'd only feel more uncomfortable. When I changed the subject, I hoped it would stay changed.

"How was dinner?"

Kegan's uneasiness disappeared beneath a smile. "The chicken wings were fabulous. The ice cream sauce was superb. But maybe you already know that, huh? Did you get to taste any of it?"

I laughed when he did. "Unfortunately, none of it landed in my mouth. How about the corn? How was that?"

"Perfect. And so was the rum punch. That's a great recipe."

That only left one thing.

"The flowers?" I asked.

He made a face. "He wasn't happy," Kegan said, and instantly, I knew which *he* we were talking about. Rather than explaining, he looked toward the table where he'd been sitting, and I saw the single iris bud that had been dropped into a too-big vase. It leaned to one side, sad and alone.

"Brad's not big on ambiance," I said. As if I had to tell Kegan. I lowered my voice and leaned closer to him. "I didn't think he was too big on being friendly, either, but I guess that should teach me not to judge people too quickly. It's nice of him to help out."

Kegan looked thoughtful. He bent his head closer to mine. "I've been wondering about him. You know, all those questions he was asking before class. Do you think—"

The kitchen door swished open, and Brad strode into the restaurant. Like people do everywhere when they're caught talking about people who suddenly show up, Kegan and I leapt back from each other and pretended to be talking about nothing at all.

"Hey! Glad you're still here." Brad strolled over. "I was afraid I'd missed you."

Kegan gulped. "You were?"

Brad chuckled. The sound was kind of rusty. Like he hadn't laughed in a long time. "You act like I'm a hit man lying in wait for you. Actually, I was wondering if I could buy you a beer. You know, to show my appreciation for what you did tonight. That was really pretty remarkable. If it wasn't for you, Annie here might have been as burned as her chicken wings."

I ignored the critique. It wasn't so easy to disregard the fact that if I let Brad buy Kegan a beer, I was being ungracious.

"Oh, no!" With an easy smile, I took over the way I did at the bank when a customer was unhappy about things like account balances or how long it takes for a check to clear. "If anyone's buying the beers, it's me," I said, and when Kegan looked like he was going to turn me down (no doubt because he didn't want to be singled out), I latched on to his arm.

"That includes drinks for Marc and Damien and you, too, Monsieur!" I said, and I waved Lavoie over. "You all helped out tonight, and I really appreciate it. How about that martini bar over on Saint Alphath's?" I suggested to Monsieur. "You can meet us over there after you lock up."

Monsieur gave me a kiss on each cheek. It was his very French way of saying he'd be delighted. That taken care of, Kegan, Brad, and I left Bellywasher's together.

We stepped outside, and as much as I hate to admit it, my throat clutched and my stomach knotted. I couldn't help myself. I guess it's my own version of post-traumatic stress disorder. Every time I leave the restaurant after dark, I can't help but relive that night when a drive-by shooting pocked the restaurant—and nearly Eve and me, too—with holes.

Like I always did these days, I paused before I stepped out on the sidewalk ahead of Brad and Kegan. I darted a look up and down the street.

Of course, I knew there was no chance it was going to happen again, but still, when a car turned the corner and drove past, I tensed.

When it kept right on going, the tension inside me uncurled.

That was then and this was now, I reminded myself. And now, I told myself what I'd been telling myself ever since

I'd solved the murder of Sarah Whittaker, I wasn't going to get involved in anything mysterious or dangerous. Not ever again.

I meant it, too.

Nothing weird. Nothing strange. Nothing out of the ordinary or—

"What was that?" An odd sound from somewhere behind me interrupted my thoughts, and I stopped and tipped my head, listening closely.

"What was what?" Brad asked.

I looked back into the restaurant. "It sounded like a . . . Nah!" I dismissed the whole idea. "I must be hallucinating. Maybe nearly blowing up Bellywasher's tonight affected my hearing. I've never even seen a cat anywhere around here, and there sure couldn't be one inside Bellywasher's, but I could have sworn I heard a cat meow."

BY THE NEXT DAY, I'D FORGOTTEN ALL ABOUT THE incident. It was no wonder—I was convinced it wasn't important, and besides, we'd had a busy day at the bank, and after work, instead of heading over to Bellywasher's, I was going to Jim's to meet his cousin, Fiona. It was the first time I'd been introduced to any member of the MacDonald clan, and at the same time I was honored that Jim considered me important enough to meet his relatives, I was also nervous.

Silly, I know, but I couldn't help wondering what Cousin Fiona would tell the folks back home about me.

"She canna cook, that's for certain."

I didn't know Fiona, but I could well imagine the words coming out of her, and in an accent every bit as heavy as Jim's.

"And as far as being a fashion plate . . ." Here, I imagined, Fiona might shake her head sadly.

I told my imagination to shut up and smoothed a hand over the black blazer I was wearing along with black pants and the creamy silk blouse I'd gotten from Eve for Christmas. Whatever she'd paid for the blouse, I was sure Eve couldn't afford it, and I wore it only for special occasions. Because of the hours he put in at the restaurant and our conflicting and hectic schedules, dinner at Jim's was a special occasion.

With that thought firmly in mind, I told myself to relax and stop worrying, pulled into his driveway, parked the car, and headed into the house.

That's right. I said *house*.

I have to make one thing perfectly clear here. Yes, I've always wanted a home of my own. Yes, I was saving for one (and actually looking at some really inexpensive houses) when Peter walked out on me and took half the down payment with him. Yes, I dream of and long for and ache to have a place with a patch of garden and a picket fence, a place that is mine all mine.

But I am not—and I cannot emphasize this enough—I am *not* dating Jim just because he owns his own home.

I was already crazy about him before I ever knew that.

Was Jim's the house of my dreams?

Not really. With its gables and gingerbread, its overgrown garden and its jumble of rooms and colors, Jim's house is too rambling and just too cluttered for my taste. I prefer clean, modern lines and any number of colors—as long as they're shades of beige. Jim, on the other hand, isn't quite so picky. He knew a good deal when he saw one, so he purchased the house from an elderly woman who had what I would charitably call flamboyant tastes. Since he hadn't owned the house that long, and he'd been busy first at Très Bonne Cuisine where he taught cooking classes and now with Bellywasher's, he'd done little in the way of renovations. The living room was papered with cabbage roses and violets. The dining room was painted red. The kitchen . . . well, since I made it a rule to stay as far away from the kitchen as I could, I won't even comment on the turquoise Formica or the avocado green appliances.

Besides all that, the house is in a part of Clarendon (one of Arlington's many neighborhoods) that borders on the seedy. I might feel comfortable visiting, but I hadn't failed to notice that when I left after dark, Jim always walked me to my car. I'd never be comfortable raising a family here.

And I was jumping way ahead of myself! If I was smart, I wouldn't forget it.

The weather had turned and finally showed a promise of spring, and Jim's front porch was already loaded with the pots of herbs he'd eventually bring into the restaurant. As I neared the front door, I could see fresh young sprouts popping out of the soil.

I also saw something else I wasn't used to seeing at Jim's house.

Toys. Lots of them.

I threaded my way between a pink tricycle and a wagon filled with stuffed animals. I stepped over two discarded jump ropes, a hot pink beach ball, and a Barbie who was dressed in a black sequined gown that looked as if it cost as much as the clothes I was wearing.

I raised my hand to press the doorbell, but I guess Jim must have seen me coming. The door popped open, he stuck his head out, and I was hit by a wave of the most atrocious sounds I have ever heard. Hip-hop music and wailing, high-pitched children's voices. All at once and each vying to be heard over the others.

"Thank God you're here." Jim's hair was mussed. His cheeks were ashen. He stepped onto the porch and closed the door behind him. The noise was muffled except for the deep, pounding bass of the music. "You've got to help me, Annie. You've got to save me."

I looked beyond him, but with the door closed, there was nothing I could see. "From your cousin?"

"From my cousin. From her children. They're hellions, Annie. They're driving me barmy!"

By this time, Jim was clutching my sleeve, and one by

one, I plucked his fingers away. Remember that gorgeous blouse. I didn't want to wrinkle it.

Nor was I willing to be drawn into the panic that edged Jim's voice.

"They've only been here twenty-four hours," I reminded him, even though I suspected I didn't have to. "How much trouble can a couple of kids be?"

"Couple?" He fixed his glassy eyes to mine. "You've no idea what you're talking about," he said. His accent was nearly indecipherable, and I knew we were in serious trouble. When Jim's feeling emotional—about anything—his accent gets as thick as Scottish beef and barley soup. "There are hordes of them, Annie. And Cousin Fi—"

Just as he said this, the front door opened, and a woman stepped out onto the porch. Cousin Fi was in her thirties. She was as short as I am, with flaming red hair that was even curlier than mine, a face that was covered in freckles, and blue eyes that at that moment were rimmed with red and as puffy as if she'd spent the entire day crying.

She was also pregnant.

Really pregnant.

"Fiona!" This wasn't exactly what I was expecting, so I hid my surprise by sticking out my hand and grabbing hers. I wasn't sure what else to do, and the way things were looking, I didn't think Jim would make the move to introduce us. I was pretty sure he was in shock. "I'm Annie. It's so nice to meet you."

"It's . . . nice . . . to . . . meet . . ." Fi sniffled and dragged a tissue out of her pocket. "It's nice to meet you, too!" she wailed. Right before she turned and raced back into the house.

"It's a curse, to be sure," Jim mumbled. "It's a punishment for something I did wrong in another life. Or a message from on high reminding me what a hell-raiser I was as a child. Mum always said it would come back to haunt me."

"It's hormonal," I told him. "Come on, Jim. The poor

woman must be miserable and uncomfortable. And I'm sure her hormones are going bonkers. When is that baby due?"

He shook his head. "I haven't asked. I don't want to know." He was hanging on to me like a limpet again. I wondered if I'd have bruises by morning. "You've got to help me, Annie."

"I can't." When Jim's mouth opened and his expression fell, I took pity on him and smiled. "Not until you let me into the house."

He opened the door, and once again, the wave of noise rose up and slapped me. I stepped over the threshold and straight into chaos.

There was a little girl jumping on the couch, and another little girl (a year or so older than the first), kicking a ball from the living room into the dining room. There were girls on the stairs, too, jockeying for position, elbowing each other and shrieking like little banshees as they fought to see who could make it to the front of the pack to get the first look at me.

Like their mother, they were all redheaded and freckled. There were . . .

"One, two, three . . ." I counted under my breath. "Seven?"

"Seven." Jim nodded and closed his eyes. He didn't have to say a word. I knew when he opened them again, he was hoping it was all a dream. That they were all gone.

They weren't.

Fiona clapped her hands together, and the noise level dropped. A little.

"This is Jim's friend, Annie," she yelled. I couldn't blame her. If anyone was going to be heard above the din, yelling was imperative. Fiona blew her nose. "Introduce yourselves, girls."

"Emma," the girl on the couch said. She never stopped bouncing.

"Lucy," said the next, and she added emphasis to the name by kicking the ball as hard as she could. It hit the far wall of the dining room, bounced back into the living room, and Lucy squealed with delight.

"Doris, Gloria, Wendy, Rosemary, Alice."

The tumble of names came from the stairway along with the girls themselves, who gathered around me, talking all at once.

"Annie's going to help me with dinner." Jim didn't raise his voice when he said this. I suspect he knew there was no use. Instead, he latched on to my hand and dragged me into the kitchen. What's that saying about any port in a storm? It says something that I stepped into that room without the least bit of trepidation.

Jim closed the door behind us, muffling the noise.

"I haven't seen her in years," he explained, even though I hadn't asked for an explanation. "I didn't know she was bringing the girls. She never told me she was pregnant or that she's on the outs with her husband."

"That's awful." I felt a pang of sympathy for Fiona. No wonder she was so emotional. And no wonder I expected the worst. I was speaking from experience. "All those girls and her expecting another baby, and he dumped her? That no-good creep!"

"That no-good creep is a fine man as far as I know," Jim said. There was a pile of vegetables on the countertop, and he started chopping. "The story Fi tells—"

"Calling again." Cell phone in hand, Fiona pushed into the kitchen. She made a face at the number displayed on her phone, then clicked it off, even though it was still ringing. "The man is addlepated, that's for certain. Doesn't he know to leave me alone?"

"You want him to leave you alone?" It was none of my business, but at that point, it hardly seemed to matter. I'd been sucked into the whirlwind that was Fiona's life. I deserved some answers. "I thought—"

Fi rolled her eyes. "Insists on doing everything for me, the man does. The washing and the cleaning and the cooking." She sniffled and dabbed her eyes. "Doesn't he know that a woman . . ." She sobbed. "A woman needs to scrub her own floors. It's a personal thing: you understand that, Annie."

I understood that if I ever found a man who wanted to do the washing and the cleaning and the (gulp!) cooking, I'd love, honor, and cherish him forever. But that, of course, wasn't what Fi needed to hear.

"Her husband, Richard, was in the navy." Jim supplied this information, leaning in close and telling it to me as if it were a secret. "The U.S. Navy. They teach those fellows to clean, right enough. Fi and Richard met when she was on holiday and he was stationed in England. Now that he's out of the service, he and Fi and the children are living in Florida, and—"

"It's just not right," Fi wailed. "I want to stand on my own two feet. I want to wash my own floors!"

When she disappeared back into the dining room, the sounds of her weeping were lost in the chaos.

"I think some serious counseling is in order," I said to no one in particular. Since Jim was the only other person in the room, he's the one who answered.

"I couldn't agree more. But it's not something I bargained for. It isn't my job."

It wasn't what he said, it was the way he said it that brought me spinning around. I eyed him carefully, and yes, my voice was tight when I spoke. I couldn't help it: the general atmosphere of bedlam wasn't something I was used to. I could practically feel my blood pressure climbing. "Are you saying it's *my* job?"

It was the wrong question. It gave him the perfect opening. He latched on to my arm again. There was desperation in his hazel eyes.

"She's staying here, Annie. At least that's what she's threatened. She's staying here until she gets things straightened out with Richard, and with the mood she's in, who knows when that may be. I've lost my home and my privacy. I'm losing my mind. You wouldn'a do that to me, would you, Annie darlin'? You'll help me out. You'll take charge of Fi and the kids."

He didn't say it like it was a question, so I didn't bother to answer.

What could I say, anyway?

Once again, Jim had pushed me out of my comfort zone.

At least this time, he hadn't asked me to cook.

Seven

✖

I HAD SIX PERSONAL DAYS ACCUMULATED AT THE bank, and it should come as no surprise that I wasn't inclined to use them lightly. The unexpected happens, even in the most well-ordered life, and I hoarded my personal time the way I kept my cupboards stocked with extra jars of peanut butter and just-in-case chocolate bars. I never knew when I'd need them. I had to be prepared.

Even so, I hadn't forgotten all the things Jim had done for me since we met. In addition to keeping me alive in that hospital room, he'd also saved me from getting arrested in a back alley where I was (technically) trespassing. Cooking classes aside, he'd given me the opportunity to stretch my wings by putting me in charge of day-to-day business operations at Bellywasher's. Jim had confidence in me. He liked me. And of course, there was the whole hunky-Scotsman-honey-bunch thing.

The next Saturday, I took the day off and invited Fi and the girls to go with me to the National Zoo.

I will not elaborate on the details. Let's just say that from that day on, *zoo* had a whole new meaning for me. I listened to more whining than I hoped to ever hear again, sopped tears, and handed out tissues. And that was just for Fi.

The girls kept me hopping, too, running me from pillar to post (or more specifically, from panda bears to tiger cubs to ferrets and back again). I'd had fruit punch spilled on me and used the Heimlich manuever to get hamburger out of Wendy's throat.

When I finally got home, I was washed up, done in, and wrung out. My mood brightened when I found Eve waiting for me—until I heard why she was there.

"I finally convinced Valerie to back off and leave Brad to the pros. I told her all about you. You know, about what a great detective you are. She's really looking forward to talking to you. I know once you meet her, once you hear the whole story about her oppression beneath the claws of the Weasel, you'll change your mind, Annie. I know you'll do everything you can to investigate Brad and find something we can pin on him."

As promised, I'd already tried to investigate Brad. I found nothing at all, useful or otherwise. I'd already told Eve that and, silly me, I thought that was the end of the matter.

I didn't know she'd commit me to meeting with Valerie. I didn't know the meeting was scheduled for later that afternoon, before Eve had to get to Bellywasher's for the dinner crowd. I didn't know why I went along with it or why, less than an hour later, I found myself in Valerie's apartment. I could only chalk it all up to the fact that I was too tired to argue.

"I'm so glad you came." Valerie was tall and gorgeous. Her apartment was small and messy. She plucked a hooded sweatshirt off a chair and let it fall to the floor before she dropped down across from where Eve and I were perched on a love seat with mushy, uncomfortable cushions. "This just proves what WOW is all about and why it's so important. One sister connecting with another sister, and that sister connecting, and so on. I can't tell you how relieved I was when Eve told me you promised you'd help."

"Eve told you that, did she?" I slanted Eve a look. She pretended not to notice. "Did she tell you that I already tried? I spent some time searching online. You know, looking for information about Brad. I didn't find a thing."

"That's because he's so sneaky." This comment came from Eve. I would have pointed out how unreasonable it was if Valerie didn't latch right on to it.

"Not only sneaky, but evil and underhanded." Valerie's hands were on her lap. Her fingers curled into fists. "I hate that man. I wish he was dead."

Seemed to be a lot of that going around.

I shifted in my seat. This wasn't my business, and I didn't want to make it my business, but as long as I'd been sucked into it, I figured I might as well strike a blow for sanity. "It won't do any good to follow him," I told both Valerie and Eve. "You're not going to find out anything, and you're only going to make Brad angry. I saw you in Alexandria the other night, Valerie. I saw you two arguing. Where did that get you?"

Valerie jumped out of her seat. "It almost got me exactly what I wanted. I wanted Brad to get mad. I wanted him to confront me. I figured if I pushed him hard enough, he'd snap." She threw back her shoulders and lifted her chin. "That would give me the perfect excuse to pop him in the nose."

I scrubbed my face with my hands. I was talking logic. Eve and Valerie were speaking from pure emotion. There was no way we were ever going to understand each other. Of course, I tried, anyway. "A physical confrontation isn't going to get you anywhere, either," I pointed out, even though I shouldn't have had to. "Listen to yourself, Valerie. You've got to let this go. It's eating you up."

Valerie paced across the living room and back again. "Easy for you to say," she snarled. "That Weasel didn't ruin your life."

"No, he didn't, but—"

"But nothing!" There was a pillow on a nearby chair, and Valerie picked it up and chucked it across the room. She was a beautiful woman with clear skin and eyes as blue as the spring sky outside the window, but just now an unbecoming shadow darkened her features. "You want to know what a schmuck he is?" she asked, and I guess she figured I did, because she flopped into the chair across from mine again. "Brad used to be a journalist. Did you know that?"

"Which doesn't automatically make him dishonest."

"Of course not." For a second, Valerie's eyes cleared, and I saw the intelligent, sensible woman she could be if only she could keep the angry, bitter Valerie at bay. Her brows dropped over her eyes. "But that's not the whole story. A couple of years ago before he started working in retail, Brad was a reporter for the *Washington Star*. He didn't leave voluntarily."

I didn't *want* to care. Honest. But I was too exhausted to fight. Before I even knew it, I tipped my head, anxious to hear the rest of the story. "Fired? Because of sexual harassment?"

A satisfied smile brightened Valerie's expression. "Fired because he made up quotes and sources for an article he published," she said. "That pretty much proves it, doesn't it? It proves he's an underhanded Weasel."

There was nothing I wanted more than to get home, jump into bed, and pull the covers up over my head. I slumped back against the love seat. "Absolutely," I said because maybe if I went along with this whole Brad-as-Satan scenario, it would make both Valerie and Eve happy, and then I could leave. "Brad is underhanded. I couldn't agree more. But how did you find all that out, anyway? I didn't see anything online about Brad. And if you're investigating, why do you need me?"

"To follow up on all this." Valerie jumped out of her chair, went into another room, and came back holding a single sheet of paper, which she promptly handed to me.

"Phone numbers and names," I said, looking it over. "All female. I assume these are the women . . . er . . . sisters," I corrected myself because I didn't want to agitate Valerie further. "These are the sisters who Brad has done wrong."

She nodded. "Every single one of them."

I was tempted to say, *So what?* I might have, too, if Eve and Valerie weren't both looking at me as if I held the key that would crack the case that wasn't much of a case.

And if Eve, in her own little, sweet, Southern belle way, didn't add, "Think of it this way, Annie. It's your way of standing up for sisters everywhere. You know, in the name of the Weasel who ruined your life."

At least Eve didn't lay out the details of my failed marriage for Valerie to examine. Then again, maybe she didn't need to. The way Valerie looked at me—her eyes bright with the knowledge that we shared in the sisterhood—I had a feeling she already knew all about Peter.

"All right, I admit it!" I yawned when I said this, which pretty much took the enthusiasm level down a notch. That didn't stop both Eve and Valerie from scooting forward in their seats. "I am intrigued," I said. I tapped a finger against the paper Valerie had handed me. "All these women? All with a grudge against Brad? If they feel about him the way you two feel about him, I'm surprised someone hasn't fitted him for a pair of cement overshoes and dumped him into Chesapeake Bay." I hesitated before I asked the final question, but let's face it, committed is committed. And I'd already committed.

"What do you want me to do about it?" I asked.

"Now we're talking." Eve patted me on the back.

Valerie grinned. "We want you to do your detective magic," she said. "After everything Eve has told me about you, I know you can investigate anything. The way she describes you, you're Wonder Woman!"

Yeah, I must be.

Because right about then, I was wondering what I'd just gotten myself into.

* * *

I CAN'T CALL WHAT I HAD A PLAN. NOT EXACTLY, anyway. It was more of a planette, the germ of an idea that might—or might not—get us someplace.

Not that I knew where we were headed.

Or what we would do when we got there.

No matter. I had made a promise, and I never go back on my word. I spent the next day at home catching up on bills and laundry and coming up with a strategy of sorts. The day after, a Monday, I refined my planette. I was anxious to run it by Eve, but though I tried her phone a dozen times, there was no answer. Since Eve and her cell phone are never parted, this was odd, but I wasn't worried. Maybe Eve had met a new guy and had better things to do than talk to me. I hoped so. After everything she had been through in the romance department, she deserved a break.

With no sounding board, I was on my own, and over and over again, I practiced what I'd say to Brad in cooking class that night.

"Were you really fired from your job at the *Washington Star*?"

"Does that prove you're a dishonest creep who doesn't care who he steps on, on his way to the top?"

"How many women's lives have you ruined, and what do you intend to do about it?"

"Are you really a Weasel? I mean, come on, Brad, come clean. If you'd just write a letter of recommendation for every woman whose reputation you've trashed, you'd do a lot toward righting all these wrongs. Need a list? I just so happen to have one, right here."

I am not completely delusional. Even as I stood in the kitchen of Bellywasher's waiting for our students to arrive that evening, I realized I couldn't exactly come right out and say all that to Brad. Not in those words, anyway. But that didn't mean I couldn't be subtle about it.

I'd assigned Brad to drinks that night and paired him up

with Kegan again. I know, I know . . . I'd promised Kegan I wouldn't, so this really wasn't fair. Even though we went out for a drink after the last class, Kegan and Brad never really hit it off. Brad was loud and pushy. Kegan was jumpy and ill at ease. I was uncomfortable on his behalf and Marc, Damien, and Monsieur weren't any happier; they left as soon as they could.

I soothed my conscience by promising myself I'd make it up to Kegan and looked at the bright side. If I just so happened to stop by while they were working, on the pretense of talking to Kegan about the ideas he had for saving money for the restaurant . . .

If I just so happened to include Brad in the conversation and somehow come around to the topic of his background . . .

If I could only get him to fess up, then I could explain about the sisterhood that was gunning for him (not in those words, of course), and I might be able to help Eve and the other women of WOW.

The thought firmly in mind and my stomach doing backflips, I nodded hello to our students and waited for Brad to show up so I could put my plan in motion.

By five minutes to seven, he was still nowhere in sight.

And now that I thought about it, neither was Jim.

I had just decided to tell Marc and Damien that I was quitting and moving to a state far, far away so that I could not be conscripted into teaching another class when the kitchen door bumped open, and Jim stumbled into the room.

His hair was a mess. There were dark circles under his eyes. His clothes, usually so neat and clean, looked like they'd been slept in. I recognized the stain on the front of his shirt—fruit punch leaves a telltale sign. I didn't want to alarm the class, so when I hurried over to him, I kept my voice down.

"What on earth happened to you?" I grabbed his arm and dragged him to the far side of the kitchen, up against the walk-in cooler where no one could hear us. "You look awful!"

"You're an angel for taking them to the zoo on Saturday." Jim kissed my cheek. "Can they live with you?"

I would have laughed if he was kidding.

"No chance of them leaving anytime soon, huh? And no sign of Richard?"

Jim sighed. "Fi's husband calls. Ten, maybe twelve times a day. She refuses to pick up the phone. Then again, it's a wonder anyone can hear her phone ringing at all. Between her bawling and those horrid children . . ." A shiver snaked over his broad shoulders. "I'm not getting a wink of sleep. If they can't live with you, can I?"

Time and again over the course of our relationship, I had imagined the knee-melting, heart-pounding, blood-sizzling way Jim might someday ask me about cohabitation. This was not it.

"Marc and Damien have everything set up," I said instead. I grabbed an apron hanging on a nearby hook and looped it over Jim's head. Before he could object, I reached around him and tied the apron behind his back. While I was at it, I gave him a hug. "Time to get going."

Just as I expected, nothing gets a chef's mind off his own troubles and back on task like the mention of work.

One look at the mound of shrimp set up on the worktable along with all the spices for tonight's marinade, and Jim shook off his stupor. Back in full kitchen mode and ready to roll, he looked around the kitchen. "Everyone's here but Brad," he said. "You've got him and Kegan on drinks, right? Would you mind helping the lad? Not that he couldn't handle things on his own, but we're making Bloody Marys tonight, and they can be a bit tricky. He strikes me as a bit of a klutz."

I'd take mixing Bloody Marys over the chance of getting asked to stand in front of the class and help Jim any day. I didn't wait around long enough for him to change his mind.

I hurried over to Kegan's workstation, and he welcomed me with a cautious smile.

He was dressed in the same wrinkled khakis and a navy sweater that had a hole in one elbow. His dark hair had been trimmed since last I'd seen him. "This is perfect," he said. "I'd much rather work with you than with Brad."

It's not like I missed Brad or anything, but since I'd screwed up the courage to talk to him about his past and his dirty dealings with the Weasel bashers, I was anxious to get it over with. I glanced at the door, hoping to see him stride into the kitchen. When he didn't, I shrugged. "Maybe he just forgot about class."

"I don't think so."

This comment came from Marc, who was handing out the night's recipes. He slid two packets of papers onto the table in front of us. "Brad stopped in Saturday afternoon. He said he forgot what he was supposed to bring to to-night's class. We were slammed, no way anybody had time to help him. I just told him to come into the kitchen and showed him the bulletin board where Jim hangs the recipes and the instructions. I'll tell you what, we were so busy that afternoon, we didn't know which end was up. I don't even know how long he was here. All I know is that last I saw him, Brad was writing down the list of things he was sup-posed to bring tonight."

"Celery salt, tomato juice, Tabasco." Reading from his own list, Kegan emptied his cotton market bag. There was already a bunch of crisp, green celery on the table, and he laid a hand on it. "It's just as well Brad isn't here. I'll bet he didn't buy organic celery."

"I'll bet he didn't, either. But still . . ." Against my better judgment, I'd promised Eve and Valerie that I'd investigate Brad. That didn't mean I was comfortable with the situa-tion. Or that I'd ever talk myself into doing it again. I looked at the door one more time and whispered words I thought I'd never hear myself say: "Come on, let's get this over with. Get in here, Brad."

And for one, incredible moment, I thought my fervent prayer had actually worked. The kitchen door swung open, and a man swaggered into the room.

It took only a second for me to realize it was the wrong swagger. And this was definitely the wrong man.

Oh yeah, right then and there, I knew those weren't the only things that were wrong.

Because the man who walked into Bellywasher's kitchen that night was none other than Tyler Cooper.

 HERE'S THE READER'S DIGEST CONDENSED VERSION of the whole, ugly story.

Eve used to be engaged to Tyler. This isn't any big news, of course, because over the years, Eve's been engaged to a lot of guys (including the senator who tried to kill us). I have any number of unworn matron of honor gowns in the back of my closet to prove it. But I digress.

The big deal about Eve and Tyler's engagement is that, unlike all those other engagements and not counting the fiancé who wanted us dead, Eve isn't the one who broke it off. Tyler broke up with her. And believe me, it wasn't pretty.

Since then, we'd heard through the grapevine that Tyler was engaged again, this time to a woman named Kaitlin Sands. Eve pretends not to care, but remember, I'd known Eve since the day in kindergarten when we were assigned to be each other's bathroom buddy. She might talk the talk, but she didn't walk the walk. Not when it came to Tyler.

Tyler Cooper was Eve's own personal human version of poison ivy. He was in her system, and until she found the right antidote, the itch would never go away.

One look at Tyler sent all of those thoughts spinning through my head, along with the realization that I was glad Eve wasn't anywhere near the restaurant that night. Until I realized that Tyler Cooper—Lieutenant Tyler Cooper of the Arlington Police Department—didn't have any reason to be barging into a cooking class in Alexandria.

Not unless something was wrong.

In one, heart-stopping instant, I remembered all those phone calls I'd made to Eve earlier in the day, and all the times she hadn't answered the phone. My mouth went dry. There was a lump in my throat. I was up at the front of the room even before the kitchen door stopped swinging and—who could blame me—I didn't bother with the niceties. I was suddenly too nervous, and besides, when it came to nice, Tyler didn't know the meaning of the word.

"What happened?" I asked him. "What's wrong?"

I hadn't seen Tyler since we did the final wrap-up of our investigation into Sarah Whitaker's murder. He didn't look any happier now than he had been then. Then, the fact that I'd out-investigated him and solved a murder he couldn't had soured his already acid personality even more. Now . . .

"Miss Capshaw." The way Tyler said it and the way he tipped his head in my direction wasn't so much a greeting as it was simply his way of saying that seeing me again was his cross to bear. "I can't say I'm surprised to find myself here again. There's something about you and dead bodies—"

Dead?

The word sank way down deep into me and froze me from the inside out. But before I had a chance to ask what he was talking about—who he was talking about—Tyler turned toward Jim. "Can we talk somewhere? Privately?"

"Sure." Jim wiped his hands on a kitchen towel, turned the class over to Damien, and assured our students (who were more than a little curious) that he'd be right back. "We can go out into the restaurant." He led the way.

Tyler didn't follow. He couldn't, because I was still hanging on to him.

"Looks like you're coming, too," he said.

"I am. I will." My blood was rushing so hard and so fast inside my ears, I could barely hear my own voice. "Only tell me, is it Eve? Did something . . . did something happen to Eve?"

"Miss DeCateur?" In as long as I'd known him, I don't think I'd ever seen Tyler smile. He didn't smile now. He sort of smirked. "Why, I haven't thought of Eve in months. You really don't think I'd come all the way over here from Arlington to talk about her, do you?"

I let go the breath I hadn't realized I was holding. Until another thought hit. "But if it's not Eve, why are you here?" I did a quick mental inventory. Jim was alive and well, thank goodness. So were Marc, Damien, and Monsieur Lavoie. I'd talked to Heidi, our only waitress, about a glitch in her paycheck earlier in the day, so I knew there was no reason Tyler would be here about her. That only left—

"Brad?" OK, the name came out of me a little too loud. As if they'd choreographed the move, our students leaned forward.

When he saw them staring, Tyler rolled his eyes. "That's right," he said and because he realized that whatever he wanted to say in private wasn't going to be private much longer, he raised his voice. "It's Brad Peterson I'm here about. I'll talk to you all about him in a bit, when I'm done with Miss Capshaw here. Just so you know: Mr. Peterson, he's not just dead. Heck, that would be too bad, but it wouldn't be any of my business. This is. You see, this morning Brad Peterson was murdered."

Eight

 THERE IS SOMETHING ABOUT THE WORD *MURDER* that demands attention.

It certainly got mine. My stomach went cold, and my breath caught. I'd be the first to admit that Brad Peterson was no prize, but to think he'd been killed . . .

The shock hit and, like a rock tossed into a deep pool, it caused a ripple of awareness that shivered through me along with thoughts I barely dared to consider.

I wrapped my arms around myself and listened to Jim's voice echo through my head as he told the class we'd be stepping out for a few minutes and that they should get busy with the night's recipes. But even when he put an arm around my shoulders and tugged me toward the door, I found it hard to move. My memories kept me frozen to the spot.

Valerie Conover said she wished that Brad was dead. So did Eve.

Now he was.

And Tyler was here at Bellywasher's asking questions.

I tried to gulp down the sour taste in my mouth. Until I had time to think through everything that had happened and listen to whatever it was Tyler had come to talk about, I had to be careful. I knew Tyler well, and I knew that one mispoken word would send him chasing off in the wrong direction. Not that I cared a whole bunch. Unless that direction happened to be toward Eve. Until I knew what he was up to and why he was there, I had to play my cards close to my chest.

Easy to say. Not so easy to do when I found Tyler watching me closely. OK, I knew he couldn't read my mind. But Tyler's got those cold, neon blue eyes. That square, chipped-from-granite chin. That etched-in-stone expression that never wavers, the one that just about screams, *If you think you can get away with anything, you're crazy.*

I've got Eve, I reminded myself, and Eve is the best friend in the world. She's the kindest, gentlest soul I know, and yes, she can get a little operatic now and again, but unless someone did something to hurt Doc—or me—there's no way she'd ever resort to violence. Not even where a Weasel was concerned.

I knew this as certainly as I knew my own name, and I told myself not to forget it, pulled back my shoulders, and walked out of the kitchen at Jim's side. He might be the one in charge, but the way I saw things, I had the most at stake here (namely, one best friend). I was also the one with the insatiable curiosity, not to mention something of a background in this sort of thing. Before Jim could say a word, and before Tyler could take over and manuever the conversation where I didn't want it to go, I slid onto a barstool and got down to business.

"What happened?" I asked Tyler.

"I'm the one who's supposed to ask the questions."

Didn't it figure. If I expected that Tyler would ever cooperate, I was kidding myself. He looked down his Roman nose at me. "I'm following a lead, chasing down some details. I can't say it's a big surprise that they led me here."

No big surprise, huh? As in, *You, Annie Capshaw, are*

involved in murder far too often? Or as in, *I know Eve had it in for Brad*?

Tyler sent a laser look around the restaurant. "No Miss DeCateur tonight?"

It was a good thing Jim answered, because at this mention of Eve's name, my tongue stuck to the roof of my mouth. "We're closed on Mondays," he said. "So naturally Eve is off. She doesn't help with our cooking classes. If you like, I can tell her you sent your best."

Big points for Jim. When it came to Eve and Tyler, he knew what was what. He also knew that Tyler wasn't going to bite. At least not until hell froze over.

Just as I expected, Tyler ignored the offer. "When did this cooking class start?" he asked, and though I think the question was meant for Jim, I stepped up with the answer.

"This is the third class. Out of eight."

"And Brad Peterson?"

I shrugged. "He's not a very good cook. And he hates doing the flower arrangements."

"Which isn't what I meant." Tyler took a small, leatherbound notebook from his pocket, flipped it open, and reached for a pen. "Did you ever meet him before?"

Jim and I exchanged looks. "Not until he walked in here the first night," Jim said.

Tyler's gaze swiveled to me. "And you?"

"Never set eyes on him before."

True, even though it was technically not the whole truth and nothing but. Tyler never asked if I'd heard about Brad, so I didn't have to say that Eve had once worked for him. He didn't ask if I'd seen Brad between classes, so I never had to tell him about the day Brad was out on the street arguing with Valerie. At least until I understood more about what had happened and why Tyler was here, he was on a need-to-know basis. This, he definitely didn't need to know.

"How about the other members of the class?" Tyler asked. "Think anyone will be able to give me any information?"

Again, I was home free in the truth department. Since Tyler had specifically asked about members of the class and neither Eve nor Valerie was in the class, it was easy to dodge this particular bullet. "A group of us went out for drinks after class last week, including Brad and Kegan," I told him. Knowing Tyler, he was going to find out eventually, anyway, and it was better if he heard it from me. "Kegan is Kegan O'Rouke, the tall, skinny kid who's in charge of drinks tonight. If you ask him, I'm sure he'll say the same thing about the experience that I do. Brad was loud and pushy and rude to our waitress. He didn't talk about anything but himself. He practically put me to sleep babbling about the years he lived in Colorado. It was boring, and I was uncomfortable. I could tell Kegan was, too. We had one drink and hightailed it out of there. Last I saw him, Brad was trying to pick up the waitress, and he wasn't having any luck."

"And you haven't seen him since?"

"I haven't. But Marc told me that Brad stopped in last Saturday. He came by to get the list of ingredients for tonight's class. I guess you were busy." I turned to Jim, because as far as I knew, he wasn't aware of Brad's visit. "Marc says Brad copied the list and left."

"And you can be sure I'll confirm that with this Marc guy." Tyler made a note of it. He flipped his notebook closed.

I should have breathed a sigh of relief and left well enough alone; Tyler wasn't going to ask about Eve or WOW or Valerie Conover. But remember what I said about insatiable curiosity? I couldn't help myself: the whole situation was peculiar, and I had to know more.

"I don't get it," I admitted. "How did you even know that Brad was a student here?"

If not for the memory of those murder investigations I'd conducted—cases Tyler never would have closed if not for my help—I think he would have brushed off my question. Instead, he gave me a begrudging look. "You wouldn't believe me if I told you that the police know everything, would you?"

"Of course not." I slipped into private investigator mode even before I realized it and stepped through what must have been Tyler's thinking process. "If you found that list of drink ingredients in his apartment, it wouldn't tell you a thing except that he was making Bloody Marys. And Brad couldn't have been killed anywhere near here, because we're in Alexandria, and you're on the Arlington force. That means you're not just checking with the locals up and down the street to see if anyone can help. He was killed in Arlington which, the way I remember it from his class application, was were he lived. So what was it . . . one of our newsletters left in his kitchen? Or maybe a receipt?" I saw the momentary flash in Tyler's eyes, and I knew I hit on the right answer. "You found a receipt for the class. In his apartment, right?"

"Got you there." There was a little too much satisfaction in Tyler's voice and in the tiny smile that played around the corners of his mouth. "Mr. Peterson didn't have an apartment. He lived in a town house. Over near the Clarendon Metro station. That's where we found the receipt."

"In his town house."

"At the Metro station." Tyler had already turned to head back into the kitchen, but I wasn't going to let him cut me off so soon or so completely. There was still plenty I wanted to know.

I slid off the barstool and stood in his path.

"You found the receipt for Brad's cooking class at the Metro station? That doesn't make a whole lot of sense."

"It does if the receipt was in Brad's pocket. Or should I say, the receipt was in what was left of his pocket."

I didn't like the sound of that. While I thought it over, I stood there at a loss for words. Of course, that's the reaction Tyler was hoping he'd get out of me: dazed and confused. That's why he left the information dangling.

He didn't expect me to, but it's also exactly why I bit.

"What was left? That must mean there was some kind of accident. But you said he was murdered. Are you sure?"

As long as I'd known him, Tyler had never been Mr. Open-and-Sharing. It was one of the things that made him such a good cop and such a bad everything else. But since I hadn't cringed at that *what was left* comment, I guess he figured he owed me the details.

"He died at the Clarendon Metro station, all right. But it wasn't an accident," Tyler said. "Somebody pushed Brad Peterson off the platform. Just as the nine o'clock train was pulling in."

I tried not to picture the scene. It wasn't easy. I knew the station well, and I could imagine the press of early morning commuters, the surge forward as the train approached. I shook my head.

"Like I said, it must have been an accident." I could see no other explanation. "Why do you think—"

"Kind of hard to avoid the facts. And the tape from the security camera . . . well, I'll tell you what. I don't think that's anything you could stomach, Annie, but it is one cold, hard fact."

Jim must have sensed that I felt light-headed. He rubbed my back with one hand and asked what I would have asked, if only I wasn't imaging what had happened and feeling a little queasy because of it.

Jim nodded thoughtfully. "You've got the murder on tape, then. That must make your job easier. Why come around looking for details if you know who did it?"

Tyler's smile was sleek. "We've got the murder, all right. But not the murderer. The tape shows a person in a beat-up hoodie who follows Brad into the station. That same person stands behind Brad and shuffles forward a little at a time. When Brad is close to the edge of the platform . . ." His palms flat, Tyler pushed both his hands out in front of him. "By the time the police got there in response to the frantic calls from the people waiting for the train, it was too late. Brad Peterson was dead, the hooded sweatshirt was in the nearest trash can, and now here I am, following one of the threads of my investigation. I'll just take a couple minutes and talk to the people in your class." He didn't ask permission for this, just edged past me and went into the kitchen. "While I'm here, I might as well find out all I can."

It was too late to stop him, and what was the point, anyway? Tyler got what Tyler wanted. He had the badge to make sure of it.

The closer we got to the kitchen, the more we heard the excited buzz of conversation. No big mystery what everyone was talking about. I heard Brad's name mentioned and someone say, "He wasn't such a bad guy."

Obviously, it was someone who didn't know Brad well.

The moment we stepped into the room, the place went dead silent.

Tyler waved a dismissive hand toward the class. "You can continue doing what you were doing. I'm going to come around to talk to each one of you. Anything you can tell me will be helpful."

Margaret Whitemore had been deep in conversation with Jorge and Kegan. She turned toward the door and wiped her hands on her apron. Don't ask me how I knew she was going to say something she shouldn't; just believe me when I say I saw it coming. Otherwise, my heart wouldn't have banged like a pile driver. My knees wouldn't have turned to jelly. Before I could come up with a way to stop her, Margaret stepped forward.

"We've been talking about it, of course," she said. She looked around the room to include her fellow students. "And we've decided that you don't need to take your time to talk to each of us. We can help you right now. We know who did it, you see." As if she was giving a presentation, Margaret clutched her hands together at her waist. "It was that Eve girl. The one who was here the first night of class. You remember . . . all of you . . ." She looked around, and as one, the students nodded. "It must have been Eve. She knew Brad, and she came right out and said it. She said she wanted him dead."

"DON'T BE SO HARD ON YOURSELF. I KNEW EVE AND Brad Peterson were acquainted before I ever walked in here."

I suppose Tyler was trying to make me feel better when he patted me on the back.

It didn't work.

When our students were finished cooking—and done telling Tyler everything they remembered about Eve's appearance at class that first night—I volunteered to stay in the kitchen and clean up. I was less than thrilled when Tyler stayed with me.

I slanted him a look. "You could have told me right from the start."

He grinned. "What fun would that be? Besides, I was interested to see how far you would go to stick up for a friend. Are you willing to go all the way to prison for Eve?"

"That's ridiculous." It was, and I reminded myself not to forget it and not to get bullied into believing anything else. That was the only thing that kept me from collapsing beneath the weight of my worries. "You know Eve would never kill anybody."

"I know that normally, Miss DeCateur wouldn't be inclined to kill. But if she had a strong motive . . ." He whistled low under his breath. "There's no telling what a girl like that would do if she felt she'd been wronged."

"She didn't kill you when you broke up with her."

"Oo-wee!" Tyler threw back his head and laughed. "You have changed from the days when Miss DeCateur and I were seeing each other. You wouldn't have dared speak up like that back then. Maybe that's because you had a husband around then to keep you in line, huh?"

With a nasty look, I warned Tyler to back down. Just in case he didn't get the message, I was sure to tell him loud and clear. "You're not doing anything to endear yourself to me. If you expect me to help you with this case—"

"Hold on. Right there." Tyler was a traffic cop when he first joined the force, and I guess old habits die hard. He held up one hand to stop me. "You don't actually think I'm here to ask for your help, do you?"

"There's no other reason. It certainly can't be because of Eve. She'd never resort to violence, and you know it."

Tyler leaned in close. "Not even when Brad Peterson made it impossible for her to get that job she really wanted?"

So Tyler knew about that.

I shrugged like it was no big deal. I hoped it looked more convincing to him than it felt to me. "She's way over that," I said. "She told me just the other day that she realized that if she had gotten the job in that boutique, she wouldn't be working here. She said Bellywasher's is the best thing that ever happened to her, and she wouldn't trade it for anything. So you see, Brad Peterson did her a favor."

"Uh-huh. That's why . . ." Tyler had his notebook tucked in his pocket, and he took it out and opened it. He flipped through a few pages before he found what he was looking for. "Ah, here it is. You say Brad Peterson did Eve a favor. Is that why on Monday, just two weeks ago, she raced into the kitchen here, pointed a finger at the man, and told him that if she had a gun, she'd shoot him dead?"

I didn't appreciate Tyler's smile, and I glared at him just so he didn't get the idea that I did. "That's not the way it happened, and you know it," I told him.

"Then how did it happen?"

I shrugged again. This time because I knew there was no avoiding the truth. "She walked in here, yes. And she was surprised to see him. That's all. She spoke in the heat of the moment."

"Only she didn't threaten him until after class was over and the students were eating. And that was what, an hour or two later? Hardly the heat of the moment."

"She didn't threaten him at all." I'd had it with standing still and listening to Tyler vilify Eve. I grabbed a nearby towel, wet it at the sink, and went from workstation to workstation, removing the pans and utensils the students had used, carrying them to the sink, then wiping off each table. "All she said was—"

"I hate his guts. I wish he was dead. He's going to be sorry he was ever born." Tyler read through the witness statements our students had given.

I was wringing out my cleaning cloth and I leaned against the sink, my back to Tyler. "Actually, it was, 'I'd like to kill that man.' "

"Got that one a few times, too," he replied. "Since I heard it from a couple different people, I figured that was the one closest to what she actually said."

"And you know it doesn't mean a thing." I tossed down the rag and spun to face him. "People say angry things all the time. That doesn't mean anything."

"Not when the people they say angry things about go right on living. But when they're murdered . . . well, that's a whole different story, isn't it?"

"It is. But come on, Tyler, think about it." I scrambled for anything I could come up with and hit upon it in one aha moment. My eyes lit, and for the first time since Tyler had butted his way into our cooking class, I smiled. "It couldn't have been Eve," I told him. "And you know that as well as I do."

"I do?"

"You do. Because you know Eve as well as I do. Or almost as well. When was the last time you saw her, Tyler? Whenever it was, I'll bet she was dressed as if she just stepped out of the latest issue of *Vogue*. She's always dressed that way. Eve would never be caught dead in a hoodie, beat up or otherwise."

It was a brilliant deduction, and Tyler could have done more to acknowledge that than laugh. When he was done (it took him a while), he bent forward and looked me in the eye. "That's the whole point," he said. "When people don't want other people to know who they are, they wear something people don't usually see them wear. That's why it works. That's why it's called a disguise."

At the mention of the word, did I gulp as loud as I thought I did?

Maybe not, because Tyler didn't seem to notice.

He didn't mention Penelope Cruz wigs or sunglasses, either. For this, I was grateful. Instead, he asked, "When did you last talk to Eve?"

I thought back to all my unanswered phone calls. "Yesterday," I said, meeting his look eye to eye just so he didn't think I had anything to hide. "We talk every day."

"But not today."

"I've been at work at the bank all day. I just got here before class started. Eve had things to do today. It's her day off."

"And you haven't talked to her."

"No. Not yet. I will."

"Have you tried calling?"

"Yes, I did." I raised my chin. "And I left her messages, but she hasn't returned them yet. And you know what that proves, Tyler? Absolutely nothing. Except that she's busy."

"Busy doing what? That's the question."

I'd had enough. I turned the water back on, rinsed my cleaning rag, and went over to the table where Marc and Damien did tonight's cooking demonstration. They were chefs, not dishwashers (at least not unless we desperately needed them to be); they left the table a mess. I set the rag down and started stacking measuring cups and spoons in the big pottery bowl Jim had pulled out of the storage closet for marinating the shrimp. I am not usually the type to abandon a friend in need, and I felt guilty for even thinking what I was thinking. Until I reminded myself that Valerie Conover wasn't a friend. And Eve really needed me.

I lifted the bowl and cradled it in my arms. "Eve isn't

the only one who had it in for Brad," I said. "If you know what Brad did to Eve, you probably know that, too."

Tyler tipped his head, encouraging me to say more.

"There's this whole group, Women Against Weasels, and—"

"Weasels?" Leave it to Tyler to find another place to laugh inappropriately. "You're kidding me, right?"

"I'm telling you what you need to know in order to find out who really killed Brad Peterson. There are other sisters . . . er, women in the group who hold a grudge against Brad. I've got a list, if you're interested."

"Only if they're all blondes."

Tyler can be a sexist pig with the best of them, but this was over the top, even for him. I pinned him with a look that he defended with a roll of his eyes.

"Just doing my job," he said. "Not making any remarks about the way any woman looks. How many of them are blondes do you suppose? You know, like Eve?"

I have to admit, at this point, I didn't see where he was going. Because I'm inherently honest, I think everyone else is, too. Mistake number one. I figured that because I was willing to be up front with Tyler, he'd return the favor.

I should have known better.

"I can't possibly say which ones are blondes and which aren't. I've only met one of them." I thought back to our visit to Valerie Conover's apartment. I remembered how messy it was and how before she sat down, Valerie had plucked a sweatshirt off the chair. I grasped at the straw of this information and refused to let go. "One of them is named Valerie Conover," I told Tyler. "And I know for a fact that she owns a hoodie. I saw it in her apartment."

He was interested in spite of himself. "And is she a blonde?"

I nodded. "You want to tell me what difference it makes?"

Tyler scribbled something in his notepad before he answered. "Makes a huge difference," he said. He turned and pushed open the door that led into the restaurant. "Because you see, that hooded sweatshirt our perp wore on the secu-rity tape, the sweatshirt we found in a trash can? There wasn't a speck of forensic evidence on it that anyone could see. Not a speck. Except for one long, sleek and shiny blond hair. You know, just like Eve's."

Nine

❖

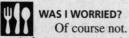 **WAS I WORRIED?**
Of course not.
At least not too much, anyway.

Tyler was nothing but bluster, and the evidence he claimed to have . . . well, it didn't really prove much, did it? At least not when it came to Eve. Besides, like I said, Eve didn't have a felonious bone in her body and not one unkind thought in her head. Not one she'd act on, anyway.

Then again, Tyler did mention that the murderer was disguised. And lately, Eve was all about disguises.

I banished the thought with a shake of my head and quickened my steps. It was a soft spring evening, and it seemed like everyone within walking, driving, and flying distance of Alexandria was taking advantage of it. The streets of Old Town were packed with shoppers, gawkers, and folks out for a stroll, and parking (bad, even on good days) was at a minimum. The only spot I could find was blocks away from Bellywasher's and, anxious to get there, I sidestepped around a group of tourists taking a photo in front of the local McDonald's and hurried on.

It was the day after Tyler had been to Bellywasher's to

question us and, being a Tuesday, Bellywasher's was open for business. Of course, being a Tuesday, I had to work my day job at Pioneer Savings and Loan, and since it was the middle of the month, we were slammed with the Social Security crowd. I didn't have a minute to myself and no chance to call Eve.

And she'd never returned my calls from the day before.

My steps drifted to a stop as I mulled over that fact. The surge of people walking behind me parted to get past, mumbled their displeasure, and walked on while I stared at my own thoughtful reflection in the window of a buritto place.

Why hadn't Eve returned my calls?

What had she been up to yesterday?

She couldn't . . . she wouldn't . . . she didn't have anything to do with Brad Peterson's death. Did she?

There was only one way to find out.

My mind made up, I started toward Bellywasher's again. The sooner I got there, the sooner I could finally talk to Eve, and the sooner I did that, the sooner I'd put my fears to rest.

Except that I never counted on Bellywasher's being packed.

I squeezed through the front door and deflected the angry looks of the people waiting in line with a quick smile and an, "I work here, honest." I waved to Jim, who was behind the bar mixing a frozen margarita, and got out of Heidi's way—fast—when she jetted out of the kitchen with a loaded tray of food on one shoulder. Eve was just seating a group of eight at our biggest table near the front window, so I ducked into my office and kept an eye on her. As soon as she was done, I waved her in.

"Can't. Not right now." Eve glanced at the line of people still waiting to be seated, and I knew she was right. My curiosity might be killing me, but business came first.

Keeping the thought firmly in mind, I got down to my own business, going over the day's invoices, preparing a deposit slip for the afternoon's receipts, and darting into the kitchen just long enough to stay out of everybody's way while I made sure the linens we'd ordered had arrived before I cut a check to pay for them.

By the time I was done, I figured the crowd would have cleared.

Wrong.

When I peeked out the door, the restaurant was just as busy as ever, and patrons were three deep at the bar. One of them was Kegan. When he saw me, his face lit, and he wound his way through the crowd and came over to my office.

He was dressed in jeans and an untucked oxford shirt. The sleeves were pushed above his elbows. The buttons were done up wrong so that the shirt hung longer on one side than the other. I was all about neat-as-a-pin, but the disheveled look worked for Kegan. Something about it emphasized his little-boy charm.

"I didn't want to bother you," he said. "Not when I saw that your office door was closed. I hope you don't mind that I stopped in."

"Of course not." I held the door open so that he could step into my office. "Sorry about the mess." My office wasn't messy at all, at least not by most people's standards, but I was self-conscious about the to-be-filed pile that sat on one corner of my desk. These days, it was starting to resemble Mount Everest. Filing was something I used to save for Monday evenings when there was no one around and I had the luxury of taking my time and making sure everything was done just right. Since cooking classes had started and I'd been conscripted into helping, my time was at as much of a premium as the parking outside.

Kegan had a glass of Pepsi in his hands, which he juggled as he asked permission before sitting down in my guest chair. "I didn't have a chance to talk to you much yesterday. I mean, not with the excitement and all." He didn't elaborate. He didn't have to. I knew exactly which excitement he was talking about, and believe me, it had nothing to do with marinated shrimp. A shiver snaked over his scrubby shoulders. "I can't stop thinking about it. Brad wasn't easy to get along with, but picturing what must have happened to him . . ." He offered me an apologetic smile. "I'm sorry. It's probably no easier for you to deal with this than it is for me. I'll bet you're trying not to picture it, either."

"You got that right." I sat in my desk chair. "Good thing our involvement in the whole thing is over. Not that I'm callous or anything," I added, because of course, that's exactly how I sounded. "I mean, if he has one, I feel terrible for Brad's family, and it's always sad to think about a life cut too short. But other than that . . . well, at least we can put the matter behind us."

"Unless that detective was right, and your friend had something to do with Brad's dying."

I guess the look I shot Kegan was more pointed than I realized. His cheeks turned a shade of red that reminded me of the Cabernet Jim bought from a vineyard in Barboursville. The next second, every bit of color drained out of his face. "I'm so sorry. I didn't mean to upset you." He clutched his glass in both hands. "I was just thinking . . . you know . . . I mean, that detective, he seemed awfully interested in what people remembered about the first night of class. You know . . ." Now that he'd begun, Kegan knew he had to finish what he was saying, but that didn't make it any easier for him. He rushed through the rest of it, his voice so low, I could barely hear it. "About how your friend, Eve, said she wanted to kill Brad."

"The only thing Tyler is interested in is making Eve's life difficult." I felt duty-bound to point this out, since Kegan didn't know the ins and outs of the whole, ugly Eve/Tyler soap opera. "Trust me, there's no way he believes what he heard. He knows Eve better than that."

Kegan's expression cleared. "I'm so glad. I like Eve. I was talking to her earlier. I was here for a while, then left to run some errands. I just came back a bit ago. Anyway, when I was here the first time, it wasn't so busy. Eve was telling me all about how you're a detective, too. She said she was sure you could solve this case."

"She's wrong." I didn't mean to slap my hand against my desk to emphasize my point; it just sort of happened. It wasn't like me to display so much emotion, and I was embarrassed. I crossed my arms over my chest. "I'm leaving this one up to the professionals."

Kegan took a drink. He studied me over the rim of his glass. "That's what Eve said you'd say."

"Eve remembers what it's like to be shot at. She hasn't forgotten the feeling of having a giant flower arrangement rigged to come down on us, either. She's a smart woman."

"She also said that you're really good at being a detective. She called it your gift. She said you'd solved two cases that the police never would have cracked on their own. She told me about the gun smugglers and that whole thing about the senator and his daughter-in-law. I remember reading about that in the papers, of course. It was a huge scandal! I just didn't know you were involved. Talking to you is like talking to a celebrity. Or a crime-solving genius. You know, like Sherlock Holmes."

Yeah, I was flattered. But I am also practical down to the tips of my toes. And practical people do not allow their heads to be turned so easily. "Hardly," I told Kegan. "We helped out the cops, sure, but it just sort of happened. It's over and done with. It's not like I've hung out a shingle and I'm looking for new cases."

"Even if Eve is in trouble?"

Kegan's question so closely resembled the one that had been pounding through my head all day, I had no choice but to stop and consider it. No matter how much I would have preferred not to.

"Eve's not in trouble. She didn't do it." Did I say this to convince Kegan or to soothe my own conscience? From out in the restaurant, I heard Jim's voice as he called to Marc to bring more ice out to the bar. "Besides, he hates it when I investigate."

I didn't realize I'd said the words out loud until Kegan responded. "You mean Jim. So, I was right! I figured you two had a thing going. I mean, just watching you together . . . well, it's pretty obvious. Pardon me for sticking my nose where it doesn't belong, but he doesn't seem like one of those macho, overbearing cavemen guys."

For the second time in as many minutes, I was embarrassed. I wasn't the type who discussed personal matters with strangers. Still, Kegan had a way of making me feel comfortable. Though we hadn't known each other long, I already thought of him as a friend. "Jim isn't overbearing," I told him. "What he is, is overprotective."

"He doesn't want to see you get hurt."

"And so far, I haven't been. This time, that is. Still, he'd rather I put the whole private eye thing behind me."

"And what would you rather do?"

I didn't expect that kind of probing and personal question from Kegan. I guess that's why it forced me to think. "I'm not looking for excitement," I told him. This was something I needed to set straight, just so he didn't think I was some kind of adrenaline junkie. "It's the puzzle of a mystery more than anything else that fascinates me. And the realization that if I don't look into things and do what I can do to make sure the truth comes out, there might be a miscarriage of justice."

"So you would investigate. I mean, if things looked bad for Eve."

"Which they don't." I had to convince myself of this once and for all, or I'd go stark, raving mad. To emphasize my point, I rolled back my chair and clutched my hands on the desk, signaling that I was officially changing the subject. "You said you wanted to talk. Let me guess; you've got something to tell me about greening up the restaurant."

Just as I hoped, Kegan got the message. And he knew better than to waste a golden opportunity. He set his drink down on the blotter on my desk and sat forward. "Recycling is the key," he said. "I know that sounds trite. I mean, we've been hearing it for so many years, I think most people just turn off when they hear the word *recycling*. But think about it, Annie. You can use recycled paper here at the restaurant for things like menus and napkins and promotional items. Think of all the good you could do for the environment."

I was not about to dismiss the idea out of hand, but it would take more than that to convince me. Apparently, Kegan knew it.

"If Bellywasher's recycled the cardboard, glass, plastic, and paper it uses every day, you could save between thirty and forty percent on trash removal fees."

Now we were getting somewhere! Interested in spite of myself, I encouraged him to tell me more. It was just what he needed to be off and running. Kegan talked about things like putting up an air curtain around the front door to keep warm-in-the-winter or cool-in-the-summer air from escaping when patrons entered or left the restaurant. He told me about the advantages of using all-natural beef, pork, chicken, cheese, and produce from local organic farmers. He explained about something called "zero waste initiatives" and how by recycling, reusing, and reducing waste, we could also cut operating costs.

I listened, and I was still listening I don't know how much much later when there was a tap on the door. It opened, and Eve stuck her head into the room.

"Why, there you two are! I was beginning to think you'd run off someplace together."

"Is it that late?" It must have been. My back was stiff from sitting too long in one place. I stretched, stood, and leaned to one side to see around Eve and into the restaurant. "Things have quieted down out there."

"It was quite a night!" Eve stepped farther into the office and closed the door behind her. "You talked to her?"

I don't think I need to point out that she asked this question of Kegan. I also don't need to point out (I hope!) that I'm no dummy. I knew exactly what she was asking about.

I chose to ignore it.

"Kegan sure has talked to me," I told her. "We've talked about recycling and reusing and what's that other thing? Oh, zero waste initiatives. It's fascinating stuff, Eve, and if we can do half of what he thinks we can, we might be able to save a lot of money around here."

Eve was not impressed. Nor was she easily deterred. She tapped the pointy toe of one stiletto against the floor. "And you know that's not at all what I'm talking about. I'm talking about our case."

"We don't have a case."

"We could, and you know it. And you know exactly where we need to start, too. With Valerie."

I saw the way Kegan's ears pricked, so before he could ask, I explained about WOW and Valerie and how she'd given us a whole list of women who might have had it in for Brad.

"That's a perfect suggestion." Kegan's eyes were bright with excitement. "Talk to the WOW women and see what they have to say. One of them probably offed Brad."

"Offed him?" I didn't want to offend Kegan, but I had to laugh. "You're talking like you're on *CSI*."

He had the good sense to blush. Eve, though, had no such qualms. "You have to admit," she said, "it's a fascinating mystery. I've been reading the papers. I know that Brad was killed in front of a whole train station full of people. And every one of them swears they didn't see a thing."

"Except for the person in the hooded sweatshirt," Kegan added.

"That's right." Eve nodded. "And no one knows who it could have been or why the person wanted Brad dead. Of course, first I heard about it, I thought of that list Valerie gave us. I mean, really, Annie, how many detectives are lucky enough to have the list of suspects even before the crime is committed?" Her golden brows dropped over her eyes, and Eve's expression grew serious.

"Not that I think any of my WOW sisters could have

done it. You understand that, don't you? But I read over that list. There are some names on it that I don't recognize. It could be one of them. Even so . . ." She paused, thinking. "I can't imagine planning a murder like that. I mean, really, if you're going to kill a man, there are cleaner ways of doing it. And easier ways of not being detected. I mean, really, a disguise? How silly is that!"

She did not notice my razor-sharp look. Or maybe she did, and she chose to ignore it. Either way, I didn't have a chance to point out that just a couple weeks before, she'd thought disguises were the best things in the world. Before I could, Kegan spoke up.

"Disguises, yeah, that was one of the first things that detective asked about yesterday," he told Eve. "He asked each one of us if Brad ever said anything about being followed."

Eve's eyes got wide. She looked at me. "A detective was here? Yesterday? He asked about stuff like that?"

It was my duty as official best friend to break the news. "Not just a detective," I said. "Tyler."

"Oh." Eve sank into the chair I'd just gotten out of. "Nobody told him about what I said, did they? I mean the whole thing about wanting to kill Brad. Nobody told Tyler—"

"It may have come up." This seemed a kinder way of explaining than telling Eve that Margaret and some of the other students had practically tried and condemned her. "Tyler also questioned me. He asked if I knew where you were yesterday. I couldn't tell him. You never returned my calls."

"Oh."

This *oh* was different from the first one. That was a sinking-feeling kind of *oh*. This one, accompanied as it was by Eve looking at the floor and biting her lower lip, packed a whole different meaning. One I didn't like at all.

"Oh? What do you mean, oh?" Because Eve refused to look at me, I crouched down on the floor in front of my desk chair to catch her gaze. "Why did you say it that way? That wasn't an *oh* like oh boy, am I glad. Or oh, I can't wait to tell you. That was a guilty sort of *oh*. What were you up to, yesterday, Eve?"

"Oh, you know . . ." When Eve stood, I had no choice but to get out of the way. I pulled myself to my feet, and I just about got beaned when she waved a hand in the air. "This and that."

"This and that isn't going to satisfy Tyler. It isn't an alibi."

"Do you think she needs one?" This question came from Kegan, who was suddenly on his feet, too. Two people in my office is a crowd. With three of us standing there toe-to-toe and eye to eye, it bordered on claustrophobic. Kegan rubbed his hands together. "I mean, gee, Eve, I don't want you to worry, but we were talking about it. Me and Annie. Before you came in. You told me what a great detective she is, so I figured I'd get her input. I asked her what she'd do if the cops really were looking at you as a suspect, but I never thought . . . I mean, it was sort of a game, wasn't it, Annie? Just sort of a hypothetical situation. I wondered how she'd handle it . . . you know, being a detective and all. I mean, I wondered what she'd do if it turned out that the cops really believed what everyone in class said about how you threatened Brad. I never thought we were really talking about you actually being a suspect. About . . . about how you might need a really strong alibi."

I shut him up with a look and concentrated on Eve, who was suddenly as green as the blouse she was wearing with a black thigh-high skirt and a nipped-at-the-waist jacket.

She ran her tongue over her lips. "You don't think . . ." She couldn't bring herself to finish.

I put a hand on her arm. "Of course not. But what I think and what Tyler thinks are two different things."

"Doesn't it figure he'd be the one investigating this case." Eve had a way of snorting that was ladylike and dismissive all at the same time. "If he shows up here, I'll just give that boy a piece of my mind, that's what I'll do."

"You'd be better off telling him where you were yesterday." I pointed this out even though she already knew it.

When Eve was overwrought (and I could see from the slightly dazed look on her face that we were definitely skirting the edges), it was wise to try and keep her on track. "I called you a dozen times, and you never answered. You didn't return my messages, either. I'm curious, Eve, but Tyler's going to be more than that. He's trying to establish a timeline for everybody involved with this murder, and right about now, he's thinking you might be involved. He's going to need to know where you were, and you'd better have somebody to back you up. Come on, Eve, just tell me. Where were you yesterday? Shopping? Then it's no big deal; you'll have receipts to prove it. Your salon? Your masseuse will vouch for you. The hairdresser's? I know Paulette, the woman who does your hair. She'll speak up for you, too. Don't tell me you don't remember where you were yesterday, Eve. Come on, time to come clean."

Only she didn't. In fact, all Eve did was stand there and chew off her lipstick.

Let it be known that I have a lot more patience than Eve ever will. I was ready to prove it by standing there until closing time and beyond, waiting for her answer. I would have done it, too, if Jim hadn't rapped on the door. When he saw that we were packed into my office like sardines in a can, he didn't bother to step inside.

"Tyler Cooper's here again," he said. His gaze settled on Eve. "He wants to talk to you."

I have seen Eve as cool and as calm as the proverbial cucumber in front of hundreds of people in a beauty pageant audience. I've watched her maintain her composure when pageant judges questioned her about things like world peace, her vision for a new tomorrow, and why she thinks it's important for a woman to always look her best. Heck, I was sitting in the front row the time she did her talent competition with flaming batons, started the stage on fire, and made it look like part of the act by stamping out the flames to the beat of the music.

I have never, ever seen her look so nervous.

Before she could step into the restaurant, I reached for her arm. "Are you sure there isn't something you want to tell me? I mean, before you go out there and have to tell Tyler?"

"Whatever are you talking about, Annie? Tell Tyler what?" There was a sheen of tears in Eve's eyes. She sniffled, grabbed a tissue from the box on my desk, and dabbed her nose. When she was done, she pulled back her shoulders. The attitude would have been more convincing if her chin didn't quiver. "I don't have a thing to worry about," she said right before she headed out the door.

Someone at the bar called for a drink, and Jim had to hurry over. That left Kegan and me.

I didn't have to turn around; I could feel him behind me, and I knew he was looking right where I was looking. Together, we watched Eve stroll over to the table where Tyler was waiting. She dropped into the seat across from his. "Think she's right?" Kegan asked. "You know, about having nothing to worry about?"

I shook my head. After all, I could see exactly what Kegan could see: though Eve claimed she didn't have a thing to worry about, she didn't look like she believed it. In fact, as I watched, Eve clutched her hands in her lap and shredded the tissues into tiny pieces.

"Just like he's going to rip her flimsy excuses about yesterday to shreds."

Luckily, Kegan knew exactly what I was talking about. "What are you doing to do, Annie?" he asked me.

I didn't have to answer. Kegan knew my answer as well as I did.

There was no way on earth I was going to allow Tyler to consider Eve a suspect, and that meant I had to find him some real suspects.

It was time to start investigating.

Ten

✖

LUCKILY, THE WOMEN OF WOW HAD A MEMBERSHIP roster that included phone numbers and places of employment, just in case they needed to contact each other for an anti-Weasel shoulder to cry on. I stopped at Eve's that night, looked through the list, and found out that Valerie Conover worked at a gym in Falls Church.

Abs of Iron, Buns That R Fun wasn't exactly the Department of Labor, but as I approached it the next day on my lunch hour, I saw that the building was new and impressive. It featured lots of gleaming glass and metal, sleek lines, and a photo of a man and woman that hung above the front doors, as big as a billboard. They were linked arm in arm, the better to show off bodies that were fit, trim, and so well-proportioned, one look at them was enough to convince any normal person who was not so fit, not so trim, and nowhere near as well-proportioned that this was not a place he (or she) would be caught dead in workout clothes.

With a glance at the sensible shoes I was wearing with sensible khakis, a sensible cotton blouse, and the navy blue cardigan I'd bought specifically because it was long enough to hide my hips, I stepped inside. The door hadn't even closed behind me when a stick-thin girl in a burgundy-colored velour warm-up suit stepped out from behind the front reception desk and chirped a greeting. She wore a name tag that identified her as Cindie. "Welcome! I'll bet you're here for buns that are fun!"

"Actually—"

"I know. I was nervous my first time, too. But that was only three months ago. Look at me now!" To make sure I did, she twirled around. When she was done, Cindie looked me up and down. "Might take a little longer for you, of course, but we guarantee results! Just step into one of our assessment rooms." She waved me toward a long hallway where I saw a row of offices, each staffed with an eager membership consultant dressed in a warm-up suit identical to Cindie's. "We'll give you a personal evaluation and a training plan designed just for you. We'll have you working out in no time at all."

"That's great, but I'm not here to work out."

"You're not?" Cindie wrinkled her nose and gave me another quick once-over. "Are you sure?"

I was before I walked in there.

I told myself I'd have the luxury of feeling unattractive later. Right now, I only had my lunch hour, and time was ticking away. "I'm here to see Valerie Conover," I told the girl.

"Valerie . . ." Cindie hurried around to the other side of the desk and consulted her computer screen. "She's just finishing up a tennis class." She pointed toward a glass wall. Beyond it was a maze of machines that looked like they came straight out of a medieval torture chamber. "You can go over to the courts and meet her. That way, you'll get to see a little of our facility. I'll bet when you do, you'll change your mind about joining."

I, on the other hand, bet I wouldn't.

I thanked Cindie and pushed through the door that led into the workout area, my steps punctuated by the sounds of metal chunking against metal. I excused my way around two sweaty guys who were talking to each other and got outside to the tennis courts just as Valerie was telling a group of middle-aged women to practice, and that she'd see them next week.

When she went over to a bench for a towel and a bottle of water, I stepped into Valerie's path.

I reminded her who I was and made sure I mentioned that I was a friend of Eve's, and of WOW. "I was hoping you'd have a few minutes to talk."

Valerie was dressed in a blindingly white tennis skirt that skimmed her thighs and a sleeveless white shirt that showed off perfectly muscled arms. Because of the sunshade she was wearing over her golden hair, her face was shaded, but even so, I saw her blush.

"Not exactly the Department of Labor, is it?"

Her question was so close to what I'd been thinking on my way in, I blushed, too. Being the perpetual fixer-upper that I am, I did my best to lessen her embarrassment. "You must be a great tennis player. I mean, you'd have to be to teach."

"Good thing." Valerie's smile was tight. "If I didn't have this, I'd be sleeping in a box under a bridge somewhere. Thanks to Brad Peterson, it's the only damn job I can get."

I whispered a silent prayer of thanks. Since she'd already brought up the subject of Brad, I wouldn't have to try to ease my way into it. "Funny you should mention him," I said. "That's what I stopped to talk to you about."

Valerie's eyes lit. "You found out something. Something about Brad. Eve said you'd come through for us! Whatever it is, I hope we can use it to nail that bastard to the wall. Then maybe when I apply for a real job and employers call him, he'll stop giving me a lousy reference."

"Oh, I don't think he'll be giving you any more bad references." I managed to keep my words casual, but I was careful to watch her as I spoke. Her expression was blank. She didn't have a clue what I meant.

She was either a really good actress or a really bad suspect.

It was my job to find out which.

Just to be sure we wouldn't be overheard, I looked around. There was a couple playing tennis on the far court, but other than that, Valerie and I were alone. "Have you seen him lately?" I asked Valerie.

"You mean Brad? No, thank goodness. Not since that day I followed him over to Alexandria." She twisted the cap on the bottle of water and took a long drink. "I was thinking about what you said, you see, and I realized you were right. Following Brad isn't something I should do. I need to leave that up to the experts. You. And Eve."

This was a bit of information I hoped Valerie wasn't eager to share with anyone else. Tyler for instance. I looked at my watch. "I really appreciate you helping me out," I told her. "I've got to get moving and head back to Arlington to get to work. Are you familiar with that area?"

She shrugged. "Been there, of course."

"I just moved there a few months ago." It was a blatant lie, so I made sure I didn't look at Valerie when I said it. I have one of those honest faces that make it impossible to tell a fib. "I've got relatives coming in from Wisconsin this weekend, and I need to give them directions. You know, to get around town and over to D.C. They're hoping to see the cherry blossoms."

Valerie squinted at me. "You came all the way over here to talk to me about cherry blossoms?"

I laughed. It was either that or admit I was the world's worst interrogator. I wasn't ready to throw in the towel. Not yet, anyway. "No, actually, I came over here to talk to you about Brad. But I wondered, you know, about the cherry blossoms. I'd hate to see Aunt Sophie and Uncle Ben get lost. Can you help me with directions from the Clarendon Metro station?"

"Clarendon Metro? Never been there." Valerie looked at me closely. "And you know what? Eve might be right, and you might be a good detective. But you're a lousy liar."

I could have debated it, but then I would have been lying again. And that only would have made things worse.

I sank down on the bench, and Valerie sat next to me. "It's that obvious, huh? I thought I was doing better than that."

"Don't take it personally." She wiped the back of her neck with the towel and tossed it into a gym bag. "It's just that once you've met enough Weasels, you have radar for that sort of thing. So you don't really have relatives in Wisconsin?"

"Not a one."

"And they don't really need to go see the cherry blossoms?"

I shook my head.

"So why do you want to know about the Clarendon Metro station?"

Since lying was getting me nowhere, I had no choice but to stick with the truth. "You haven't seen the papers? You don't know? Brad Peterson was killed at the Clarendon Metro station on Monday."

Even a good actress couldn't make the color drain out of her face like it did out of Valerie's. She sucked in a breath. "Killed? You mean, like an accident?"

"I mean killed. Like murder."

"And you think that I . . ." She hopped off the bench, and her hands curled into fists. "That's crazy."

"I know it is." I was lying again, but this time, she was too irritated to notice. "It's not like I suspect you or anything, but you have to admit, it's pretty convenient. You wanted Brad to stop giving you lousy references. Well, you got your wish."

"That doesn't mean I had anything to do with him dying."

"No. Really, it doesn't." I said this with all the oomph I could muster because I hadn't found out nearly enough, and I couldn't afford to alienate Valerie. "Look," I told her, "I'm not accusing you of anything, I'm just looking for the truth. To do that, I need to follow every lead. You have to admit it, Valerie. I heard you say it. You said you wanted Brad dead."

"I did. I do. Brad Peterson is . . . was . . . a vile, no good son of a bitch. But just because I hated him doesn't mean I killed him. Lots of people wanted Brad dead."

"And I'm going to do my best to talk to every single one of them."

"But you started with me."

I could have lied—again—and said I'd made the decision based on the WOW women I'd met. But really, my reasons were simpler than that.

"You have a hooded sweatshirt."

"What?" Valerie was far taller than me, and when she looked down at me, her eyes flashed. "Of course I have a hooded sweatshirt. I've got a few hooded sweatshirts. And what does that have to do with Brad, anyway?"

It didn't help when it came to the height department, but I stood, anyway. At least that way, I didn't feel like a little kid getting lectured by an adult. When I spoke, I was careful to keep every scrap of emotion out of my voice. "There's a security camera at the Metro station. It shows a person in a hooded sweatshirt pushing Brad off the platform. The cops, they found a blond hair inside the hood."

"And you think—" Valerie nearly choked on her fury. "You've got a lot of nerve. Eve said you were a detective, but she didn't bother to mention that you were stupid. And Eve . . ." Thinking, she narrowed her eyes. "That's it, isn't it? I wanted Brad dead. But so did Eve. I'm a blonde. But so is Eve. You're playing favorites, Little Ms. Detective. You're trying to clear your friend."

"Yes, of course I am. Eve didn't do it."

"Well, neither did I."

It wasn't like me to be shifty, but except for the fact that I was pissing Valerie off, I was getting nowhere fast. I had to try to trip her up.

"Do you have an alibi for the time Brad died?"

Valerie tipped her head. With her top lip curled, she wasn't nearly as pretty as I remembered her to be. She managed to keep her voice down, but even that wasn't enough to hide her anger. Her words were sharp. "I don't know. When did he die?"

Damn, if she'd produced an instant alibi after telling me she didn't even know Brad was dead . . .

With that route closed to me, I stuck to the facts. "Monday morning, about nine o'clock."

"An alibi, huh?" Valerie grabbed her gym bag and strode toward the building. "Will the first lady do?"

I was still wondering what she meant when I scrambled to catch up. I followed Valerie into the women's locker room. She stopped at a locker to the left of the door and spun the dial on the lock. When she yanked the door open, I saw that she had a newspaper clipping taped inside.

"There. Is that good enough for you?" Valerie pointed. I didn't bother reading the article but concentrated on the photo that went along with it. It showed the first lady visiting with an elderly woman at a nearby hospital. I noticed the date at the top of the picture was Tuesday's and that the caption clearly said the photo had been taken the day before, Monday morning. The same morning Brad had been killed.

When it comes to egos, mine is as low-maintenance as they come. Still, it wasn't easy playing at being a detective, then having to admit I didn't have a clue what Valerie was trying to show me.

My blank expression said it all.

"Look. There." She stabbed a finger at the photo. In the background was a line of people, eagerly waiting to greet the first lady. Valerie was in the front row. She was standing right in front of a clock that clearly showed the time: 9:10.

"My grandmother is in the hospital," she said. "I stopped there Monday morning to visit her. I got there around eight, early enough to talk to her doctor when he did his rounds. With all the security and all the news cameras that came along with the first lady, I didn't manage to get out of there until just after noon. So you see . . ." She slammed the locker shut and stood with her back to it, her arms crossed over her chest. "I say three cheers for whoever killed Brad. But if he died Monday morning at nine, it sure couldn't have been me."

WHEN I STEPPED INTO BELLYWASHER'S THAT NIGHT, I knew instantly that something was different.

That might have been because of Doris, who was standing on the bar trying to reach the picture of the Loch Ness monster that hung on the wall nearby. Or Emma, who had gotten hold of the kilt that should have been draped over the sandalwood screen that separated the entryway from the seating area of the restaurant. She had it wrapped around her shoulders and was zooming through the place proclaiming herself to be a superhero. Wendy, Gloria, Lucy, Alice, and Rosemary were at one of our tables, bickering over the last bite of a hot fudge sundae. It didn't take an expert in children's behavior to see that things were about to get physical.

Thank goodness it was pouring outside, and traffic was at a minimum. The restaurant was empty of customers except for Larry, Hank, and Charlie, regulars who were sitting at the bar, sharing a pitcher of beer, and taking it all in stride. Jim was behind the bar, and even as I watched, he reached a hand out to catch Doris before she fell and broke either the Nessie picture or a couple of bones, reminded the girls at the table to mind their manners and keep their voices down, and told Emma, in no uncertain terms, that if she "didn'a stop that rollickin' and settle down, she wouldn'a have a place to sleep that night but in the yard."

I didn't bother to say hello. I figured Jim was too busy to notice, and besides, I never had the chance. I don't know where she came from, but as soon as she saw me, Fi had ahold of my arm.

"A boy! Can you believe it? Oh, Annie." Tears streamed down Fi's cheeks, and she wiped them away with the back of her hand. "What on earth am I going to do with a boy?"

Call me psychic, I knew she was talking about the baby. Or maybe that's because while she imparted this information, she had one hand on the bulge of her stomach.

I smiled and raised my voice to be heard about the din. "That's wonderful news," I told her. "I'll bet Richard is thrilled."

Fi's lower lip quivered. "Haven't told him. Just found out myself this afternoon. A boy!" Her carroty-colored curls quivered when she shook her head. "I don't know a thing about raising boys."

"Richard will be happy to help you with all that." I hadn't been able to get through to her with logic—maybe a little empathy was what she needed. I patted her arm and kept my smile firmly in place. "I'll bet he's always wanted a boy, right? And think about it, Fi, think about how much fun it will be. Soccer and baseball and tadpoles and trucks." I have to admit, even as I tried to convince her, it sounded like fun to me. "The girls will love having a little brother."

"And I . . ." Fi's tears burst. "I don't even have any boys' names picked out!"

Overcome, she disappeared into my office and closed the door behind her.

So much for the work I had planned for that night.

I went over to the bar, plucked Doris off of it, and set her on the floor. "How's your day going?" I asked Jim.

His tight-edged smile said it all. "And yours?"

"Well, my first suspect didn't pan out." I wasn't worried about telling Jim about my investigation. Sometime between when I figured out that I had to look into Brad's death and when I went to see Valerie, I also figured out that one of the reasons Jim had been opposed to my previous investigations was that I hadn't let him in on all the details. He worried about me because he was left in the dark, and naturally being worried, he did his best to try to make me mind my own business. I wasn't going to make that mistake again; I valued our relationship too much. This time, I had vowed to clue him in from the start. I climbed onto a barstool. "I need to talk to Eve about the rest of the names on that list Valerie gave us. Is she around?"

"Out back." He tipped his head that way. "Walking Doc."

The fact that Jim spoke without the least bit of rancor said a whole lot about his mood. Then again, I could hardly blame him. With little girl voices bouncing off the walls and the sounds of Fi's incessant sobbing coming from my office, it was hard to think straight. Otherwise, Jim wouldn't be taking Doc's visit in stride.

I cringed at the memory of the last time the dog had made an appearance at Bellywasher's, and the same worries I had then came back in spades. If a health inspector happened to see the dog . . . If a customer happened to complain . . . If anything went wrong and anyone found out that there was a dog in our kitchen . . .

I was off the barstool and looking for Eve and Doc in no time flat.

I found them just as they were coming in the back door.

"Little Doc was a good little doggy-woggy." Eve cooed and lifted the dog into her arms so she could take off his yellow rain slicker and matching boots. She kissed the top of his head. "He's my sweet-ums!"

"He's going to be the reason this place gets closed down."

She didn't looked worried. "It's just for tonight. My dog walker has strep, and I couldn't leave Doc all alone without his dinner-winner or a chance to go for a little walkie." She lifted the dog long enough to rub noses with him. "He's going back into my tote bag, and my tote bag is going into the storage room for the night. I'll check on him when I take my break. Don't worry, Annie. This time, nothing's going to go wrong."

"That's what you said last time."

Her grin was short-lived. "It was kind of funny. Except that Doc ended up with a tummy ache. Besides, this time . . ." As if it had been timed, we heard a crash from out in the restaurant, and the squeals of seven little girls. Eve rolled her eyes. "Doc could walk out there and start mixing drinks at the bar. Who would notice?"

She was right. And even in four-inch heels, she was also faster than me. With Doc still in her arms, Eve pushed through the kitchen door, and I trailed behind her. We found Doris, Gloria, Wendy, Rosemary, Alice, Emma, and Lucy gathered around the shards of the sundae dish they had knocked on the floor. Gloria was snickering. She was the only one who thought it was funny. Wendy, Doris, and Rosemary were on the verge of tears. Emma, Alice, and Lucy had apparently learned a thing or two from their mother. They were sobbing to beat the band. Cousin Jim was standing over them, his fists on his hips and his eyes flashing fire.

"You're naught but little hellions." Jim's face was flushed. His voice shook. "If you were my bairns, I'd put each and every one of you over my knee and—"

"Well, of course they're being bad!" As if it was nothing, Eve strode into the middle of the chaos. She stepped between Jim and the girls. "These poor little darlings are bored. And who wouldn't be in this place all night?" She somehow managed to ensconce herself in the center of the circle, and she looked at each girl in turn. "If y'all can behave . . ." While she let this statement sink in, she gave each of them another careful look. "I will let you talk to Doc."

"The puppy?" Emma's tears dried up instantly. She looked at her sisters for confirmation and nodded furiously. "We'll behave. We promise. Can we hold him?"

"I will hold him. At least until you can prove that you won't be rough with him. Doc is a very special dog. Has Jim told you that story? Why, once, Doc saved the life of the vice president of the United States."

The girls might not have known much about politics, but instinctively, they picked up on the undertone of Eve's voice, the one that told them in no uncertain terms that what she was talking about wasn't just important, it was downright incredible. She sat at the table and, their tears drying and their voices hushed, they gathered around her and waited almost patiently for a turn to pet Doc.

I put a hand on Jim's arm. "You need a drink of water?"

"I need a drink of something stronger than that." He turned to head back behind the bar. "I will refrain, though. A beer or two in me, and I'll be at the airport, buying tickets for the whole brood of them to go back to Florida. I can't afford that."

"They've got to leave eventually." I tried my best to sound as if I believed this.

"If my mother and Fi's mother weren't so close . . ." Jim shook his head. He poured an iced tea, handed it to me across the bar, and poured one for himself. "We've got to do something to take care of this muckle, Annie. I'm losing my mind."

I offered him a smile. "It will be OK," I said, and he actually might have believed it, at least for a while, if Eve hadn't hopped to her feet.

"You pinched his ear!"

I couldn't tell which girl Eve aimed the accusation at. It didn't matter. Every single one of them started crying.

Eleven

✖

IT WAS CLASS NUMBER FOUR—FINGER FOODS night—and as good as that normally would have sounded to me (it should come as no surprise that I am a sucker for potato skins with plenty of cheese and sour cream), I was not in the mood. I'd spent the better part of the past week talking to the women on that list Valerie gave us. As for results . . . well, I guess my not-so-good mood said it all. Sure, every one of them had something bad to say about Brad. And not one of them was sorry he was dead. But as for uncovering viable suspects . . .

Jim was out at the bar getting things ready for an early luncheon scheduled for the next day, and I was setting up for class. When I sighed, it had nothing to do with the ten-pound bag of potatoes I was carrying to his worktable and everything to do with the fact that every single woman I'd talked to had a verifiable alibi for the day and time of Brad's murder. Believe me, I knew. I'd checked every one of them out.

And every one of them checked out.

Every one except Eve.

The thought niggled at me now like it had every minute

of every day since the Monday before when Tyler first showed up at Bellywasher's to break the news about Brad and point an accusing finger at Eve. Now, like every other time I thought about it and my doubts reared their ugly heads, I told them to shut up and got back to trying to make sense of the case. If none of the other women on the list were possible suspects, and Eve wasn't either (I knew this in my heart), then I was obviously missing something. Or someone. The solution to this problem was simple: I had to think about it more. I had to work harder.

The truth of this really hit home when I got to Belly-washer's that night and Jim informed me that Tyler had stopped in the night before just after I left. It was no big surprise to hear that he'd come to have another chat with Eve.

According to Jim, it was very low key, and no one heard what Eve and Tyler said to each other. But Jim is a pub keeper, remember, and if there's one thing pub keepers know, it's human nature. He couldn't help but notice that when Tyler walked out, his expression was stonier than ever, his shoulders were rock steady, and his jaw was stiff. Like he'd made up his mind about something, and he wasn't about to change it, come hell or high water.

As for Eve, Jim didn't want me to worry, so he tried to downplay the whole thing, but he eventually came clean. No sooner had Tyler walked out the door than Eve said she had a headache and had to go home. When she left, she was crying.

Of course, as soon as I got the scoop, I tried to call Eve. Is it any big surprise that there was no answer? In the spirit of trying harder and working more, I set down the bag of potatoes and reached for my phone again. Before I had a chance to dial, the kitchen door swung open.

"I hope you don't mind that I stopped in early." Kegan was apologizing practically before he was all the way in the kitchen. "I had lunch here on Saturday, and I ducked into the kitchen to say hi to Marc and Damien. Damien mentioned that his roommate had a bad sore throat. I know it sounds like I don't have a life . . ." He rolled his eyes. "But all I could think about yesterday was how awful it would be for you and Jim if Damien got sick, too. Without him, you folks would be busier than ever. I can't even imagine how you'd handle it." Kegan held up his market bag. "I brought Damien some horehound tea and organic honey. That ought to help him out. Now how about you? Do you need any help?"

I could have mentioned the investigation that was going nowhere fast, but that wasn't what Kegan was talking about. Besides, the kid thought I was the goddess of private eyes. There was no use bursting his bubble. I put him in charge of gathering the ingredients Jim would need to make nachos.

Kegan hurried over to his workstation (he'd be making mozzarella sticks for the class that night) and set down his bag. While he grabbed an apron, I went over to our one and only kitchen window to look through the pots of herbs for the mint Jim would use in his mojitos. I found the pot and set it nearby so Jim could reach it easily when it came time to demonstrate how to make the drinks, and Kegan washed and then chopped tomatoes.

"I've been thinking about our case." Kegan's words so closely mirrorered what I'd just been mulling over, I turned and stared at him in wonder. He didn't notice. He was too busy concentrating on the tomatoes. "Are you getting anywhere with it?"

I could have pointed out that it wasn't *our* case. But technically speaking, it wasn't *my* case, either. Kegan had as much right to know what was going on as anyone else did.

He looked up briefly. Maybe the way I shook my head told him everything he needed to know.

"That bad, huh?" He scooped the chopped tomatoes into a bowl and rinsed the cutting board. When he brought it back to Jim's workstation so he could start on the scallions, Kegan's expression was thoughtful. "You know what I was thinking? I mean . . ." He busied himself wiping off

the cutting board and setting it in place. "Not that it's any
of my business, of course, but I have to admit, I've never
been this close to a murder investigation, and it is pretty
exciting. Just like on TV. I was thinking, that's all. I mean,
sort of pretending that I was the one in charge of the case
instead of you. And wondering, you know, what I'd do
next. If I were you." Just as I expected they would, Kegan's
cheeks turned the color of the tomatoes in the bowl. "Not
that I have any business telling you how to do things."

"Maybe you do." I pulled a tall stool up to the table
where Kegan was working and plunked down on it.
"Maybe you're a genius, and you're not giving yourself
enough credit."

I didn't think it was possible for him to get any redder,
but he did. "You think so? You mean, you think I might be
a good detective, too?"

"Well, I can't say. Not until you tell me what you've got
planned. But I can say this, I'm getting nowhere on my
own. It's time for me to get a little outside input. So what
do you think, Watson? What's your theory?"

"My theory? Oh, my!" Kegan couldn't contain a smile.
"I'm honored you asked. I mean, I think it's wonderful that
a detective with your credentials would actually care . . . I
mean . . ."

I got the picture, and before his flattery went to my
head, I encouraged him to keep talking.

"Well, it's like this." Kegan grabbed a bunch of scallions and set them on the cutting board. "You're not getting
anywhere doing what you're doing, right?"

I couldn't deny it.

"So you should probably do what you haven't been
doing."

This seemed right on, too. I propped my elbows on the
table, my chin in my hands, and listened.

"I was thinking that if the answers you're looking for
aren't with the women of WOW, then maybe they're with
Brad."

"Only Brad's dead."

"But the way he lived isn't." Kegan wrinkled his nose. "I'm sorry, I'm not explaining this well. What I mean is that if you're going to find out more about what happened to him, you need to find out more about Brad. It seems only logical that you'd check out the place he worked. And maybe the place he lived, too."

I had thought of the work angle, of course, but as for snooping around Brad's house, that was beyond the scope of Annie Capshaw, girl detective.

I was all set to explain this to Kegan when Eve walked into the kitchen.

"There you are!" I honestly didn't think that she'd run off to some sunny island where there is no extradition agreement with this country, but a wave of relief shot through me, anyway. It was followed immediately by a shot of good ol' why-have-you-been-avoiding-me. My phone was on the table, and I picked it up and waved it in the air. "Don't you ever answer your calls these days?"

She set down a paper shopping bag that made a clinking sound, and I remembered that Eve had promised Jim she'd roll silverware in napkins for the luncheon that was scheduled for the next day. "I've been kind of busy," she said.

"Kind of busy ignoring me?"

"No, silly." Eve was wearing sunglasses, and she didn't take them off. I wasn't fooled. She might sound flip, but I knew she was still upset about her interview with Tyler the night before. I suspected her eyes were red and swollen. "Just . . . you know . . . busy."

"We're going to be busy, too." Kegan was finished with the scallions. He put them in a bowl and hurried over to Eve's side. "We're going to start a new avenue of investigation. We're going to take a look around Brad's house."

How things had gotten to the *we* stage was beyond me, but right about then, that was the least of my worries. At the first mention of Brad's house, all the color drained out of Eve's face, and she reached back to brace one hand against the sink. I didn't have to be a detective to see that Kegan had hit on a nerve, and I knew I had to act fast, before Eve regained her composure.

I had to act fast before she fainted, too.

I jumped off the stool and hurried over to prop one hand under Eve's left arm. Kegan already had ahold of her right. Between the two of us, we kept her on her feet. She pulled in a breath to steady herself. "Funny you should mention Brad's house," she said.

"Funny, huh?" Standing that close gave me the perfect chance to look up and try to catch Eve's eye. I would have known if it worked if she took off her sunglasses. When she didn't, I had no choice but to raise my chin and pin her with a look that I hoped was intimidating. "What have you been up to, Eve?"

She drew her arms to her sides and stepped away, her back to us. "Nothing. Really. Not . . . not recently, anyway."

"But you were up to something." I didn't say this like it was a question, because there was no doubt in my mind that I was on to something. Guilt practically dripped from Eve's words. "And that something that you were up to has something to do with Brad. With Brad's house." An idea struck, and a cold chill spread in the pit of my stomach. "Oh, Eve, you didn't—"

"I couldn't help it, Annie." Eve turned and rushed toward me. She stripped off her sunglasses and tossed them down on the nearest table. Her eyes were red and swollen. New tears filled them. "It made so much sense at the time, don't you see? And it seemed like the perfect opportunity. I never thought . . ." A tiny sob escaped her, and she pressed a finger to her lips. "I didn't know someone was going to kill Brad. Now . . . Well, I think maybe . . . I mean, I'm afraid . . . Oh, Annie," she wailed. "I think I really screwed up!"

Panic nibbled at my brain and soured my stomach. Still, I tried not to let it get the best of me. Easy to say. Not so easy to do. Especially when Eve was having a full-blown meltdown and Kegan was looking from one of us to the other, completely confused.

Dealing with him—and the logic of the situation—was easier than trying to figure out how to handle Eve's over-wrought emotions and the stampede of terrifying thoughts that pounded through my brain. The ones that told me that the situation wasn't just bad, it was worse than bad and heading toward critical.

I kept my eyes on Kegan. It was better than watching Eve wring her hands, and maybe if I stuck to the facts, I wouldn't be swallowed whole by the fear that threatened to knock me off my feet.

"Lesson number one," I told him. "You want to be a detective, follow my train of thought. Here's pretty much how it works. You mentioned Brad's house. Eve got upset. I asked what she's been up to. She said nothing—recently. That's the key here. That one word: *recently*. Because remember, Eve doesn't have an alibi for the day Brad was killed. Not one she's willing to talk about, anyway. Put it all together, Kegan. Think like a detective. What do you come up with?"

He tried. Thinking hard, Kegan squeezed his eyes shut. When he opened them again, he didn't look any more enlightened. He shrugged. "Eve's been up to something. That much is clear. But we still don't know when and where."

"Sure we do." When I said this, I turned back to Eve so I could watch her closely. "You were at Brad's house the day he died, weren't you? That's why you don't want to tell Tyler where you were. You know it makes you look even guiltier."

She sank down on the stool I had gotten up from just a few minutes before. "You think so, huh?" She sniffled. "I mean, about the guiltier thing?"

"I know so. Eve . . ." I closed in on her. Moving gave me a way to use up some of the energy that was building inside me and ready to burst. "What were you doing there? How—"

A tear slipped down her cheek. "That's how he showed

he was interested in me. Back when we still worked together. Brad sent me flowers and a note, telling me to stop by for dinner. He enclosed the key to his house. I meant to throw it out, I just never got around to it. When I found the key again, I thought . . ."

Eve's voice faded. Just as well, since I probably wouldn't have heard what she said because I gulped so loud. "Key? You have a key? You mean to tell me, you weren't just there, taking a look at the house or watching to see when Brad left and where he went? You were inside? His house?"

"Well, I didn't know that was the day somebody was going to kill him!" Eve jumped up from the stool, which was a good thing. My knees were mushy, and I sat right down. "I was just looking for evidence, you know, trying to find something the WOW sisters could use to prove that Brad was a creep. That was Monday morning. Just about the time he was killed. Then when I found out he was dead . . ." Enough said. She shrugged.

"That's why you didn't return my calls that day. You didn't want me to know where you'd been. And you can't tell Tyler . . ." I drew in a deep breath that did nothing to still the crazy beating of my heart. But I couldn't control my curiosity. "Did you find anything?"

"Nothing useful."

"Then we're in big trouble here—"

"For nothing."

"Or maybe not."

At Kegan's comment, I looked up. I was just in time to see him grimace as if he knew he'd crossed the line. Maybe so, but like I said, I was more than willing to listen to suggestions, especially now that things were looking worse than ever. With a nod, I encouraged him to keep talking.

"Well, it's like this. Or at least this is how it looks to me." Unsure of himself, Kegan clutched his hands together at his waist. "I mean, to me, this looks like the perfect opportunity for us to do a little sleuthing. Remember what we were talking about just a little while ago, Annie. We said it would be useful to take a look at Brad's things, at his life. Now, we've got a key to his house! It's a gift from the gods! We could go there and have a look around. We're not going to take anything, so it wouldn't be illegal. Not exactly, anyway," he added this last bit quickly, apparently reading the objection I was all set to make. "We don't even have to touch anything. We'll just look. You know, for something that will tell us more about who might have killed him. The cops couldn't be mad about that, could they?"

"Only if they find us."

My sarcasm was lost on both Brad and Eve, who had decided he was right and was all set to buy into his plan.

She nodded so fast and so hard, she looked like one of those bobble-head dolls. "We could go at night so nobody sees us. And we could wear disguises."

"Enough with the disguises!"

Do I need to point out that I am the one who injected reason into this little slice of insanity? Kegan was far more easily intimidated than Eve would ever be, so after I stared him down, I turned back to her.

"You're not going," I said, my words as firm as the look I gave her. "You've already taken a chance, and it's too dangerous for you to be there again. We don't need to make you look even more guilty than you already do."

There are plenty of people who are fooled by Eve's good looks and Southern girl charm. They underestimate her. I knew better, of course, and knowing what I know about her, I could practically see the wheels turning in her head. When they rolled to a stop and the truth dawned, her eyes went wide. "I'm not going. But you didn't say you weren't. Annie, are you telling me you'll do it? You're going to Brad's to investigate?"

Call me crazy. Call me desperate. Call my anything but dishonest, because dishonest is something I am definitely not. Even when I tried to talk myself out of the plan, I knew I couldn't. And I knew why, too. No matter which way I looked at the situation, I always saw the same thing: Eve in an orange prison jumpsuit. No way I was going to let that happen. Not if I could do anything about it.

"I'm going," I said, and when I held my hand out, she knew what I wanted. She dug into her purse and handed me the key to Brad's house. The next thing I did was push an order pad to her and hand her a pen. When she was done writing down Brad's address, I folded the paper, put it in my pocket, and just so nobody got the wrong idea, I looked again from Kegan to Eve. "And I'm going alone."

"But—"

Before she could say another word, I cut Eve off with a look.

"But—"

If I wasn't going to cave in to Eve, I sure wasn't going to give in to the pleading look in Kegan's eyes, either.

"It's too dangerous," I told them at the same time I tried not to listen to my own advice. "I'm going alone."

Before I had the chance to say another word, Eve locked me in a bear hug. "Annie," she burbled. "You're the best friend anybody ever had!"

I MIGHT HAVE BEEN THE BEST FRIEND ANYBODY EVER had, but I wasn't stupid. No way I was going to tell Eve and Kegan more than I already had. Sure, they agreed to my plan. Sure, they saw the wisdom of me investigating at Brad's on my own. Or at least they said they did.

But I knew Eve better than to think she'd give up without a fight. I didn't know Kegan hardly at all, but I saw the ain't-it-fun-to-investigate gleam that shone in his eyes every time we talked about Brad's murder. I wasn't going to take the chance of having to fend off both of them at the same time I worried that Brad's neighbors (or—heaven forbid—the cops) might find me at his town house.

Before I could talk myself out of what I should have been smart enough not to talk myself into, I decided to get it over with. The next night, a Tuesday, I stopped at Bellywasher's after work and tried to act normal and look unconcerned like a person would if she wasn't planning on illegally entering the home of a recently murdered man in order to find something that might exonerate her best friend who was suspected of the crime.

Yes, in retrospect, it sounds crazy, but what choice did I have? I had to help Eve. And yes (again), getting my act together and acting like I had nothing up my sleeve, no flashlight in my purse, and that no one would notice that I'd deliberately dressed all in black that day (the better to blend in with the night) was nearly impossible, but I managed. Even though my insides were thrumming like a hive of bees, and my brain was buzzing along with them, I did all the things I usually do when I stop at the restaurant in the evening. I organized my office. I went through the day's receipts. I prepared the bank deposit.

Oh yeah, and I slipped out of the restaurant just as the eight o'clock rush arrived, too.

No way Eve could follow me when she was busy seating all those customers.

Who could blame me for feeling mighty satisfied with myself? I timed my exit perfectly, and when I stepped outside, the coast was clear.

Or at least it should have been.

"I knew it!"

When Kegan stepped out of the shadows between Bellywasher's and the building next door and directly into my path, I screeched. He pointed an accusing finger in my direction. It might have been easier to be mad at him if he sounded annoyed rather than hurt. "I knew you were going to go to Brad's tonight. I just knew it."

Since I was pretty sure he couldn't read my mind, I wasn't about to fall for his blatant attempt at getting me to come clean. "I'm on my way home," I told him.

"Uh-huh. That's why you changed from your work shoes to your sneakers."

I *had* changed into the sneakers I kept in my office for

those days when my schedule was hectic and my feet couldn't take another step in pumps, no matter how sensible. I was surprised Kegan noticed such an insignificant detail. Maybe he was more of a detective than I gave him credit for.

I kept walking. "It was a long day," I said. "My feet hurt."

"Yeah, and that explains why you grabbed that digital camera that Jim keeps in the kitchen, too."

I had hoped no one noticed when I scooped up the camera during class the night before. I saw it peeking out of my purse and sighed. "You were supposed to be busy with your mozzarella sticks. Besides, I could be using the camera for anything. Pictures of Fi and the girls. Pictures of spring flowers. Pictures of—"

"Whatever it is we're going to find at Brad's."

Another sigh. It was getting to be a bad habit. I stopped and turned to Kegan. "I can't ask you to do this. It could be dangerous."

"Only if we're not prepared."

"I am prepared. Prepared to do this on my own."

"But I could help."

Who was I to break the kid's investigatin' heart? While I tried to find the words to let him down softly, Kegan spoke up.

"I've got everything we need," he said, and he lifted the paper shopping bag he had with him. I saw that it came from International Spy Museum.

I didn't want to think what might be inside. "Thanks, Kegan. Really. I appreciate you wanting to help, but—"

"But you don't have a tape recorder, do you?" He patted the shopping bag. "I brought one, and it could come in handy. We could talk as we walk through the place, then listen to our recording later. You know, just so we don't forget anything."

"We could, but—"

"But if you start walking around Brad's property with a camera, you're likely to be noticed. Am I right?" Good thing Kegan didn't give me a chance to answer. I wasn't in the mood to admit he was right and I was wrong. Before I could, he dug into the shopping bag and brought out what looked to be a pair of ordinary glasses. He perched them on his nose. "Camera," he said, pointing to the glasses. "Nobody would ever guess."

"No, they wouldn't. But—"

"And a security camera." He brought this out, too, still in its box, and showed it to me. "We can leave this outside the door. You know, just in case anyone happens to show up. I don't know what we'd do if that happened." His laugh was nervous. "But at least we'd know they were coming."

"We would, but—"

"And this is the best!" Again he reached into the bag. He brought out a—

"Remote control car?"

"Not just a remote control car. A spy car. We let it take a look around the place before we even walk in."

"But—"

"But nothing. This is really cool. See." He pointed. "It's got a little built-in camera, and I'll hold on to the monitor. We can look around Brad's place without stepping a foot inside. If something doesn't look kosher, we won't take any chances."

"But—"

I paused, waiting for him to interrupt me yet again. When he didn't, I pulled in a breath and launched into my objections. "I don't want to get you in trouble," I said. "I don't want you to do anything that isn't ethical. I don't want to feel guilty if something happens and you end up with a record because of me. I don't want you to feel as if you have to do this."

"But I do. Don't you get it?" Kegan looked at me carefully. "Eve is your friend, sure, but she's my friend, too," he said. "I've got to help her. And I've got to help you, too, Annie. You guys at Bellywasher's . . . well, you're all special to me. I know it sounds corny and old-fashioned, but heck, ever since Grandpa Holtz died, I've been pretty much on my own. Then I started coming to class here . . . well, you're all like family. I can't let one of the family down. Not if there's any way I can help."

Like I was supposed to find a way to argue with that? Or the puppy dog look that went along with Kegan's statement?

I told him to stow his spy toys and bring them along.

Twelve

✖

BRAD THE IMPALER LIVED (I GUESS I SHOULD SAY *used to live*) in a well-groomed town house in a well-groomed part of town. His home was redbrick and Georgian in style, with neat flower beds on either side of the short front walk, a tiny but perfectly manicured lawn, and outside the first-floor windows, planting boxes filled with yellow and purple pansies.

Call me cynical, but I decided right then and there that there must have been a homeowners' association for this row of town houses and the identical ones that faced it from across a visitors' parking lot. And that the association must have taken care of the outside of the buildings. No way could I picture Brad in the garden on his hands and knees.

Which was exactly where Kegan was. Kneeling on the tiny porch just to the left of the front door, he finished positioning the camera that came with his spy security system and rose. Since he was wearing his camera glasses and the heavy, dark frames made it hard for him to see, standing up wasn't as easy as it sounded. He put a hand on one of the window boxes to boost himself to his feet.

It was the first I noticed that sometime since we'd gotten out of my car, he'd put on a pair of latex surgical gloves.

"What?" When he saw me staring at his hands, Kegan raised his eyebrows, then looked down. "Oh, these. I almost forgot. I was watching an old episode of *Matlock* on cable last night. That's what made me think of the gloves. The bad guy used them when he burglarized a house." I guess this was supposed to make me feel better, because Kegan grinned. "No use taking any chances. I brought a pair for you, too." He dragged the gloves out of his pocket and handed them over.

Of course he was right to think of the precaution, and had I been operating like a real detective instead of like a bank teller who was terrified of being caught at the home of a recent crime victim, I might have thought of it myself. I drew on the gloves at the same time Kegan stepped back. All the while, he kept an eye on the security monitor he held in one hand.

When he pointed, I peered over his shoulder and saw the two of us pictured side by side on the screen. Even though the evening was cool and none of the neighbors were likely to have their windows open, he kept his voice to a whisper. "See? This is perfect. If anybody gets this close to the door, we'll see them for sure. No matter where we are in the house. We'll leave the camera right here when we go inside. Just in case, you know?"

I did know, and it was the *just in case* part I didn't want to think about.

With that in mind and eager to get this over with, I looked over my shoulder one last time. The sidewalk was empty, and though the blue light of a TV flickered from a window next door, there was no sign of activity. And no sign of neighbors, either.

Praying it stayed that way and with hands trembling inside my very own pair of burglar-approved latex gloves, I unlocked Brad's front door.

Anxious to play with his new toys, Kegan had the Spy Museum shopping bag opened on the floor practically before

I had the door closed behind us. He flicked on a flashlight. With its hands-free stand and halogen bulb, it was way more high-tech than the flashlight I always carried in my purse. With the help of the beam of pure, white light, he positioned his security monitor on a table in front of the window and got busy with the spy car.

I left him to it, turning on my own little pathetically un-complicated flashlight and clutching it in my left hand as I slowly made my way through the living room and into the dining room beyond.

"The place is neater than I expected." I whispered, too, just like Kegan had done outside, though come to think of it, I probably didn't need to. I arced my flashlight across the dining room and a china cabinet where crystal wine-glasses were displayed along with a silver serving platter and a decanter that contained what looked to be whiskey. "That should teach me not to judge so quickly. Since Brad was so rude, I guess I just expected—"

"What?"

Since I hadn't heard Kegan come up behind me, I had every right to squeal. Instinctively, I clamped my left hand over my mouth and the beam of my flashlight swung wildly across the ceiling.

In the crazy play of light and shadows, Kegan's eyes were black puddles behind the clear lenses of the camera glasses. "Sorry. I didn't mean to scare you. I wanted you to know that I'm going to start up the car so you wouldn't be surprised by the noise."

Fortunately, the noise was nothing more than a gentle whirr. With Kegan working the joystick controls at the same time he peered at the tiny monitor screen, the car zipped over the hardwood floor, climbed the lip of an Oriental rug under the dining room table, and took off down a hallway on our left. The spy car monitor in both hands, the security camera monitor tucked in his pocket and with the camera glasses down on the end of his nose so he could see where he was going, Kegan headed off after it.

I have to admit, I was relieved. With Kegan busy playing spy, I could get down to some honest-to-gosh detecting.

I peeked into the kitchen but decided right away that chances were slim I'd find anything useful in there. Instead, I looked around for a stairway and climbed. If Brad had secrets, my guess was that he kept them in his bedroom.

Unlike the neat-as-a-pin downstairs, in Brad's bedroom, my light slid over clothing piled at the end of the bed, newspapers scattered on the floor, and an open, half-empty bottle of beer on the dresser. The nearly surgical cleanliness of the first floor had lulled me into thinking my search was going to be impersonal, and as devoid of emotion and full of logic as every investigation should be. Now, these signs of life— a life that had ended horribly and brutally—made my stomach clutch. I wasn't fooling myself, and I sure wasn't trying to fool anyone else; I'd never liked Brad. I had never pretended I did. Brad was pompous and ill-mannered and if half of what the women of WOW said about him was true, he was underhanded and so testosterone-driven that he let his sex drive rule his common sense. None of that explained the sudden knot that blocked my breathing. Especially when I saw that the bed wasn't made. The sheets were pulled back and rumpled from where Brad had lain on them. From where he'd spent his last night on earth.

I guess I'm just a sucker for justice. And getting pushed in front of a Metro train . . . well, not even a Weasel deserved that kind of justice.

I swallowed the lump in my throat and turned my back on the bed. It was time to get down to business.

There was nothing of interest in or on Brad's dresser. Nothing that held a clue to who might have killed him in the piles of papers next to his bed or in his closet or anywhere in the tiny bathroom off the bedroom. Of course, Brad didn't know he was going to leave the house that Monday morning and be murdered. Is that what I expected, some sort of trail of bread crumb clues that would prove that someone other than Eve had done the deed?

Absolutely!

Disappointed I hadn't found it, I went out into the hallway and looked over the railing. "Kegan!" My voice was a stage whisper that was barely louder than the whirr of the spy car from somewhere in the dark downstairs. "Kegan, I'm not having any luck. Have you found anything?"

No answer.

Reluctant to raise my voice, I trooped down the stairs. I aimed my flashlight into the living room. I pointed it into every corner of the dining room. I checked out the kitchen again.

There was no sign of Kegan anywhere.

Still, I heard the whirring sound of the spy car, and I followed it to another bathroom. I found the car caught up under the lower lip of the vanity cabinet, its motor running, its wheels spinning, going nowhere.

I picked it up, turned it off, and tucked it under my arm. What was that I said earlier about wanting to be analytical about this investigation? That'll teach me, because for all its benefits, being analytical has a downside, too. Like right then and there, as I analyzed the situation with all the logic of a real detective:

If Kegan was paying attention to the car monitor screen, he should have seen that the toy was stuck and that now, it was turned off.

Which meant he wasn't paying attention.

Which was weird, considering it was his idea to bring along the spy car in the first place.

My logic *kachunk*ed along, and before I knew it, my heartbeat was speeding as fast as the thoughts that raced through my head.

If Kegan wasn't paying attention to the spy car, it meant he was busy doing something else. Or that he wasn't able to pay attention.

Which might mean he was in trouble.

Which suddenly had me very worried.

"Kegan!" My voice was hushed in the dark, but even I

couldn't fail to hear the note of fear in it. I raced as fast as I could through the dark, retracing my steps through the house as I pictured every disaster imaginable. Most of them included police cars outside, their lights spinning, and uniformed officers closing in on the house to take us into custody.

With no sign of Kegan on the first floor, I hurried back upstairs. "Kegan, where are you?"

"Over here!" He popped out of a doorway on my left, and for the second time in an investigation that should have been all about silence, I let out with a yelp. Kegan didn't hold it against me. He poked a thumb over his shoulder into the blackened room he'd just stepped out of. "Come on. You've got to see what I just found."

What he'd found was Brad's home office. The beam of my flashlight washed over a desk where piles of paper were mounded precariously, a computer, a file cabinet with bulging drawers, and a credenza where more papers— stacks and stacks of papers—were heaped in little mountains that looked as if they'd topple at the slightest touch. It was just the sort of treasure trove I'd been hoping for, so I couldn't hold it against Kegan for being so distracted by it that he hadn't kept track of his spy car. But realizing what it meant, my shoulders drooped.

"It will take us forever to go through all of this stuff," I grumbled.

"But I don't think we have to." Kegan stepped back and trained his light on the wall behind us. One look, and my breath caught.

I was eye to eye with a photograph, and even with no light to go on but the soft glow of my flashlight and the brighter, clearer beam of Kegan's, I would have recognized the blue eyes that looked back at me anywhere. Oh yeah, there was no mistaking the sleek, blonde hair, either. Or the upbeat smile.

"What on earth?" The words whooshed out of me, and

my stomach filled with ice. I'd come to Brad's home specifically to prove that his death was in no way, shape, or form
connected with Eve, and instead of finding something that
would exonerate her and point the finger of guilt at someone else, I'd found her framed photograph hanging on his
office wall. No wonder Tyler had reason to be suspicious!
Though he was a royal pain in the butt, Tyler was also a
good cop, and no doubt, he'd been here before us and had a
look around. No way he could have missed the picture of
Eve. No way he wouldn't have jumped to the conclusion of
what it might mean.

"Darn." There I was, grumbling again, and I didn't even
care. I reached out a hand and clutched Kegan's arm, eager
for comfort and because I knew that, left to their own de-
vices, my knees just might give out. "This is exactly the
kind of thing we didn't want Tyler to find. You know what
this will mean to him, don't you? He's going to make a
huge assumption. He's going to think it proves there was
more to Eve and Brad's relationship than she says there
was. Oh, Kegan . . ." I realized that even as I looked at it,
Eve's face got blurry. That's because my eyes filled with
tears. "This is terrible."

"Maybe not so terrible." Kegan wrapped an arm around
my shoulder so he could turn me just enough to see the rest
of the wall. The light of his flashlight glided over more
photographs. Each was of a woman. No one could have
been more surprised than I was when I realized that I recognized them.

"That's Valerie," I told him. "And this is Grace, one of
the other WOW women I talked to about Brad. As a matter
of fact . . ." I stepped back so that my light, too, could rake
the wall. One by one, I identified the faces of each of the
women I'd talked to with regards to Brad's death.

"It's a wall of suspects," I said. "Or at least it would be
if they all didn't have alibis."

I took another look. There were one, two, three, four,

five, six framed pictures in all, and the way I remembered it, I'd interviewed—

"Five women." Since Kegan had no idea what I was talking about, I caught him up on my thought process. "I talked to five women who said they'd been wronged by Brad, but there are six pictures up there. This is the one who doesn't belong," I said, pointing to a picture that hung in the bottom row and all the way to the right. The photo was of a pretty, light-haired woman with big eyes, long lashes, and cheekbones that would have made a super-model envious. More proof that Brad had an eye for nothing but pretty women. "Who do you suppose she is?"

Kegan leaned closer. "The picture's signed, but she used some kind of silver ink. It's kind of hard to read." I trained my light where his was shining. If I squinted, I could just make out the flowing cursive.

"To the man of my dreams. Love, Gillian."

"Gillian Gleeson?" Kegan leaned in for a better look, but he hardly had a chance. That's because I grabbed his sleeve and tugged him back.

"How do you know her name?"

He pushed his camera glasses up the bridge of his nose and snapped a couple shots of Gillian's photograph and the ones that surrounded it. "I was looking through Brad's mail," Kegan said. "Before you came up here. I saw her name in that pile." He waved in the general direction of one of the mountains on Brad's desk. "Gillian isn't a common name. It's got to be the same person. Who do you suppose she is?"

I wasn't sure, but I knew one thing: Gillian Gleeson was on Brad's trophy wall along with women who I knew for a fact he'd sexually harassed, women whose lives and reputations he'd ruined.

I was thinking like a detective, remember, and like a detective, I knew exactly what this meant. If the other women were Brad's victims, then chances were, Gillian was, too.

That also meant Gillian Gleeson was a suspect in Brad's murder.

UNLIKE THOSE OF US WHO WORK FOR A LIVING, THEN go to their other jobs when their first job is done for the day, Gillian Gleeson apparently had a life. Her chirpy voice mail message said that she was out and that I could leave my name and number. By the time I did that and waited for her to return my call, it was already the weekend. She was not so chirpy when we talked. In fact, she sounded downright gloomy. Nor was she inclined to get together with a stranger who had called out of the blue and would say only that she found her on the Internet and was looking for information. Good news, though, Gillian changed her tune when I finally realized she was being sensible and I was being mysterious for no good reason. As soon as I mentioned that I wanted to talk to her in connection with the investigation into Brad's murder, she agreed to meet with me.

I was thinking like a detective, right?

Thinking like a detective, her quick consent told me she probably wasn't a viable suspect. What suspect in her right mind would agree to meet with someone who was bound to ask all the wrong questions?

But thinking like a detective, I knew I had to give the meeting a shot, anyway. In my efforts to exonerate Eve, I could leave no stone unturned.

Gillian and I set a date and a time, Sunday afternoon, and because he asked so nicely, I agreed to let Kegan come with me. I agreed to meet him at Bellywasher's for the trip out to Middleburg, where Gillian lived.

Kegan was a little late, and the brunch crowd was gone. I knew that before the dinner hour, things would be quiet at the restaurant, so while I waited for him, I took the opportunity to finish up some paperwork. When he still hadn't shown up, I went out to the bar for an iced tea. Monsieur

Lavoie was sitting at a table near the window. I waved to him before I went over to the bar where Jim was working. I was tempted to ask him about Fi and the girls. Since there were smudges of sleeplessness under Jim's eyes, and his cheeks were pale, I played like a detective and figured things out for myself. Rather than bring up what I knew was a touchy subject and remind him of his misery, I made sure my smile was sunny.

"What's up? It feels like we haven't talked in days."

"That's because we haven't." Jim had a rag in one hand, and he wiped down the bar, even though it didn't look like it needed it. "You've been busy."

I added sweetener to my tea and sipped it. "No busier than usual."

"But busy, nonetheless. Busy detecting."

As I may have mentioned before, the subject of my sleuthing had been a sore spot in our relationship. That's why I'd been aboveboard about every phase of this investigation. (Well, except for the part about going to Brad's home. Discretion, as they say, is the better part of valor, and I figured it was smart to keep the details of that little adventure to myself. There was no use making Jim a part of our little conspiracy. If the question came up—like from Tyler—I knew Jim would lie to protect me. Since I couldn't ask him to do that, it was better to say nothing at all.)

I took another sip of tea. "I've been detecting, all right. But I haven't found out a thing."

"Still, you keep trying."

"I have to. If Tyler thinks Eve had anything to do with Brad's murder—"

"I understand that." Jim reached across the bar and squeezed my hand. Since he'd just been cleaning the bar, his hand was damp and cold. "It's just that . . ." He pulled his hand away and turned around, and I saw his shoulders rise and fall. I guess I know Jim well enough to know what that meant. He was making up his mind about something, something important. When he turned back to me, his shoulders were rock steady, his chin was firm. He looked me in the eye. Have I mentioned that his are the most incredible shade of hazel? Caught in their tractor beam, I looked deep into his eyes.

"Have I ever told you that you are . . ." Jim's voice was hesitant, but only for a second. He looked past me and over my shoulder and whatever he saw there, it seemed to give him encouragement. When he looked at me again, his voice was as unwavering as his gaze. "You are light and sunshine," he said. "Flowers in the spring. A soft breeze and a . . . a warm fire."

This was, to say the least, a remarkably romantic thing to hear from a man who was always warm and wonderful but who had never been known to be the hearts-and-flowers type. I was flattered. And bewildered. My natural reaction was a spontaneous, "Huh?"

Jim was not deterred. He went right on. "You're the stars in my night sky," he said and he grabbed both my hands and held them in his. "You're the warm splash of sunlight in a garden. You're—"

"Sorry I'm late! The cherry blossoms are blooming, and traffic is a bear!"

I had been so busy listening to Jim sound like a greeting card, I hadn't heard the front door of Bellywasher's open and close. Kegan called his greeting from the door and closed in on us.

"Hey, what are you guys up to?" he asked.

"Nothing now." Jim grumbled below his breath. This was as much not like him as poetry, and it caught me so off guard, when he turned away, I naturally got defensive.

"Kegan and I have an appointment," I said.

"Of course you do." Jim walked into the kitchen, and I sat back, as confused now as I had been when he was spouting what sounded like country song lyrics.

Kegan plunked down on the barstool next to mine. "You two fighting?"

"I didn't think so." My answer was knee-jerk. Then I

remembered the poetry. "Not fighting," I said. I was sure of it. I think. "Just . . ." I shrugged.

Apparently that was enough of an explanation for Kegan. He jumped off the stool. "Ready to go?" he asked.

I was, and I followed him to the door.

I was ready to talk to Gillian Gleeson and ready to get this investigation off dead center.

I was ready to clear Eve's name, because maybe once I'd done that . . .

Just before I walked out the door, I glanced back toward the kitchen. I saw Jim looking out the window toward me.

I waved. He didn't wave back. I stepped out into the sunny Virginia afternoon with one thought on my mind: maybe once I had this case cleared up, I could get my life back on an even keel.

Right where it belonged.

Thirteen

✖

WHEN GILLIAN GLEESON TOLD ME TO STOP BY, SHE failed to mention that she lived smack in the middle of Virginia horse country and in an elegant home as big as my apartment building. Did I say home? The place was an antebellum plantation mansion, pure and simple, from the white pillars along the front porch (or was it called a portico on a house like that?) to the acres of rolling, beautifully tended land around it. When I rang the bell, I expected a uniformed and gloved butler to answer the door.

But nobody did.

Kegan and I waited for what seemed a polite amount of time. Then I rang again.

When we got the same response, Kegan's shoulders drooped. Poor kid. He was so excited about investigating. He was learning the hard way that a lot of a private investigator's time is spent just watching. And waiting.

"She's not home." His words echoed exactly the same, disheartening thing I was thinking. "So what do real detectives do when something like this happens, Annie? Do we break in?"

I guess my wide-eyed look of horror told him that, well-intentioned or not, his question was out of the question. That's why he stammered, "Well . . . I just . . . I mean, we came all the way out here. And it's important for us to talk to Gillian. I mean, she is . . . she is a suspect, right?"

"We don't know that. We don't know anything about her. We won't. Not until we have a chance to talk to her." I'd brought my cell phone with me and had Gillian's number programmed in. (Another lesson for Kegan: a detective is always prepared, especially a detective who, in her real life, as a bank teller/restaurant business manager plans for every contingency, envisions every possibility, and looks—a dozen or more times—before she ever even thinks about leaping.) I called Gillian. And got no answer.

This time, it was my shoulders that drooped.

Thinking about the best way to handle things, I looked around. There was a window to the left of the front door, and I pressed my nose to the glass. I was peering into a study, and I saw a huge mahogany desk, walls of bookcases, and a plush carpet. What I didn't see were any signs of life. Baffled, I drummed my fingers against the sill.

"We could come back another time."

Kegan's words were reasonable, but I wasn't ready to throw in the towel. I was anxious to talk to Gillian and not so anxious to spend the gas money to get out to the country again. I was also curious. Why would Gillian invite me to her home, then not be there to talk to me?

Unless she had something to hide.

My imagination—and my suspicions—fueled by the thought, I decided right then and there that I wasn't going to give up.

"Come on," I told Kegan, and I headed around to the back of the house.

Of course, being a sensible person, this sounded like a sensible plan to me. On the off chance that Gillian was somewhere where she'd heard neither the doorbell or her phone, I'd look around in the hopes of finding her. But being sensible, I had no concept of how big grand old plantation homes can be. By the time we were nearing the place where we could head to the right and come up behind the house, we were threading our way through magnolia trees covered with flowers and a maze of rhododendrons that looked as if they'd be bursting with spectacular blooms in just a few more weeks, and I was out of breath.

I'd like to think that's why I gasped when I finally rounded the corner and nearly slammed into a tall woman wearing dirty jeans and a ratty sweatshirt.

She was uncommonly pretty, with big eyes, long lashes, and cheekbones that would have made a supermodel envious. Yeah, I recognized her, all right. Even though in that picture that hung in Brad's office, her eyes weren't swollen, her face wasn't drawn, and there wasn't a gray pallor to her skin.

Gillian Gleeson jumped back and pressed a hand to her heart.

And me? Sensible person that I am, I apologized as quickly as I could. "I'm so sorry to have startled you. When you didn't answer your doorbell . . ."

Gillian stared blankly for a moment, then the light dawned. She pulled out the earbuds attached to her iPod and gave me a weak, embarrassed smile. "I do apologize," she said. I've lived in Virginia all my life, and I'm used to what Yankees call our accent. But Gillian's was different. Her vowels were long and drawn out, her enunciation was perfect. Every word dripped culture. Oh yeah, and old money. "It seems as if I lost track of the time. You're the one who called. About . . . about Brad."

"That's right, Annie Capshaw." I stuck out my hand, and while I was at it, I introduced Kegan.

Gillian pulled off her gardening gloves and shook both our hands. "I get so wrapped up when I'm out here gardening. I just love puttering in the soil, and after all that's happened . . ." Her voice drifted along with her gaze, and I looked around, too. The garden was bright with yellow and

white daffodils and hyacinths in shades of pink and purple
that made the air sweet and heavy. It was a perfectly manicured space, with the flower beds laid out precisely amid a
labyrinth of stone paths and gurgling fountains.

No big surprise, the orderliness appealed to me. But it
was the sheer beauty of the garden that caused me to gasp,
"It's gorgeous." I wasn't trying to ingratiate myself to
Gillian. For all I knew, she was a murderer. But heck, I
couldn't help but be impressed. "I live in an apartment and
don't have a garden to work in, but if I did . . ." Another
look around, and I was convinced. "I'd sure want it to look
like this."

I could tell she was proud of her work, because her eyes
gleamed, even if her smile wasn't convincing. "It takes a
great deal of time and hard work," she explained. "Of
course, now that it's the only thing I have to do . . ." Her eyes
filled with tears, and she turned away.

Kegan and I exchanged puzzled looks, but the instant it
looked like he might say something to try to soothe the
awkward moment, I sushed him, one finger to my lips. Little did he know he'd just stepped into another lesson in the
fine art of detecting: sometimes it's best not to speak, because sometimes, in those quiet moments, a suspect starts
talking.

Lucky for us, that's exactly what happened.

Gillian tossed her gloves down on a nearby bench and
invited us inside for a drink. She led us through French
doors and into a spacious sunroom furnished with white
wicker furniture. "I've been so distracted lately," she said
on the end of a sigh. "But then, I'm sure you understand.
When you called, you told me that you knew Brad."

"Yes. He was in my cooking class." All right, so it
wasn't exactly *my* cooking class. It was easier to say it was
than to try explain that I was really just Jim's sometime assistant who was really the business manager who was really a bank teller who was really—

I snapped myself out of it before I got too carried away.

"Maybe Brad mentioned the class? It's at Bellywasher's, a restaurant in Alexandria."

"Cooking class!" I guess Gillian felt about cooking the way I feel about cooking; a single tear glided down her cheek. There was a box of tissues on the coffee table between the couch where Kegan and I sat down and the chair she took for herself. She plucked out a tissue and dabbed her eyes. When she laughed, her voice was watery. "Did he confess?" she asked, and when I gave her a blank look, she shook her head. "No, I didn't think so. That was just like Brad. If you knew him at all, you must realize that. He didn't have the slightest interest in learning how to cook."

That explained a lot. At least a lot about Brad's attitude in class. Rather than point that out, I made myself comfortable against the lavish blue and yellow floral cushions. Since I didn't know where the conversation was headed, I toed the line between saying too much and hoping to draw Gillian into saying more. I tucked my hand down between the cushion I was sitting on and the one next to it. Just so Gillian couldn't see that my fingers were crossed. "Brad tried his best," I said.

She nodded. "Of course. He always did. And he was learning to cook for me, you know. Because he knew I would appreciate the effort he was making. That was so like him."

"You knew him well." This was far more politically correct than pointing out that if she thought Brad was trying his best as he groused and grumbled his way through class, she must not have known him well at all. I tried for the sisterly WOW approach I knew would make any Brad victim spill her guts. "I'm sorry. The whole thing with Brad . . . that must have been very difficult for you."

"Yes, of course." She sniffled in a genteel sort of way. "It was such a shock."

"So you never met any of the other women?"

The look Gillian turned on me was nothing less than icy.

And suddenly, I began to wonder. Oh, not about Brad. I knew we were talking about the same thing: Brad's murder.

I just questioned whether her take on Brad's death and mine were the same.

"Oh." Was that my voice, small and ill at ease? It must have been, because when I looked toward Kegan for support, I saw that his face was as red as a beet and his hands were clutched together on his lap. I wasn't the only one getting the message from Gillian. Now if I could only figure out what it meant!

Certain it was time to stop beating around the bush, I leaned forward. "I'm here because I'm trying to figure out who killed Brad," I said.

Relief washed over Gillian's expression. "And I'm so glad! In my opinion, the police aren't doing nearly enough. You said something about women. Other women. Do you think one of them might have killed my Brad?"

OK, call me slow on the uptake. It took that one moment and that one phrase—*my Brad*—to make me see the light. I sat back, the better to let the icy claw in my stomach uncurl. "You're sorry Brad's dead," I said.

Gillian's eyes brimmed with tears. Her voice teetered on the brink of hysteria. "Sorry? Of course I'm sorry. Brad was the love of my life, my soul mate. We were engaged to be married."

IT WAS THE MOTHER OF ALL UNCOMFORTABLE moments, but luckily, Gillian didn't stay around long enough to hear me stammer out an apology that wouldn't have made any sense unless she realized I had been thinking of her as a suspect. Which, come to think of it, would have been just as embarrassing. She hopped up, mumbled something about splashing cold water on her face, and left Kegan and me to sit there in stunned silence. That's the way things stayed for a minute or so. Then he hopped out of his chair, too.

"Come on," he said. "Let's go have a look around before she comes back."

"You're kidding me, right?" He'd already started toward the door, and I had no choice but to leap off the couch so that I could clap a hand on his arm and keep him from leaving the room. "We can't just go snooping through the woman's house. That would be terrible."

"It would be terrible if she wasn't a suspect."

"But we don't know if she is a suspect. In fact, she might be the only nonsuspect we've met. She's the only one who actually cares that Brad is dead."

"And I think that makes her look more suspicious than anyone else."

In its own, crazy way, Kegan's theory actually made sense. Unfortunately, I thought about this for a moment too long. By the time I was willing to admit that he might be right and suggest that instead of ransacking the house, we conduct the rest of our interview more carefully, Gillian was back, and Kegan was saying something about finding the bathroom and heading out in the direction where she pointed.

All of which, of course, left Gillian and me with nothing in common and nothing to talk about.

Except Brad, of course.

"I'm sorry for your loss," I said, and it wasn't a lie. I had never liked Brad but, believe me, I recognized pain when I saw it. Gillian might have questionable taste in fiancés, but that did nothing to ease the hurt. "If there's anything I can do—"

"You said you were trying to find out who killed him. That's the best thing you could do for me. Do you have any suspects?"

I shrugged. "We thought we did. Nothing's panned out."

"So you want to know more about Brad, about his life. You think that might help you figure out who did this terrible thing to him."

"That's right." I settled myself back on the couch, glancing at the doorway as I did and hoping that Kegan really was in the bathroom and not wandering around the house playing detective. "What can you tell me?"

Gillian's smile was soft at the edges. "I can tell you that a lot of people were jealous of Brad."

"You mean—"

"That what you may have heard about him, none of it is true."

"Except that I've heard the same sorts of things from a lot of people."

Gillian hadn't sat down when she came in, and now she paced to the far end of the sunroom and back again. "You're talking about those women. The ones who are trying to trash his reputation."

"They say he harassed them."

"Like he'd need to!" For a cultured woman, Gillian's snort was monumental. "Why would a man as handsome and as charming as Brad need to beg a woman for sex? Don't you see? Those women, they said what they did about him because they were the ones who were after him. When he rejected them . . ." It was her turn to shrug. Her gesture was much more regal and dismissive than mine. "There are so many jealous people in the world. That explains what happened at the *Washington Star*, too. Those other reporters weren't nearly as good as Brad. They weren't nearly as talented. They made up lies about him."

"That he phonied up sources."

"That's right." Gillian's chin was high and steady. "He told me they were jealous."

"And you believed him?"

Her eyes flashed and, honestly, if I wasn't so anxious to get a handle on this case, I would have let her go right on being mad at me. She deserved it for believing that line of bull Brad had handed her. But I couldn't afford to alienate her, not when I was desperate for answers.

"It's not that I'm doubting you. Or him," I hurried to say. "It's just that . . . well, been there done that, when it comes to the cheating significant other. I know that guys don't always tell the truth."

"Maybe that's true of some men. Brad wasn't one of them."

Good thing Kegan chose that moment to come back in the room. I didn't know how I would have responded. Instead, I looked Kegan's way, and I was instantly sure that he'd actually been in the bathroom, that he hadn't taken a quick look around. How did I know? Nobody as honest as Kegan could look that innocent if he had something to hide.

I admit it, I was disappointed. I didn't approve of the snooping plan, but I wouldn't have objected if he'd found something interesting. I also wasn't going to let that stop me.

When I asked my next question, I watched Gillian closely. "What about the other women, then? The ones whose pictures are in Brad's office?"

"You've been inside?"

I realized my mistake the moment she asked the question and was all set to scramble with a lie about how the police had let me go to Brad's with them when they searched his home. But the next moment, Gillian spoke, and I knew I'd panicked too soon. She wasn't questioning what I'd been doing in Brad's house, she was talking about his home office.

"We were in his office. Yes." I did my best not to sound as guilty as I felt about this. "There are pictures of six women there on the wall. You're one of them. The other five are women I've talked to. Women who say they were harassed by Brad."

"No. It isn't possible." Gillian sank into the nearest chair. "He told me none of that was true. But he never—" She chewed her lower lip, and I knew she was trying to decide if she could trust me. When she looked at me through her veil of long, lush lashes, I knew she'd made up her mind. "He never let me in his office. He always kept it locked. He said there was nothing in there but boring papers for work."

That explained why Eve hadn't seen her own picture on Brad's wall. He kept his office locked, and it wasn't until after Brad died and the cops looked around his house that it was left open.

"Then I'm sorry, but he lied to you. I've talked to the other women, and they each have an alibi for the day Brad was murdered." Could I be blamed for leaving out the part about Eve? I think not. I went right on. "When we saw your picture, we didn't know who you were, and we thought—"

"That I killed Brad?" The color washed out of Gillian's face. Tears streamed down her cheeks. "I could never. I loved Brad. With all my heart."

I didn't bother pointing out that this was probably one of the dumbest things she'd ever done. Eventually, Gillian would figure that out on her own. For now, I had to stick to the facts. "Then maybe you can help me find out who killed him," I said.

"Anything." Gillian clutched her hands together on her lap so tight, her knuckles were white. "Ask me anything, and I'll try to answer. If one of these other women—"

"We don't think so." It was the first thing Kegan had said since we walked into the house. For this, I was grateful. I was feeling my way through this interview, and I didn't need to worry that he might say the wrong thing before he even realized it was wrong. I sent him a look to thank him for his help and took over before he could say another word. I remembered something Gillian had mentioned earlier.

"You were right when you said we needed to learn more about Brad's life. Now that we know you were close, I know you're the perfect person to ask. Had he been acting odd lately?"

Her shrug said it all. "Brad never acted normal. I mean, normal is boring, isn't it? And Brad was anything but. He was dynamic. And exciting. Though now that you mention it . . ." Her eyes clouded, and she tipped her head, thinking.

"He told me he was going to come into some money," she said.

"Did he say how?"

"No. He just said it was a kind of bonus. He was very excited about it, though, so I assumed it had something to do with his work. And oh . . ." She stopped to think again. "He said something about sending a package here to the house. He addressed it to himself, he said, and I had strict orders not to open it."

At this, I could practically hear Kegan purr with excitement, and I couldn't blame him. I, too, was captured by the intriguing idea of a mysterious package that came along with the caveat to leave it unopened. It might not mean anything at all, of course, in terms of Brad's death. Then again, it might be a significant clue.

I scooted closer to the edge of the couch. "Has the package arrived yet?"

"No." Gillian rose. "In light of everything that's happened, I forgot all about it until right this moment. But Martha, my housekeeper . . . if the package had arrived sometime while I was out, she would have put it on the desk in my study. Especially if it was addressed to Brad and not to me. She knows how much he meant to me."

A fresh stream of tears poured down Gillian's cheeks, and this time, she didn't even attempt to wipe them away. "Oh, Brad!" Her shoulders heaved, and she sobbed. "I miss him so terribly. You've got to help me find out who killed him, Miss Capshaw. You have to help me find justice for Brad's killer."

"It's what I want, too." I knew we'd get nothing else out of her, not when she was that upset, so I rose and put a hand on her shoulder. "You can help," I told her. I handed her one of my Bellywasher's business cards. "When that package arrives, give me a call, will you?"

She looked up at me, and her eyes shone with tears. "You mean, you think there's something in that package that will tell us who killed Brad?"

I couldn't make those kinds of promises. Instead, I told her we'd find out when the package arrived. A moment later, we showed ourselves out.

I didn't dare say a word to Kegan until we were in the car. "So?"

He looked out the window. "So, nothing. She was telling the truth about the package."

I wheeled my car along the long, curving drive. "And you know this, how?"

"Because I looked around, of course. While I was supposed to be in the bathroom. I checked out her study. And her bedroom and—"

"Kegan!" I was appalled. I kept one hand on the wheel and pressed the other to my heart. "You didn't!"

Kegan laughed. "Of course I did, Annie. That's what real detectives do. And we're real detectives, aren't we?"

Fourteen

✖

IT WASN'T AS IF I FORGOT ABOUT GILLIAN, IT WAS just that in spite of Kegan's twisted logic to the contrary, I didn't think she was really much of a suspect. She loved Brad Peterson.

Go figure.

And though, thanks to Peter, I had learned from first-hand experience that love could turn sour, go wrong, go bad, and just plain shrivel up and die, I couldn't wrap my brain around any scenario that would have morphed Gillian, devoted and supportive as she was, into the one who had shoved Brad into the path of that Metro train.

Except for that wall of photographs in Brad's office, of course.

Gillian said she'd never seen the pictures. She'd acted surprised to hear she was just another of Brad's trophies. But was she? Surprised, I mean. What if she knew about the other women? About Brad's reputation? The other women had their careers ruined by the man, but what if it was even more serious for Gillian?

What if Brad had broken her heart?

I knew exactly how that felt. Though I'd never plotted

Peter's demise (except in the blackest of moments, and even then, I knew it was only a stress reliever and not an actual plan), I could well imagine that a woman's hurt could grow and swell beyond anger and all the way to a hate that might make her kill.

Was Gillian one of those women?

It was a tantalizing thought, and I promised myself I'd consider it—as soon as I had time. Believe me, over the next few days, I didn't have time to think about Gillian or much of anything else. Not when I had Fi to worry about.

Fi had a doctor's appointment and needed someone to watch the girls while she was gone. Jim insisted the restaurant was busy that afternoon (the daily receipts did not bear him out, but I didn't know that until after the ordeal was over) and begged me to please, please, please babysit on my lunch hour.

Fi had to go shopping for boy's clothes and desperately wanted someone along who was focused enough to keep her out of the pink-clothes aisle and firmly in the blue.

Fi needed moral support and a shoulder to cry on. Boy, did she need a shoulder to cry on. By the time it was all over, three days had flown by, and I was too tired to care who had killed Brad. As long as it wasn't Eve.

I guess that's why I forgot all about that package Brad said he sent to Gillian. Or at least I forgot that she was supposed to call and let me know when the package arrived.

In fact, I wouldn't have remembered it at all if not for Kegan mentioning it the next Monday after class (Veggie Night, but don't worry, it wasn't nearly as healthy as it sounds, considering that the menu included homemade potato, sweet potato, and root vegetable chips; onion rings; and fried mushrooms). I'd just stepped into my office, and he was right behind me.

"Seems weird, don't you think?" He scratched a hand through his short-cropped hair. "Gillian said she'd call, and she hasn't. I've been trying to think like a detective, and I think this makes her look guiltier than ever. I'll bet the package from Brad arrived, and there's something incriminating in it. That's why she doesn't want us to know."

I was looking through the day's mail and only half listening, but that didn't dull my logic. "Or it means the package hasn't arrived. Or it has, and Gillian hasn't opened it. Or she did open it, and it has nothing to do with Brad getting killed, or—"

Kegan laughed in an embarrassed sort of way. "I get the message. I'm jumping to conclusions, and that's one thing a detective should never do. No wonder you're so good at this, Annie. You're—"

Something he said struck a chord—now, if I could only figure out what it was. My head came up, and I looked at him hard. "What was that you said?"

Thinking, he wrinkled his nose, and since he didn't know what I was getting at any more than I did, he hesitated. "I said . . . I said I was jumping to conclusions. At least that's what I think I said. I said . . . I think I said that because you don't jump to conclusions, it proves you're a good detective and I'm just a rookie."

It didn't click. "Not that. Before that."

"I said . . ." He thought some more. "I think I said I got the message."

"That's it!" I tossed down the pile of mail and grabbed my phone. It had a little red light on the side of it that flashed when there was a message waiting. It wasn't flashing. Did that stop me? I connected to my voice mail, put in my password, and heard a computer-generated voice tell me that I had one saved message.

Yes, it was from Gillian. She said was calling just like she promised she would. The package had arrived, she told me. Since whatever was in the package might be important and might help solve Brad's murder, she was waiting for me to come back out to Middleburg before she opened it.

According to that same computer voice, the message had arrived a couple hours before.

When I was helping Jim in class.

It didn't take a detective to figure out who had picked it up. At the time, Eve was the only one in the restaurant. She was helping arrange the flowers we'd ordered for a retirement party the next evening. Eve—the only one around there besides Jim, who knew my voice mail PIN.

I think even before I clicked off the phone, I was already grumbling. That would explain why Kegan looked a little worried.

"I'm not mad at you," I told him because he was so darned cute and he looked so darned concerned that he'd said something to offend me that I felt I owed him. I guess slamming the phone down on its recharger didn't exactly prove my point. "It's Eve. She's got to be the one who picked up the message. You know what this means, don't you?"

Of course Kegan didn't. That didn't stop him from following me when I grabbed my purse. Jim was behind the bar, and I didn't stop to explain where I was going. I waved good-bye and pushed out the door.

"She wants to help," I told Kegan. "Eve always wants to help."

He scrambled to keep up. "And that's a bad thing because . . . ?"

"Because Eve is Eve. Because Eve is a suspect. Because Eve hated Brad, and she shouldn't be one-on-one with the woman who loved him. Not without someone there to run interference."

I unlocked my car, and Kegan and I jumped in. I knew he was still trying to work his way through the problem, because he was quiet for a couple minutes. It wasn't until we were on the Capital Beltway and heading west that he spoke. "So why would Eve take a chance?" he asked. "I mean, why make things more complicated? She must know it would just be better for you to handle this whole thing with Gillian. Why does Eve want to get involved?"

I was changing lanes, and I waited until I was safely where I belonged before I answered. Then again, a sigh isn't much of an answer. "Maybe she's feeling left out," I said. "She's seen that we've been investigating together and, knowing Eve, she feels like she's missing out on the action. She wants to be a part of it. Maybe she's just trying to save me the time and money of driving all the way to Middleburg again. That would be just like her, going out of her way to save me a couple bucks when she can't afford it any more than I can. Maybe she thinks now that you and I are friends, I'm pushing her out of my life. Who knows!" I took my hands off the wheel just long enough for a gesture of utter frustration.

"So you think that she's . . . ?"

"Gone out to Gillian's on her own? I'm sure of it."

"And you're worried?"

"Do I look worried?"

"Well, you are speeding."

I was. I let up on the accelerator. "Eve knows better than to do anything stupid," I told Kegan and reminded myself.

I actually might have gone right on believing that if when we arrived at Gillians's, the place wasn't teeming with police cars and if in the pulsing glow of their lights, I didn't see Eve being led away in handcuffs.

THE MIDDLEBURG, VIRGINIA, POLICE STATION IS A nice enough place, but believe me when I say that I wished I was anywhere but. Kegan and I waited while they processed Eve (though they refused to tell us what they were processing her for) and thank goodness he was there with me. Sure, I'm graceful under pressure. In most situations, anyway. Yes, I'm logical, reasonable, and rational. But none of that applies when it comes to watching my best friend get arrested.

I was a basket case, pure and simple, and Kegan—bless his little environmentally friendly heart—was a trooper. He brought me hot chocolate and apologized because it was in a foam cup. He called Jim because he said I was too upset to talk (he was right) and explained where we were and what was happening. He sat at my side, and he held my hand, and when a fresh-faced officer finally came out to the waiting room and told me I could go back and talk to Eve, Kegan came along, too. But only as far as the doorway.

"I'd better wait here." Kegan peered into the hallway beyond the front desk. "Eve's probably upset. She needs a friend more than she needs me poking my nose where it doesn't belong."

See what I mean? When it came to knowing what to say and when to say it, the kid was darned near perfect. He even gave me a pat on a back to buck me up.

It worked. A little. My breath tight in my chest and my heart beating double time, I went toward where the officer pointed, rounded a corner, and saw immediately why we'd had to wait so long.

No doubt, it took Tyler Cooper a while to drive out there.

He wasn't any happier to see me than I was to see him, but that didn't stop me from closing in on Tyler and grabbing on to his arm with both hands. Any port in a storm, as they say, and at times like that, a familiar face is a familiar face, and a familiar face offers at least a little comfort.

"They arrested her, Tyler." My words bubbled around the tears I'd refused to let fall when I was out in the waiting area. "They've got her locked up somewhere. What's happening? What did Eve do?"

He gave me that enigmatic look of his, the one that was so annoying. It made me want to scream. "You don't know?"

"Would I be asking if I did?"

Tyler had been leaning against the wall, and when he straightened up, I let go of his arm. He worked a kink out of his neck. "Did you know Ms. Gleeson?" he asked.

"Gillian?" I hadn't been thinking straight. I hadn't been thinking at all. For the first time, I realized I hadn't seen Gillian there at the station, and that if Eve had been accused of something—like breaking into Gillian's house or refusing to leave when Gillian asked or upsetting Gillian enough for her to call the police—I would have thought she'd be there filing her complaint. Then again, maybe people with money get to do that sort of thing from the comfort of their own homes.

"I've met her," I told Tyler, because I knew until I told him what he wanted to know, he'd never tell me anything at all. "She was engaged to Brad Peterson, you know."

He nodded. "And you care about this, why?"

"Because Eve didn't kill Brad." Just in case Tyler really was that dumb, I pinned him with a look when I said this. "I thought if I talked to Gillian, I could find out more. You know, about Brad. About his life. About what he did and where he went and who he knew. About who—"

"Who might have killed him?"

I shouldn't have been embarrassed to admit it. Still, when Tyler put it so bluntly, it did sound like I was talking about a case that was completely out of my league. Then again, I had already solved two cases that had baffled Tyler and the rest of the Arlington force.

I raised my chin. "That's right. I thought Gillian might know something about Brad's death."

"And did she?"

My shrug was as noncommittal as my words. "She doesn't know about the other women. You know, the ones who Brad has wronged. Or at least she says she doesn't. And if she's lying . . ." I was hedging my bets again, guessing there was no way Tyler could be so dense, but I couldn't take any chances. Eve's freedom might be on the line; I had to be sure he understood.

I looked Tyler in the eye. "If Gillan's the jealous type, she's definitely a suspect."

"No, she's not."

I wasn't willing to concede the point this soon, but I knew arguing it would get me nowhere. I regrouped, pulling in a deep breath while I tried an end run around Tyler's argument. "All right. Let's say Gillian's not a suspect. That doesn't change the fact that Brad sent a package to her home. A mysterious package."

"Mysterious, huh?"

Was that a gleam of interest I saw in Tyler's cold, blue eyes? It was enough to make me think the man was almost human.

Encouraged by the thought, I went right on. "Yes, mysterious. Because he sent it to Gillian's house, but he addressed it to himself. And he told her not to open it until he was around. So you see, the package might be important."

"It's not."

Do I need to point out that by this time, I was getting a little frustrated? My words were clipped by my gritted teeth. "But we don't know that. Not for sure. Since Brad couldn't open the package—he's dead, remember—I asked Gillian to call me when it was delivered. And—"

"Did she?"

"Call me? Yes, just this evening. Which is why I came out to see her, only when I got there—"

"Eve was already there."

I threw my hands in the air. "Well, if you already know everything, why are you bothering to talk to me at all?"

"You're the one who started the talking."

"And you're the one who hasn't told me one, blessed thing. What's happening, Tyler? What did Eve do? Because you know as well as I do that she doesn't have a nasty bone in her body. If Gillian says—"

"She doesn't."

"Then if Gillian thinks—"

"She doesn't do that, either."

This time I didn't even try to contain my screech. Though I did make sure I kept it down so the cops out front didn't know I was being driven to distraction by the most annoying man ever to carry a badge. "What are you talking about?" I demanded of Tyler. "What's going on? Tell me now, Tyler, or I can't be responsible for what I might do to you. What did Eve do?"

I don't think it was my threat that got him to talk. In fact, for a fraction of a second, I actually thought Tyler was going to laugh. His expression faded as quickly as it came, and the next thing I knew, his eyes flashed, and his jaw was so tight, I swear I could hear the bones grinding against each other.

"What did Eve do? Well, you're going to have to ask her that. I'll tell you what she was arrested for. The murder of Gillian Gleeson."

I DON'T KNOW HOW LONG I STOOD THERE AFTER Tyler walked away. I was frozen to the spot, my insides icy and shivering as much as if I was out in a snowstorm without a coat. I guess it was when I wrapped my arms around myself to keep warm that I realized where I really was. And what I had to do.

I swiped the tears off my cheeks, pulled back my shoulders, and opened the door to the room where Eve was waiting.

The second I saw that she was crying, I started all over again, too.

"Oh, Annie!" She fell into my arms, which isn't easy, since she's so much taller than me. With her hanging on, I back-stepped across the room over to a table and chairs. I pressed her down into one of the chairs and took the one next to it. Just in time, too. From the way they were shaking, I knew my legs weren't going to hold me much longer.

"What happened, Eve?" We were holding hands, but I couldn't tell if she was clinging to me or I was clinging to her. I guess it didn't matter. "Tyler told me . . ." I choked on the words. "He said . . ."

"That I killed Gillian." Eve's voice was breathless. Her skin was ashen. Now that she was sitting opposite me, I noticed that there was a maroon-colored smudge across the front of her pink mohair sweater. I knew instinctively what it was, and instinctively I pulled my hands away.

Eve's eyes welled with fresh tears. "You think I did it, too. You think—"

"No. Really." I felt as guilty as a best friend can who's just let a best friend down but, try as I might (and believe me when I say I tried), I couldn't pull my gaze away from the macabre stain. "It's just that—"

"I found her, Annie." Eve's words were nearly lost beneath her sobs. "I went to Gillian's because . . . because I hated sitting around doing nothing while you and Kegan were doing all the work. I figured I'd help you out in the office, and that's why I picked up the message. And then when I heard it was from Gillian . . . well, I wanted to help with the case. And I went to her house and the door was open and I walked into her study and . . . and . . ."

I patted Eve's arm. "How did it happen?"

She made a face. "Someone stabbed her."

"And you called the police?"

"I didn't have a chance." Her shoulders rose and fell along with her voice. "I knelt down on the floor to see if she was still alive. And the knife was right there. And I knew I shouldn't pick it up, I mean, that's what all the stupid people in the movies do, right? They pick up the murder weapon and get their fingerprints all over it. So I knew I shouldn't, but . . . but I did anyway, and just as I did . . . the housekeeper walked in."

The ice water in my veins solidified. It was hard to breathe. "She called the cops."

Eve nodded. "Only I didn't do it, Annie. I didn't kill Gillian. I didn't even know Gillian. I never talked to her. I'd never even seen her before. Not until I saw her dead. I just thought—"

"I know." I chafed Eve's hands between mine. "You just wanted to help."

A wave of panic engulfed her, and she dropped her face in her hands. "I didn't do it, Annie. I swear I didn't do it."

She was still crying when Tyler and the young officer walked into the room.

"Ms. DeCateur, you're going to need to stay here tonight. Until you're arraigned." The officer was almost apologetic. "We'll get you to a cell and—"

"Annie, you've got to help me!" Eve's plea cut across the policeman's voice. "You've got to!"

"I will," I promised. "You know I will. And we'll get you out of here first thing in the morning. I'll stay in Middleburg tonight," I added, just as the officer took Eve out of the room. "I'll be in court tomorrow morning. You can count on it."

"That's what real friendship is all about."

I didn't bother to honor the comment from Tyler with a reply. At least not until Eve was out of the room. Then I turned both barrels on him. "You think this is funny, Tyler Cooper? Then you really are as much of a cold-hearted bastard as Eve always said you were. You know this is a crock. No way did Eve kill someone. She didn't even know Gillian. Doesn't that prove anything to you?"

For a moment, I thought I was actually going to get a reasonable response out of Tyler. That's how thoughtful he looked. But the moment didn't last long, and the next thing I knew, he shook his head.

"You just don't get it, do you? Eve didn't have to know Ms. Gleeson to be jealous of her."

"Jealous?" I have to admit, this was one scenario I had never even considered. That was because it was impossible.

I propped my fists on my hips. "You're nuts," I told Tyler and, since my voice was loud enough to wake the dead, I guess I didn't care who heard me. "First you thought Eve killed Brad because she hated him. Now you think she killed Gillian because she was jealous because Brad and Gillian were getting married. Make up your mind, Tyler. You can't have it both ways."

A smile came and went across his somber expression. "Sure I can." He sauntered out of the room. "Eve wants

Brad, Brad doesn't want Eve. Brad chooses someone else,
Eve gets more jealous than ever. It's a sad story, but it's
nothing new. We both know how bitter Ms. DeCateur can
get when she's dumped."

Fifteen

✖

"I OWE YOU. YOU KNOW I DO. I'LL DO ANYTHING I can to make it up to you."

Since Eve was saying this to Jim and not to me (who'd not only stayed in an old country inn I couldn't afford the night before when Eve was in the Middleburg jail, paid for a room for Kegan, too, and had taken the day off from the bank because I was so worried about paying for those rooms, I hadn't slept a wink), no one could blame me for being a little miffed. Especially since I didn't know what they were talking about.

"What's going on?" I was done playing games; it was easier just to come right out and ask. "What do you mean you owe Jim? For what?"

Since she'd gotten out of jail on bond, Eve had been more emotional than ever. Her eyes filled with tears. "Why, for the—"

"It's not but nothing." The bar didn't need to be cleaned, but Jim swiped it with a wet cloth, anyway. "She's just being burbly. You know, on account of her having a felony record and all."

He was going for funny. It didn't work. The waterworks burst, and Eve dropped her head into her hands.

Jim's expression fell. "I didn't mean to—"

"Of course you didn't." I grabbed the rag out of his hand and tossed it back on the sink. "Now, would somebody please tell me what's going on?"

"No." This from Jim, at the same time Eve lifted her head and said, "Yes."

Of course I was more curious than ever. Luckily, the phone rang. The lunch crowd was gone. We were the only three people in Bellywasher's, and I made it clear that I wasn't going to answer the phone, so Jim had no choice. Once he was gone, I dropped into the chair across from where Eve sat.

"What are you thanking Jim for?"

"Don't you know?" She sniffed and gently dabbed her nose with a tissue. She'd done so much crying since the night before when she was arrested, her nose was raw and red. "Well, of course you don't. He wouldn't tell you, would he? He's not like that, not looking for praise or anything. Which only goes to show that he—"

"Eve!"

She glanced toward where Jim was still on the phone and lowered her voice. "I promised not to tell."

"But you're going to, anyway."

It was proof of her weakened condition that she didn't argue. "It's how I got out on bail. I know, I know . . . I told you I got the money from my parents, but that's not true. They couldn't come up with enough, and I know you tried, too, but there's no way you have that much money. And he made me promise I'd lie about it, but . . . Jim . . ." Eve sniffled, and a fresh cascade of tears started. "He put up Bellywasher's as collateral."

I was surprised. Only I really wasn't. It was just like Jim to come to the aid of a friend and then not make a big deal out of it. My heart squeezed with affection, and when he finished on the phone and hung up, I didn't give him a chance to say a word. I raced over and gave Jim a big, sloppy kiss.

Obviously, he knew Eve spilled the beans, but he wasn't very good at pretending to be mad about it. A smile threatened to destroy what he thought was an angry expression. "Well, I don't know what I did to deserve that."

"You certainly do."

Jim rolled his eyes. "It was naught. And I told her not to tell you, besides."

"But she did tell me." There was no use wasting the chance of being that close to Jim. I gave him a hug. "Have I told you lately that you're the greatest guy alive?"

Jim wrapped his arms around my waist. "You have not. But I'm more than willing to listen, if you'd like to tell me now."

"Didn't I just do that?"

"Not in so many words. But I've been thinking, with all the stress of what's happening, if we could get away . . . just the two of us. There's little happening here at the restaurant tomorrow that Marc and Damien can't handle, and you do have vacation time coming, don't you? We could—"

Believe me, when I was standing that close to Jim, and he had his arms around me, it wouldn't have taken too long to convince me to do anything. No matter what his plan. Unfortunately, I never had a chance to get the details. The front door flew open, and Fi and the girls paraded in.

Jim's expectant smile vanished, and he glanced toward the phone on the back of the bar. "That was her on the phone. She called to say they were just parking the car. She's got another doctor's appointment," he said, keeping his voice down so Fi wouldn't hear him. As if she could. The girls were making so much noise, I could barely hear him. And he was right there next to me. "I'll lose my mind with these wee bairns here."

"Only maybe you don't have to." After I gave him another peck on the cheek, I pulled away from Jim and signaled to Eve. "You want to know what you can do to thank

Jim for bailing you out of jail?" I guess the look I gave the girls made it easy for Eve to read my mind.

Good sport that she is, she clapped her hands and spoke nice and loud, like she was up on stage talking to a dozen beauty pageant judges and the hundreds of people who watched from the audience. "Girls! Let's get our acts together." She breezed through the room and in a jiffy; she had the girls lined up, oldest to youngest, near the door. "We're going out," she told them. "And you're going to behave like the little ladies you are. Every single one of you."

Did I believe they would? Honestly, no. But I knew we'd found a solution to Jim's problem and a perfect way to keep Eve occupied, too. With the girls under her wing, she wouldn't have any time to think about her own troubles.

That taken care of, I brushed my hands together and waited for them to march out of the restaurant. Once they were gone, it was time for me to get down to some work of my own.

I kissed Jim one more time, then ducked into my office to call the Arlington Police Department. Once I was connected with the right desk, I started talking, almost before Tyler had identified himself. I didn't want to give him the chance to hang up on me.

"You said it wasn't important," I blurted out. "How do you know that, Tyler? How do you know the package Brad sent Gillian wasn't important? Unless you know what was in it."

"So . . ." I could picture Tyler making himself comfortable. He'd lean back and put his feet on his desk. "You've been thinking about that all night, haven't you?"

"It was better than thinking about what I was paying for the room at that chichi inn in Middleburg." The very memory made me wince. "If I was thinking a little more clearly last night, I would have asked you then. The package was there, wasn't it, Tyler? Just like Gillian said it was. Only when she left me that message, she told me she hadn't opened it. But she obviously did after she called me. Otherwise, you wouldn't know what was inside it, and you wouldn't know that whatever it was, it's not important to the case."

I can't say for sure, but I think Tyler was going to blow me off. It was a knee-jerk reaction, and I guess I couldn't really blame him. But then maybe he thought about those cases I'd solved for him, because the next thing I knew, he was talking to me almost as if I was a colleague. "The package was there, all right," he said. "But not in the house. We found it out in the garden, ripped to pieces."

"Are you telling me Gillian wasn't the one who opened it?" I thought this over. "Then someone else did. And that someone else might have found something in it after all. Something that same someone else took because that someone else didn't want us to find it."

"I dunno." I heard his desk chair squeak, and I pictured Tyler sitting up and putting his feet back on the floor. "The package was from Brad Peterson and addressed to Brad Peterson, all right. There was nothing in it but cruise tickets and a note in Brad's handwriting addressed to Gillian. Apparently, he was going to give it to her when he opened the package."

"And it said?"

"It said he wanted to surprise her. The tickets were for their honeymoon."

"Oh." This piece of information pretty much negated my theory about Gillian being an angry suspect. If she really was willing to marry Brad . . .

I set this thought aside and got down to business. "You said the package was out in the garden. Like someone had found it in the house and taken it out there to look through it, right? And when that someone didn't find whatever he was looking for, do you think that someone confronted Gillian? That that's how she ended up being killed?"

"Someone? Or Eve?" Tyler didn't give me a chance to get mad. He went right on. "I think you're right, and that's probably what happened. Or there was something else in that package. Something the killer took."

"Either way, Eve's fingerprints aren't on that package, are they?"

There was the slightest pause while Tyler collected his thoughts. I knew what it meant, and for the first time since I saw Eve in handcuffs, the tightness behind my breastbone uncoiled. "She didn't do it, Tyler," I said.

He didn't agree with me. But he didn't disagree, either. It was another point in my favor, but I wasn't about to take it for granted. Especially when Tyler said, "Then who did?"

Thinking, I chewed on my lower lip. "That's what I'm going to find out," I told him.

"Darn it, Annie." I heard a noise and realized that Tyler had slapped a hand against his desk. "You're just not going to give up on this detective thing, are you? You know it's none of your business, right?"

"I do, but—"

"You know there are professionals with way more experience and better resources to handle this, don't you?"

"I do, but—"

"You're aware of the danger?"

I wasn't so quick to reply to this question. Oh, I knew the answer, all right, it was just that I remembered how I'd been face-to-face with the danger part of my detective avocation, and I wasn't looking forward to putting myself in harm's way again.

Except . . .

I gulped down my misgivings and cleared my throat. "We're talking Eve here," I told Tyler. "Not just her reputation, but her freedom. I'm not going to say the danger doesn't matter, because then you're going to say I'm a real dope, and if there's one thing you know about me, Tyler, it's that I'm not stupid. I am going to say that there are some things even more important than danger. Friendship is one of them. So, go ahead, tell me I'm sappy. Or just plain crazy. I'm ready for it."

I waited, and when Tyler didn't respond, I continued. "You're not going to make fun of me for being goofy?"

Again he didn't say anything, and again, I knew why: he was thinking I was the most lame-brained woman on the planet and just waiting for the optimum time to break the news.

"You're not going to tell me I'm foolish? That I'm an amateur? That I—"

"How would you like to help me out?" I was so stunned by Tyler's question, I couldn't find my voice. That's why he had to ask again. "Annie, there's something you can do to help. Will you?"

I'd been pacing my office, the better to deal with the nervous energy that always built when I was dealing with a blockhead like Tyler. But now I dropped into my desk chair. "Anything."

Like he wasn't happy about asking, he drew in a breath. "I've been to the *Washington Star,*" he said. "You know, that newspaper where Brad used to work. I talked to Ray Judson, the editor. He's a self-righteous little son of a—" Tyler coughed away the rest of his words. "Well, never mind. Let's just say that I didn't get much out of him that was helpful. It won't do me any good to go back. When people know you're a cop, they clam up. Even when they don't have anything to feel guilty about. But if someone else went over to the *Star,* maybe that someone could talk to the other folks there. And if that someone wasn't someone official, maybe they wouldn't feel so inclined to keep their mouths shut. I've got to do something to wrap up this investigation. My boss is breathing down my neck and looking for answers, and the people out in Middleburg are joining the chorus. I sure could use some help on this one. You know what I mean?"

I did, and I could barely believe it. I shook my head, convinced I was dreaming. Or hallucinating. "You're asking me to go in your place? You think I can facilitate the investigation?"

Tyler might be desperate, and his desperation might have caused him to act out of character, but he wasn't about to admit that he needed me. "It's not like I'm asking you to be an official part of the team," he said. "You understand that, don't you? You're just going to go and play dumb. You know, say you're there to find out more about Brad. Make up some reason. Like you're there because . . . because . . ."

"Because he asked me to marry him."

Tyler sucked in a breath. "That's certainly not a lie I could get away with!"

I smiled and realized it was one of the few times I'd spoken to Tyler and had that reaction. "What do you need to know?" I asked him. It should come as no big surprise that I wasn't about to trust any phase of the investigation to chance. While Tyler talked, I took copious notes.

I CALLED KEGAN AND ASKED IF HE COULD MEET ME at the offices of the *Washington Star* that day. As it turned out, he had a meeting that afternoon, something about chemical pesticides. He would have loved to come with me and hone his sleuthing skills, he told me, but he'd have to pass.

With Eve preoccupied with the girls (I hoped things were going well!) and Kegan hard at work, I was on my own and feeling a little more nervous than usual now that I was official (OK, semiofficial) and helping out the cops. On Tyler's advice, I showed up at the newspaper without an appointment. That way, he told me, I wouldn't give the folks there time to think about what they should—or shouldn't—tell me.

When a kid named Tammy who sat behind the reception desk asked why I was there, I was ready for her.

Before I left Alexandria, I'd stopped at an antique store and bought a lace-edged hankie. I touched it to my eyes (briefly, of course, since I hadn't had time to take it home and wash it). "I thought I could talk to someone about . . ."

I sniffled, and even I was surprised at how convincing it sounded. "Well, you know, about Brad, of course. Brad Peterson?"

For a couple seconds, Tammy didn't look sure. Then the light dawned. "Oh, you mean the dead guy. I just started here last fall. I never knew him. But ever since he was killed, everybody around here has been talking about him." She was a short, skinny kid with bad skin and a nose that was too big. When she wrinkled it to give me a closer look, she looked like a gnome. "You're not sorry he's dead, are you?"

I didn't have to pretend to be surprised by a question as blunt as that. I guess my wide-eyed look of outrage said it all, because the next thing I knew, Tammy was scrambling to cover her blunder.

"I'm sorry. I didn't mean that to sound the way it sounded. It's just that—"

"What?" I figured a little righteous indignation would get me a long way, and I was right. By that time, Tammy was so flustered, she would have given me the password to her bank account.

Her cheeks got as red as Kegan's always did when he was embarrassed. "I mean . . . that is . . . well, I guess you must be sad that the guy died because you look sad and all, but—"

I was barely taller than her, but when I pulled back my shoulders, she caved completely. Just like I hoped she would.

Tammy's lower lip trembled. "From what I've heard . . . I mean . . . like I said, I didn't know him but . . ." She gulped down her mortification. "I haven't heard one person around here say anything nice about him. Are you sure it's the same Brad Peterson?"

I assured her it was, and while I was at it and she was still feeling guilty about hurting my feelings, I asked to talk to the person who'd said the most bad things about Brad. Tammy had to think about this for a bit. She finally took me through a doorway and stopped at the first office on the right. I glanced at the name plate that hung alongside the door that identified the occupant of the office as Julie Arbogast, and stepped inside. By this time, I wasn't at all surprised to see that Julie was a pretty blonde.

"Miss Arbogast, thank you for taking the time to talk to me." She hadn't, of course. She hadn't even known I was coming, but since Julie was sitting at her desk playing Spider Solitaire on her computer, I figured she wouldn't mind. Before she could decide she did, I plunked down in her guest chair. "I'm here about Brad Peterson," I said.

Julie sat back. "Why? I've already talked to the cops. I told them everything I know about Brad. That isn't much."

"Of course not. But I'm not here in an official capacity." This time when I pulled out the hankie, I dabbed it to my nose. It smelled like mothballs. "I thought . . . that is, I know Brad worked here at one time. I thought you could tell me more about him."

She cocked her head. "Why do you want to know?"

Leave it to a reporter to ask all the right questions. I did my best to make it look like I was trying hard to control my emotions. "Brad and I, we were engaged."

"You've got to be kidding me!" Julie jumped out of her chair. Her office wasn't big, and she sidestepped to her window, then back behind her desk. She had pale, porcelain skin that got dusky at the first mention of Brad's name, and when she leaned over her desk for a better look at me, her eyes flared.

"You don't look like Brad's type," she said, and I didn't have to ask what type that was. I knew. Tall. Blonde. Gorgeous.

No, I was short, brown-haired, and round.

Rather than think about it, I stayed on task. "I thought maybe you could—"

"What?" Julie's snort was unladylike. "Tell you how much we all miss him?"

"Well, I don't know." I adjusted my position in the hard chair. "I just thought—"

"Oh, honey, there's nothing I can do to help. Not if you really loved the guy. Damn! You don't look nearly that stupid. You mean that bastard had you fooled, too?"

I had anticipated something like this, and I was ready for it. Rather than act like Gillian, the wounded lover (and I meant this emotionally, of course, not literally, since poor Gillian really was wounded and I hoped she rested in peace), I nodded my understanding and stifled a little sob. "So it is true. Everything I heard about Brad. I was hoping you'd tell me I was wrong." I brought out the hankie again for effect. "He lied to you, too?"

"That man lied to everybody he ever met." Now that she knew we were on the same page, Julie dropped back into her chair. "He asked me to marry him, too. A couple years ago. God, even now I can't believe it. I was all set to say yes. Then I found out what he was doing around here."

"You mean the stuff about making up sources and quotes for his stories. I'd hoped that wasn't true."

She nodded. "That, and the bit about him already being engaged to Ginny in accounting. The rat bastard!" She made a sour face. "Hey, you're not like that cop who came here, are you? The good-looking one with those incredible blue eyes? You don't think I had anything to do with Brad's dying, do you?"

I realized before I spoke that I was becoming an accomplished liar. "Yeah, Detective Cooper showed up to question me, too. But I'm not here to point fingers or look for suspects. Just for answers."

"Yeah, well . . ." Julie frowned. "If that cop thinks I'm a suspect, then he'd have to think every other woman Brad ever met is a suspect, too. Like I said, there was Ginny down in accounting, but last I heard, she was living in Mexico somewhere. Think she came back to off Brad?"

I didn't have an answer, though I was hoping to find one.

"Then there's Linda, the woman who used to run our library. He came on to her, too, even though she was happily married. She quit because of him. Couldn't take the constant harassment. Last I heard, she was working down at the National Archives."

"Is there anyone left here who could tell me more about Brad?"

Julie thought for a couple minutes before she shook her head. "He chased all the women away. All but me. I refused to give in, refused to get scared and back down. I even threatened to sue the creep, but management wouldn't stand behind me. But it wasn't just the women, you know. The guys around here, they hated Brad, too. He jumped on their sources. He scooped their stories. He acted like the second coming of Geraldo. Then when we found out that he'd really been lying about everything the whole time . . . well, even Jack Kramer, our editorial cartoonist and the nicest, calmest guy you've ever met . . . I saw him take a swing at Brad once. Even Brad's family hated him. You must know that if you were engaged to the guy. You know about his Aunt Mamie, right?"

I continued my lying ways. "I've heard Brad's side of the story, of course. But . . ."

"Oh, there are plenty of buts. And if you've heard Brad tell the story, I guarantee you haven't heard the truth. Old lady, right? And she made the mistake of putting Brad in charge of her finances. He robbed her blind. Poor old thing. I hear she's living somewhere out in Fairfax. She lost a bundle, thanks to her lovin' nephew."

"Mamie in Fairfax. Yes, of course." I nodded as if this wasn't news. "What was her last name again? Crosby or Cunningham. Something like that, right?"

"I think it was Dumbrowski." Julie thought a bit before she nodded. "Oh yeah, if there was anybody who wanted Brad dead, I'll bet she was at the top of the list."

All of this should have come as good news. I had arrived at the *Star* looking for suspects, and thanks to Julie, I had suspects galore. Everyone in the newsroom, for one thing. A couple more women Brad had once put the moves on—or tried to put the moves on. Even an old lady with a grudge and a more-than-good motive.

It looked as if everybody he ever met hated Brad Peterson.

And that didn't even count the people he'd written articles about. Or all those people he'd made up quotes from who'd never said the things Brad said they'd said.

My mood plummeted. My shoulders slumped beneath the weight of the realization that it was no wonder Tyler had asked for my help. It wasn't that he was especially impressed with my detecting skills. Tyler just knew that there was no way any one police department in the whole world could ever deal with all the people who had it in for Brad Peterson.

Of course, all those same people couldn't have hated Gillian Gleeson, too.

Could they?

I thought about the mysterious package and the fact that Brad and Gillian's deaths must have been connected. I wondered, not for the first time, what could have been in the package. What was small enough to mail along with a couple cruise tickets and a note? Newspapers, maybe? Newspaper articles?

"How long has Brad been gone from the *Star*?" I asked Julie.

She shrugged. "Three years, maybe. I can't say for sure. All I know is I went out and bought a bottle of champagne the day he got the ax."

"And he hasn't been here since?"

"No way!" Julie's phone rang, and I knew the interview was over. I thanked her and walked out.

I was almost past the reception desk when Tammy stopped me.

"It's not like I was eavesdropping or anything . . ." She looked over to the doorway and Julie's office beyond. "But the door wasn't closed and I wasn't doing anything and it's pretty easy to hear stuff and I am in journalism school. I know I always have to pay attention and be on the lookout for a good lead." She hauled in a breath. "I heard what Julie said, but she doesn't know. Brad Peterson was here. Just a couple weeks ago. I heard a couple women at the copy desk talking about it. He made sure Ray Judson wasn't anywhere around. And then he did some research."

"Research about . . . ?"

Tammy thought hard. "I remember them talking about it, but . . . oh, that's it!" Her eyes lit. "They said he was asking for copies of every article they could find about some sort of protests out in Colorado. But not new stuff, stuff that happened years ago. Weird, huh?"

Oh yeah, it was weird, all right.

Which was exactly why I was so interested.

And why I sniffled just a little more, told Tammy that if it was important to my dear, departed Brad, it was important to me, and asked for a copy of every article Brad had taken with him.

Sixteen

✕

FINALLY, I WAS GETTING SOMEWHERE!
I had two new avenues to investigate. One was Brad's Aunt Mamie, and believe me, I intended to check her out as soon as I could get over to Fairfax. The other, of course, involved the newspaper articles Tammy was kind enough (or maybe just feeling guilty enough) to copy for me.

I'd barely hopped into the car before I thumbed through the articles. One look, and I knew I needed to call in an expert.

I headed right over to Kegan's.

As it turned out, he lived not far from where I'd first encountered Jim—and murder—in a neighborhood just off the beaten path in Clarendon. Kegan's apartment building was small and homey looking. His apartment was bare-bones essential with an eye on eco-friendly fabrics and a little feng shui thrown in for good measure.

He was surprised—but happy—to see me and offered me a glass of spring water practically before I was through the front door. It wasn't until he'd brought the water over to a table that looked like it came from the secondhand store that he asked what was going on.

"These." Tammy had provided me with a file folder, and I plunked it down on the table between us. "Brad was at the newspaper office just a couple days before he died. This is what he was looking for."

"Really?" Kegan was as jazzed as a kid at Christmas. He scratched a hand through his dark hair. "You found that out? Just by going to the newspaper office? They told you all that? You're incredible, Annie."

"Not so incredible." I was sure to point this out, even though it was fun thinking it was true. "I wasn't exactly one hundred percent truthful with them."

"Who cares, if it got us what we need!" Kegan sat down and flipped open the file. He scanned the article at the top of the pile. His brows dropped over his eyes, and he flashed me a look, set that article aside and went on to the next. And the next one after that.

"Environmental protests. In Colorado." He chewed his lower lip while he quickly leafed through the other dozen or so articles. "Why would Brad—"

"I don't know." He'd carefully stacked the articles he'd already read, and I dragged them closer. "But I figured you were the man to ask. Every single one of them seems to be about the same environmental group." I rifled through the articles, looking for the name that had caught my eye back in the car, and when I found what I was looking for, I pointed.

"Here. Mother Earth's Warriors. Have you ever heard of a group by that name?"

Kegan didn't look sure, and that shouldn't have been enough to discourage me, but truth be told, it did. I had gone to his apartment hoping for answers, even though I knew it was a long shot. The articles went back six years, and the incidents they talked about had happened halfway across the continent. Still, hope springs eternal. Especially in the heart of an investigator who doesn't know a thing about ecological causes.

"Are you sure you've never heard of them?" I asked Kegan.

He was too nice to disappoint me and too honest to lie, so he responded to the imploring note in my voice by buying a little time. He read over the article in his hands and summarized as he went along. "It says here that this group known as Mother Earth's Warriors was responsible for a bunch of fires out in Colorado. They burned down some new housing developments they said encroached on what should have been protected forest land." He let go of the article, and it fluttered to the table. "That really hits home."

My stomach clenched. "You're not telling me you would—"

"Start fires? Don't talk crazy." I could practically see Kegan wrestling with his conscience. "I can understand why they'd do it, though," he finally admitted. It said a lot about our friendship that he'd trust me enough to confess even to thinking about a felony. "There are less and less places for animals to live, and that means entire species are going to be totally wiped out someday. There are fewer green spaces, more concrete. You don't think that's contributing to global warming? Developers aren't taking any of that into account, and I'll bet these . . ." He consulted the article again. "These Mother Earth's Warriors probably tried to address the issue sensibly. When the developers wouldn't listen . . . well, I've seen this kind of thing happen dozens of times. I'll bet the environmentalists tried, but they didn't get any answers. Or any help from the government. They believed they had to take matters into their own hands."

"Maybe, but it says here that a couple firefighters were killed battling one of the fires. That takes their protests to a whole new level." Reading about the fatal fires in the article I pulled from the pile and looking at the photo of windwhipped flames, a chill snaked over my shoulders. "It also says that the authorities were closing in on their leader. Look." I tipped the article so that Kegan could see the smaller photo below the one that showed the firefighters and the sky-high blaze. It was dark and grainy, and it showed a thin guy with a scraggly beard and blond hair that cascaded over his shoulders and looked like it needed not only a cut and style, but a good washing, too. "His name was Joseph Grant," I said, reading the caption. "It says that he was the arsonist. Looks like he was killed accidentally by a fire he set himself. The article is four years old."

I drummed my fingers against the table. "So why would Brad be interested in protests that happened years ago, and a guy who's already dead?"

"Well, Brad did say he lived in Colorado once." I knew this, of course, but I'd forgotten all about it until Kegan brought it up. "He was a journalist back then, remember. Maybe he wrote about the group. Or knew some of its members. Maybe he knew something about the fire that killed that Joseph Grant guy. Maybe Brad knew that Joseph Grant didn't just die accidentally in that fire."

"You mean Grant might have been murdered? And Brad knew that? And somebody found out that Brad knew it and killed Brad, too? Wow." I sat back, my head spinning. "It all makes sense, but we'd never be able to prove any of it. Unless . . ." I realized that Kegan didn't know about the package that had been found ripped open in Gillian's garden and filled him in on the details.

"Maybe Brad did find something interesting in regards to Joseph Grant. Or Mother Earth's Warriors. Maybe he was looking for a way to keep the information safe, so he mailed it to himself. Maybe . . ." I glanced through the articles again. "This Grant guy has light hair. And it's long. He looks like the type who might wear a ratty sweatshirt. You don't suppose—"

"He's dead. He couldn't have pushed Brad in front of that train."

"There is that." I sipped my water and thought through the problem some more. No big surprise, I got nowhere fast. "So let's go through it again. Brad takes a sudden interest in Mother Earth's Warriors. Brad sends something to

Gillian. Brad gets killed. Gillian gets the package. Gillian gets killed. There's got to be a connection, Kegan. All we have to do is figure out what it is."

"I'll tell you what . . ." He scooped up the newspaper articles, tapped them into a pile, and put them back in the folder. "I'll keep these and read through them carefully and do some cross-referencing on the Internet. I'll talk to my friends in the environmental community and see what they know about the group and about Grant."

"And I'll . . ." I hated to admit that I didn't know what I'd do. Right now the connection to Mother Earth's Warriors was looking like our strongest clue. But thanks to his contacts and his experience, Kegan had that covered.

"I guess I'll go check out Aunt Mamie," I said and brought Kegan up to date on that aspect of the investigation. Even as I explained, I couldn't shake the feeling that an old lady in Fairfax wasn't nearly as strong a link as the newspaper articles and the mysterious Mother Earth's Warriors. "Mamie's not going to get us anywhere," I added. "She's going to be a dead end."

"You don't know that. Not for sure." Kegan hopped out of his chair and took the file with him, carefully tucking it between a couple books on a shelf. I noticed one of them was the *Whole Earth Catalog* and the other was called *Home on the Range,* and I couldn't help but smile. Leave it to Kegan to not only practice what he preached, but read about it, too! "When will you have a chance to go out to Fairfax?" he asked.

This was not so easy to determine. I'd already missed a day of work that week, and I was on the schedule at the bank for Saturday. "Sunday," I told him. "Maybe. If Jim doesn't need me to do anything special at Bellywasher's."

"Yeah, Jim."

It wasn't what Kegan said, it was the way he said it. Like just thinking about Jim somehow bothered him.

Call it a professional hazard; I was curious. When Kegan turned away, I cocked my head to try to see his face so I could better gauge his reaction. "What's up with that? You mad at Jim about something?"

"Not mad. No." He grabbed my water glass and took it into the kitchen, and he refused to meet my eyes. That's why I followed right after him.

"You're not mad at Jim, but you don't want to talk about him."

He turned on the water. He squirted the glass with soap (I had no doubt it was environmentally friendly), washed it, and rinsed it. "Jim's a great guy."

"I know that. But that's not what we were talking about."

"We were talking about Brad and Mother Earth's Warriors."

"No, we were talking about me having to be at Bellywasher's on Sunday and you getting all weird when I mentioned Jim's name."

By now, that glass was the cleanest in Arlington. Kegan washed it again. When he finally turned off the water, he didn't turn around to face me. "I know Jim's older and more successful than me," he said. "I know he's got that whole Scottish accent thing going, and I know how women go nuts for stuff like that, but . . . well . . . I'm going to be successful someday, too, Annie." He glanced over his shoulder at me. Briefly. His cheeks flamed. "Not in a monetary way, I don't think. Not in the way Jim is going to be, because Bellywasher's is such a hit. But I'm going to be successful following my dreams and living up to the things I believe in. I think . . . I think that a woman could find that appealing. And I know I'm a couple years younger than you, but I was just thinking . . . you know . . . maybe someday if you and Jim weren't . . . you know . . . that you and I might . . . you know . . ."

I did, and at the same time I felt like a fool for not seeing this coming sooner, I also felt my heart squeeze in sympathy for Kegan. I'd already tried to ease into what I had to say with, *You're such a nice kid, Kegan,* when I realized it was exactly the wrong way to address the problem.

"I'm flattered," I said instead. The truth made a whole lot more sense than beating around the bush. "But Jim and I . . . well, I can't say we're serious, because honestly, we haven't had time to get all that serious. But we're thinking about getting serious. Right now, that's as much of a commitment as I can handle. To anyone."

Kegan nodded, but he still didn't turn around.

I showed myself out.

BELIEVE ME, IT'S NOT LIKE I SET OUT TO HURT KEGAN. It's not like I wanted to do it, or that I ever even imagined it might happen. Who would have thought he'd fall for a short, average woman with uncivilized hair and hips that were too big? I thought we were friends, and realizing that I'd hurt a friend made me feel lousy for the rest of the week. Not to mention worrying about what I'd do and say the next Monday when Kegan showed up for class, and I had to act like he hadn't laid his heart on the line— and I hadn't given it a couple of big bruises.

By the time Sunday rolled around, I was more than ready for a diversion.

When I called to ask if I could stop to talk to her, Mamie Dumbrowski wasn't in, but a woman who identified herself as Betty said, "Miss Mamie, she'll love having some company."

Good thing Betty didn't ask what I wanted to see Mamie about. Something told me that when the old lady found out the subject was her low-down, sneaky nephew, she wasn't going to love me so much anymore.

Mamie lived in a sprawling brick rambler not far off Chain Bridge Road. When I rang the bell, Betty was the one who answered. She was a heavyset, middle-aged African American woman with a glint in her eyes and a ready smile that made me feel like one of the family. She informed me that Ms. Dumbrowski had just returned from church and ushered me into a dining room with windows that looked out onto a rose garden and with a formal cherry dining table and chairs that were polished to perfection. A woman sat on the far side of the table. She was thin and aristocratic-looking with a face so full of wrinkles, it reminded me of a map. She also just happened to have a full head of long, silky hair. It was dyed a vivid shade of yellow.

I told myself this meant nothing at all—not unless Mamie Dumbrowski happened to have something to do with a wacko environmental group known as Mother Earth's Warriors, anyway. Still, it wasn't easy ignoring the blonde coincidence. Or to keep the excitement out of my voice when I introduced myself and told her what I'd come about.

"You want to talk about Brad?" Mamie's eyes were blue and hazy. That didn't keep them from being as sharp as a hawk's. When she studied me from across the table, I shifted from foot to foot. "Why?"

"I understand you weren't happy with the way he handled your finances."

Her chin came up. "Who told you that?"

"A friend."

"Not a friend of Brad's." The old lady's top lip curled. "Brad didn't have any friends."

"Yeah, I've heard that, too. He had so many enemies, it's making it hard for the cops to figure out who killed him."

"Who cares!" She dismissed the very thought with the wave of one hand. "He was a louse. You know what that is, don't you? If you have any questions, kid, take a look in the encyclopedia. Right there under the word louse, you'll see it: a picture of Brad Peterson."

"You're angry."

"You think?" The noise Mamie made wasn't so much a laugh as a cackle. "He cheated me out of a crapload of money."

I glanced around the nicely decorated home and thought of Betty who'd answered the door.

"Pardon me for pointing it out, but you don't seem to be suffering."

"That doesn't make what he did right, does it?"

"No, it doesn't."

"And it doesn't make it any of your business."

"Right again." I swallowed hard and tried for a smile that withered beneath her laser gaze. "But maybe you'll understand when I tell you that even though it's none of my business, I've got to ask about your relationship with Brad. You see, the cops think my friend Eve killed him. And his latest fiancée, Gillian Gleeson."

"And you're trying to prove she didn't."

I nodded.

"So you came here to try and prove that I did."

When she put it like that, I guess it did sound crazy. Not to mention bold-faced, shameless, and just plain un-couth. I'd already started to apologize when Mamie cut me short.

"Spare me, young lady. You're not sorry you're here looking for someone else to blame, because what you want to do is clear your friend's name. And I'll tell you what . . . I'm not sorry Brad's dead. I only wish I was the one who'd shoved him, but you see . . ." She pushed back from the table, and for the first time, I realized that she was sitting in a wheelchair.

"Car accident," Mamie said. "Back in '78. Haven't taken a step since. Oh, I wanted Brad dead, all right. But I'm sorry to say, I wasn't the one who did him in."

"I never really thought you were."

"No." Her eyes lit. "But you were hoping."

"Yeah." My smile answered hers. "I was."

Before either of us could say another word, a man walked into the room. He was tall and beefy, a big guy wearing white hospital scrubs and an attitude.

Then again, maybe he just didn't like people staring at him. And I was. Staring, that is. For the second time in as many minutes, I'd met another person with long, light hair. His was pulled into a ponytail that hung down his back.

"This is Reggie Goldman," Mamie said. "My driver and

attendant. This young lady is a private eye. She thinks I killed Brad."

"That's not true!" I figured I'd better make this clear. Fast. Especially since the moment he heard the news, Reggie's nostrils flared and his eyes sparked. "I never said that. And I'm not a full-time private eye. I'm a teller at Pioneer Savings and Loan over in Arlington and I'm the business manager at Bellywasher's and . . ." I was rambling and it was so not professional. I gulped down the rest of my lame explanation and tried to wrap things up with as positive a statement as I could make. "I never said Ms. Dumbrowski killed anybody."

"Of course you didn't!" Mamie slapped a hand against her thigh and laughed. "Just thought I'd see if I could get a rise out of you. Helps pass the time, you know, when you're old and stuck in this chair."

"Your bridge game this afternoon will help pass the time." Reggie stepped in front of me so he could go around to the other side of the room and slide Mamie's wheelchair away from the table. "You've got just enough time to get freshened up," he said. "Then I'll get you over to Mrs. Klausen's."

I don't know where Betty was through this whole thing, but she appeared instantly at my elbow. Good sport that she was, she stood and waited while I said good-bye and watched Reggie wheel Mamie away. Maybe Betty noticed that as I stood there, I narrowed my eyes, trying to imagine what Reggie would look like if his hair wasn't as neat and he sported a scruffy beard.

"What's he like?"

Betty looked where I was looking. "Devoted to her, that's what he is. Been with Miss Mamie for a couple years now. Loves her like she was his own grandmother."

"Which means he might be really pissed if someone hurt her."

If I thought Betty was going to spill some deep family secret, I was wrong. She clamped her lips shut tight.

I turned so she could lead me to the door. "I don't suppose . . ." We were nearly to the wide foyer, so I knew if I was going to find out more, now was the time. Yeah, it was off the subject. Sure, it was a gamble. But I had only one chance. I played the odds. "Is Reggie interested in environmental causes?" I asked.

Betty stopped in her tracks and looked at me hard. "How do you know that?"

"Just a wild guess. What can you tell me?"

She looked to her left and her right, just to be sure no one was around. "Always protesting some cause or another. Global warming and saving the owls and the whales and the baby seals. That kind of nonsense. Miss Mamie, she doesn't mind. She says for all he does for her, Reggie deserves some time on his own and things to keep him interested. What she doesn't know is that a couple times, the demonstrations he's participated in have gotten out of hand. Reggie, he's got something of a temper when things rub him the wrong way. Cops who get in the way of protesters . . . well, I guess he thinks that shouldn't happen. He's been arrested. Twice that I know of. But don't you go and get the wrong idea about him. When it comes to Miss Mamie—"

"Loves her like his dear ol' granny, yeah, I know." I wasn't sure how much longer Betty could talk, or what she'd be willing to say. I looked around, too, before I spoke again. "Does he live here?"

Betty nodded. "He's got rooms above the garage. Takes good care of them, too."

"And you said he's been here a couple years. Where did he live before that?"

"Came from some hospital in upstate New York where he was an orderly. Said he needed something more peaceful where he could get to know his patient better."

Or maybe he just needed a story to cover up those lost years setting fires in Colorado. I inched nearer to Betty. "And the day Brad Peterson died. Was Reggie around all day?"

This she had to think about. I knew exactly the moment she remembered, because her mouth fell open. "Took the day off. Said he had some personal business to take care of. It's not like him to do that. He's here all the time. I never thought that he might have had anything to do with—"

"I'm sure he didn't." I didn't know this for sure—in fact, I was counting on it not being true—but there was no use leaving Betty to fret about having a murderer around the house. "I'm just asking questions, that's all. It's just a coincidence."

"Uh-huh." Betty wasn't convinced. She looked at me over the frames of her wire-rimmed glasses. "You one of them private investigator types?" she asked.

"Yup." For the first time, I was't embarrassed to admit it. "I sure am," I told her. "So you can believe me when I tell you that you have nothing to worry about."

I managed to keep the smile off my face until I was back in the car. "Hot'cha!" I slapped the steering wheel. "I just cracked the case!"

Seventeen

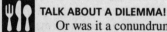

TALK ABOUT A DILEMMA!

Or was it a conundrum?

After Kegan's confession about his feelings for me, I couldn't imagine how I'd face him or what I'd say the next time we were together. I didn't want to see him.

On the other hand, I was anxious to tell him about my visit to Mamie Dumbrowski's and my theory about Reggie Goldman. I couldn't wait to get to class that Monday night.

See what I mean about a conundrum?

I guess that's what I was thinking about as I pulled out of the parking lot of the bank and headed over to Belly-washer's for the night's class: Bar Food with a Spoon? (There were three kinds of chili on the menu—turkey, one that had dill pickles in it, one made with no beans or veggies in it at all—as well as a killer lobster bisque, cheddar cheese and potato soup, and the pièce de résistance as Monsieur Lavoie might say, a banana split so loaded with syrup and fruit and whipped cream, it was sure to send every student's daily caloric intake into hyperdrive.)

Maybe I was thinking about that banana split.

Either way, when I changed lanes on the George Washington Memorial Parkway and my car bucked, I didn't think a thing of it. My Saturn was a couple years old, and I'd been pretty busy lately. I was a few hundred miles past needing an oil change and—

The steering wheel wobbled in my hands.

I'm no mechanic, but I doubted this had something to do with my poor oil-changing habits. I held on tighter to the wheel, but even as I did, I knew it wouldn't do me any good. No matter how hard I tried to keep it going straight, the car pulled sharply to the right, and since I was in the left lane at the time . . . well, I won't bother to describe how the fellow in the car next to me signaled his displeasure.

Like I cared?

Right about then, I didn't have the luxury of being offended. When he saw I wasn't going to stop, the other driver backed off and repeated the gesture he'd made the first time. Good thing, too. About him backing off, not about the gesture. I veered into the right lane and did the only thing I could think to do: I jammed on my brakes.

When my brake pedal fell all the way to the floor and I didn't slow down a bit, my stomach turned to a solid block of ice.

There I was, surrounded by rush hour traffic and completely out of control, but not like regular D.C. drivers are out of control (which they always are, but that's because everyone's in a hurry to get somewhere and to get to that somewhere before the person next to them gets there first). I knew there was something seriously wrong. I was going sixty in a car I couldn't steer or stop. Oh yeah, and I was scared to death, too.

My fingers gripping the wheel, I closed the gap on a red station wagon up ahead that was going too slow. I checked my mirrors and glanced over my shoulder. There was a black sedan in the left lane, not nearly far enough away, but I didn't have a whole lot of choice. I threaded the needle.

"I'm sorry, I'm sorry, I'm sorry," I groaned, though I knew there was no way the other driver could hear me, and I suspected that even if he could, he wouldn't have cared about my flimsy apology. Besides, I didn't have much time to worry about it. There was a furniture delivery truck directly ahead of me, slowing down, its right turn signal on. If he didn't move fast enough, something very bad was going to happen. I didn't bother with my signal (a first for me who, needless to say, always follows the traffic rules), I yanked my steering wheel to the right and slid into the lane just in front of that station wagon. Of course, that didn't help at all when the furniture truck inched to the right and moved directly in front of me.

Fortunately, though my fingers were frozen on the wheel and my heart was pounding so hard, I was sure it was going to jump out of my chest, my brain was still working. And boy, did it work! Going even faster than my speeding car, it scrambled over every piece of driving how-to I'd ever heard or read.

"Pump the brakes! Pump the brakes!" My brain sent the message, and I screamed the words, and somehow, my body obeyed. I slowed the car just enough to get over to the berm. A few more pumps, a couple more screams, and I skidded to a stop.

Good thing, too. The next second, I heard a noise like a crack, and something snapped. The right front side of the car buckled. When it hit the ground, my teeth clattered.

Never let it be said that D.C. drivers are not compassionate. The driver of the furniture truck must have seen my erratic stop in his rearview mirror. He blared his horn. The red station wagon zipped by, and that driver screamed something out his window. I was glad he was going fast and I didn't quite catch it. The folks in back of him, of course, slowed down to see what was going on, and going slow in rush hour in that city . . . well, nobody was happy about it. I got glared at. I was cursed. I had a couple fists waved in my direction.

Through it all, I hardly noticed. I sat with my hands clamped to the steering wheel, my knuckles white. My heart pounded harder and faster than ever, and I swear, I never even took a breath. My lungs felt as if they were on fire.

I guess that's how the police officer who stopped behind me found me. The lights on top of his patrol car were swirling, but I never even saw them. Not until he knocked on my window.

"You all right, ma'am?"

I don't remember doing it, but I guess I had turned off the car, because I had to turn it on again to hit the button to roll down the window.

"Something happened," I said. As if he couldn't see that.

Big points for him, the officer simply nodded and went around to the front of the car. I saw him peer at the right front tire. He bent down and took a closer look. When he stood up again, his forehead was creased, and his mouth was pulled into a thin line.

At least I had the presence of mind to check for traffic before I hopped out of the car. I carefully made my way over to where the cop stood. I was shivering and I wrapped my arms around myself.

"What is it?" I asked the officer. "Is there something wrong? I mean, I know there's something wrong. My tire went wonky. And my brakes wouldn't work. I mean, there's got to be something wrong, but the way you're looking at the car, I don't think your version of wrong and my wrong match up."

"Ma'am." He'd apparently dealt with hysterical drivers in his time. He looked into my eyes and kept his voice firm and low. Like a trainer would if he was working with a really bad dog. "Take a breath."

I did.

"Better?"

I nodded.

"You sure?"

I wasn't. I took another breath.

He watched me carefully and, don't ask me how, but he knew I was in control before I knew I was in control. When I was ready to listen and proceed, he pointed to my front right tire. It was lying on the ground next to my car. Even in my current state, I knew this was not a good thing.

"You get new tires lately?" the officer asked.

I shook my head.

"You change a tire because of a flat?"

Again, I indicated that I hadn't.

"Anybody else do it for you?"

Another shake. My head was starting to hurt. But maybe that was because the enormity of all that had just happened hit me like a ton of bricks. I staggered back against the car.

Again, the cop looked over at my tire and at the rim of the car, now resting on the ground. He shook his head. "You've got bigger problems here than just a flat tire and a bent frame," he said. "If you didn't put that tire back on cockeyed, and you nobody else did it for you . . ."

Even if I wasn't a private investigator, I would have seen where he was headed. I gulped down the sour taste in my mouth. "You're saying if I didn't do it, and I didn't ask somebody to do it, then someone else loosened it. Purposely. Without me knowing about it."

He backed up a step, and really, I couldn't blame him for being noncommittal. I was already shocky. He didn't need a fresh outburst of delirium there on the side of the road. "We can't know that for sure, and really, it doesn't make a whole lot of sense. If someone loosened your tire and messed with your brakes, that would mean—"

He refused to say it, and I knew why. I didn't want to say it, either. But we both knew what it meant.

Somebody had loosened that tire and cut my brake line, all right. Somebody who knew exactly what would happen when I left the bank.

Somebody had just tried to kill me.

* * *

BY THE TIME I WAITED FOR A TOW, CALLED A CAB from the lot where my poor car was taken, and got over to Bellywasher's, our students were already cleaning up the last of the pots and pans from the night's class. I saw that Kegan and Agatha were busy washing and drying banana split bowls, and I was glad; I was in no shape to deal with either the fallout of his unrequited love or my guilt at being the unrequitee.

Of course, Jim didn't know any of that. Or about what had just happened over on the parkway. The moment I was through the door, he stepped into my path.

"Your eyes are like starlight," he said, and honestly, who can blame me? When I heard this, I figured I must have bumped my head when I had my close encounter with nearly being the late Annie Capshaw. That was the only thing that would explain the slightly pained expression on Jim's face. And the rest of the corny words that came out of his mouth.

"Your lips are luscious, like summer strawberries."

OK, I should have said something. Anything. But remember, I was shell-shocked. And if I hadn't been before I walked in there, I would have been by that time, what with Jim talking crazy and looking deep into my eyes as if he was the hero of some really bad romance novel, and I was the brainless heroine who was about to fall under his macho spell.

In frustration, he threw his hands in the air. "What does a fellow have to do to light a fire around here?" he asked.

"Fire?" This was not the response he was expecting, but it was the only thing I could manage, and apparently (and for reasons I couldn't comprehend), it was encouraging. Back on track, he cleared his throat and paused, like an actor who'd forgotten his lines. When he found his place again, he kept his voice to a low rumble.

"The color in your cheeks is like . . ." He bent to give me a closer look. "Gads, Annie," he said, that rumble lost beneath a rush of honest concern, "there's not a spot of color in your cheeks at all. You're as pale as ashes, and you look terrible. What's happened to you?"

I guess it was the opening I was waiting for because even before he clamped a hand on my arm and led me over to the stool next to his worktable, my fragile composure cracked. The second I sat down, I burst into tears.

For a class that had already had one of its members tossed in front of a moving train and one of the people who worked at the place where they took their classes arrested for murder, it was only natural to be curious. Before I knew it, I was surrounded my our well-meaning students. Their voices overlapped when they asked, "What's wrong, Annie?" And "What can I get you, Annie?" And "What happened to Annie?" All at the same time.

The words swirled and pounded through my already aching head. I cried harder, and worried as I always do that crying makes me look like a puffer fish, with eyes so swollen I can barely see. My hearing was just fine, though, and I heard Jim loud and clear when he yelled above the babble, "Back up, people! Give Annie some room to breathe."

When they didn't move fast enough, Jim shooed them away. They left—reluctantly—and just to make sure we had some modicum of privacy, Jim stationed himself directly in front of me with his back to the class. "What is it?" he asked. "What happened?"

I told him. Not quickly. And not without stopping a whole bunch of times to hiccup, and catch my breath, and wipe my nose. But eventually, Jim heard the story about the tire and the out-of-control car and the brakes that mysteriously stopped working. In keeping with my vow to turn over a new leaf when it came to investigations, I told him about Reggie Goldman, too, and about how I was sure my recent meeting with him and the problems with my car weren't coincidental.

That's when he got really mad.

"It isn'a a good thing, that, Annie," he said, and I braced myself. When Jim's accent thickens to the consistency of peanut butter, we're in for trouble. "You'll promise me you'll na have naught to do with this Reggie fellow again. I'll na be havin' you plastered on some freeway somewhere in little pieces."

"I'm not, though." I sniffled and sniffed, and when he handed me a glass that I thought was water, I took a big gulp. It was white wine, but I didn't complain. In fact, I took another drink. "I'm fine," I told him, though I guess I really wasn't or I wouldn't have needed the wine to begin with. "I handled it just fine, too. And now that I know Reggie's involved, I'll be more careful, and I'll talk to Tyler, too, I promise I will. Really, Jim . . ." I squeezed his hand. "There's nothing to worry about."

"There's you." It was as simple as that. At least for Jim. He lowered his voice, and this time when he spoke, he didn't sound nearly as corny as he did sincere. "I canna bear the thought of somethin' happenin' to you, Annie, dear."

I was no brainless heroine (at least *I* didn't think so!), but it would have taken a stronger woman than me not to fall under Jim's macho spell. The look in his eyes was sweet and strong and more tempting than any banana split ever concocted. "I can't bear it, either," I said, and this time, my voice was clogged not with tears, but with emotion. "If I couldn't be with you, I—"

"We're here!"

Leave it to Eve to make a grand entrance that cut me off at the knees. Jim and I both looked over to where Eve stood with her back to the kitchen door to hold it open. She had Doc in her arms. Even as we watched, a neat and orderly line of little girls marched into the kitchen. It took me a moment to realize I knew them.

Doris, Gloria, Wendy, Rosemary, Alice, Emma, and Lucy were dressed in pink dresses that matched Eve's (and—not incidentally—the froufrou outfit Doc was wearing). Every single one of the girls held her head high as she walked into the room, hands at her sides. Like a chorus line of mini-Rockettes, they stopped on a dime and looked my way.

"We're on our way to get our hair done," Eve informed me. "What do you think?"

"I . . ." I glanced from girl to girl and then over to Fi, who stood near the door, beaming at them with tears of joy in her eyes. Each child twinkled like a beauty pageant queen. "I mean, I . . . Wow, girls!" I slid off the stool to get closer. "You're all beautiful, like fairy-tale princesses."

Doris, stepped forward. "We might be beautiful, but don't get the wrong idea."

"Beauty isn't nearly as important as brains," Alice added.

"And brains . . ." This came from Emma, whose ear-to-ear smile revealed dimples that wouldn't quit. "In the long run, brains will do more than beauty to earn us decent salaries."

I was speechless.

Which is exactly why Eve grinned. "I'm teaching them to stand on their own two feet," she said. "No Weasel will ever take advantage of these girls." She clapped her hands, and Doris, Emma, and Alice fell back into place. "Thanks, Annie." Careful not to squish Doc, Eve gave me a quick one-armed hug. "This was exactly what I needed. The girls are great, and working with them . . . well . . . I haven't had time to worry about . . . you know!" And before she could get emotional, too, she headed out the door. The girls marched behind her, and I was back on the stool, too stunned to do anything but watch them go.

"Ach, they're little angels, aren't they?" Fi had stayed behind, and she sniffled and smiled. "I knew they'd blossom someday. I'm so happy I brought them here, Jim. It's made a world of difference." She wrapped her arm through her cousin's. "I only wish . . ." She sniffled some more, but this time, pride and happiness had nothing to do with it. Fi's lower lip trembled. "I wish I could be as happy."

"You might be yet." Jim unwound her arm from his, but he held on to her hand. "I've got a surprise for you, Fi. That's why I asked you to stop down this evening." He signaled to Damien, who opened the back door. A medium-height, whip-thin man walked into the kitchen. He had buzz-cut sandy hair and dimples I would have recognized anywhere. The moment he saw Fi, he raced forward and took her into his arms.

"Surprise!"

Nobody had to tell me; I knew this was Fi's husband, Richard. He kissed the top of her head.

"Jim called and said it was about time we were a family again, and I knew he was right. I couldn't wait to see you and the girls. We're heading back home to Florida, Fi, all of us. Together. We've got to get things ready for our little fellow." He touched a gentle hand to her bulging belly. "I heard from Jim that you've bought some clothes, but we've still got a lot to do. We need trucks for him to play with, and cars, and speaking of that, another car seat, too. Oh, and wait until you see what I stopped and bought on my way up from Florida. It's a little bat and ball and catcher's mitt. He's gonna love to play baseball!"

Tears streamed down Fi's cheeks. "That's wonderful, Richard. But are you sure you're ready—"

"I want you back. I always have. And I've got everything ready back home. The house is spick-and-span. The beds are made. The carpets are vacuumed. The floors are washed. You won't have to lift a finger, Fi, I promise."

"You've done all the work?" New tears erupted, and Fi backed out of his arms. "You just don't get it, do you, Richard?" she bawled, and before anyone could stop her, she ran out of the kitchen.

I wouldn't have blamed Richard for being upset. Instead, he just watched her go. "Happens every time." He didn't sound happy or unhappy. He was just reporting the facts. "Fi gets pregnant, her hormones go wacky, and she gets emotional. She'll settle down as soon as the baby's born. You're a real saint to have put up with her, Jim."

"Aye." Jim didn't sound happy or unhappy, either. Like Richard, he was just reporting the facts. "It's been an interesting few weeks."

"We'll be out of your hair in a couple days." Richard slapped Jim on the back. "Until then, we've got plenty to do. We don't have boys' names picked out. And we need to shop." Excited by the prospect, he took off in the direction Fi had disappeared.

Jim turned back to me. "Well, that's one problem taken care of. I hope. Now we need to talk about you. And this investigation."

"Only not right now." An idea had struck, and I latched on to Jim's arm. Call me conceited, I knew if I played my cards right (and this involved close proximity, him and me), he'd have a hard time saying no to what I was about to suggest. Which was, "A shower."

"A what?"

"A shower. Let's have a baby shower for Fi. Here. At Bellywasher's."

Since our students had spent only part of the last few minutes cleaning up like they were supposed to be doing and the better part of the time watching and listening in to everything that was happening, it was no surprise when Margaret stepped forward. "I love showers! Oh, what fun!"

"And we could cater it! You know, as a sort of final exam." This came from Jorge, who had really gotten into the whole cooking thing (go figure) and was talking about chucking his day job at a stock brokerage to open his own restaurant. "It would be great, hands-on experience, and since there would be no labor costs, it would be economical, too."

"We could do it next Sunday. Before the restaurant opens." This suggestion came from Agatha.

Do I need point out that by this time, Jim was outnumbered, and he knew it? He gave in without a fight, and the class gathered around the table where Margaret already had out a pad and paper and was starting a list of what was needed and who would do which jobs.

"I could help, too, Annie." When I wasn't paying attention, Kegan had come up behind me. I offered him a smile that he didn't return. In fact, he looked downright uncomfortable. He refused to meet my eyes, and I didn't have to wonder why. I was embarrassed by all he'd said back at his apartment, but Kegan was doubly mortified. "I've been working on a recipe. I call it Smokin' Good Chicken Dip. I'll make it. Would that . . . Would that be OK?"

Like I was going to tell him it wasn't and stomp on his ego again?

While I was at it, I figured I'd create a little more goodwill.

"Up for some investigating?" I asked Kegan.

I could tell he didn't want to be interested, but I saw his eyes light.

"I've got a lead," I confided. "An activist named Reggie Goldman. If you could get me some info about him, we might be able to get this case wrapped up."

"Really?" He could barely control his excitement. "And you don't mind taking me along? I mean, after everything I said, you don't think I'm a dope or that I'm really lame or—"

It was time to put the past behind us and get our friendship back on an even keel. I gave him a smile. "Can't think of anyone else I'd rather have along on this investigation with me," I told him. "Besides, what do you mean, after everything you said? I have no idea what you're talking about."

Eighteen

✦

I HAD SATURDAY OFF. MOST NORMAL PEOPLE WOULD have spent an appropriate amount of time doing the happy dance in celebration, then gotten down to business doing things normal people do on their days off, like the laundry or catching up on bills. Or at least helping with the preparations for the baby shower the next day. Of course, my life was anything but normal. That would explain what I was doing out in the pouring rain, a placard in my hands. Since Kegan had put it together for me and I'd barely given it a glance when I picked him up at his apartment in the rental car the insurance company had provided me, I wasn't exactly sure what I was for. Or against. I only knew the neon-colored sign in my rain-slick hands said something about a Pollution Solution.

On his cue, I waved it in the air. The sign helped me look like I belonged in the crowd of chanting protesters in Lafayette Park across the street from the White House. And it kept some of the raindrops at bay, too.

While I was at it, I stood on tiptoe and looked around, hoping for a glimpse of Reggie Goldman. "Are you sure he's going to be here?" I asked Kegan. It wasn't the first time I'd asked, so I wouldn't have blamed him if he lost his temper. Kegan being Kegan, he did no such thing.

"I've checked around and talked to plenty of people. Reggie's got something of a reputation. He's a hothead and a troublemaker. Not the kind of guy anyone wants associated with a legitimate cause. But . . ." I'd described Reggie to Kegan, and he looked around, too. Being taller, I figured he'd sight Reggie long before I did. "People remember him, Annie. They talk about him. A couple people I asked told me that the plumes of airborne dust and pollutants from Asia that blow across the ocean to North America . . . well, according to them, that's Reggie's thing. His cause, you know? And Benjamin Rhodes . . ." Kegan looked over to the makeshift stage from which a distinguished-looking guy in a yellow slicker was getting ready to address the audience. "Rhodes is the world's foremost expert on the subject. No way Reggie is going to miss this."

A raindrop plopped in my eye. "Maybe Reggie found something better to do today. Like keeping dry."

"Better than hearing about black carbon particles?" In disbelief, Kegan shook his head. I could tell the research he'd done to get us ready for the day's protest had really fired him up. All the way into D.C., he'd filled me in on the massive plumes of pollution that make their way across the oceans. Interested or not, I already knew the plumes packed a combination of industrial emissions like soot and trace metals, and that by studying them, scientists hoped to shed light on global warming.

"Black carbon produces warming by absorbing sunlight," Kegan said, his enthusiasm for the subject taking flight, just like those plumes. "They may mask up to half of the global warming impact of greenhouse gases. I'm telling you, Annie, Reggie will be here. He has to be. This is way too exciting for him to miss."

At that point, I wished I believed it. At least if Reggie showed, and we had a chance to grill him about any connection he might have to Brad Peterson and Mother

Earth's Warriors, it might justify standing there in the rain. Even as I thought about it, a single, cold drop dripped off the brim of my hat and rolled inside the collar of my blue rain slicker and down my back. I shivered.

Kegan glanced around again. "If it wasn't so crowded, we might be able to see more."

"Or maybe we just got lucky." I latched on to Kegan's arm and pulled, and he had enough faith in me not to ask where we were going. Maybe he didn't have to. Maybe like me, he'd seen a glimpse of a bare head and the golden ponytail plastered down by the rain.

I excused us through the crowd, darting between protesters as I kept an eye on the beefy guy thirty feet up ahead. When we made our way around the technicians operating the sound system as they huddled under tarps, we closed the gap.

"Reggie!" I called his name, and when he stopped, I stepped up my pace. "Imagine seeing you here! I'm Annie," I said when he gave me that blank look designed to make me think he didn't remember our meeting at Mamie Dumbrowski's. I wondered if he remembered my front tire any better and promised myself that someday, I'd have the chance to ask. "So, you're interested in plumes of Asian pollution, too."

"Yeah." Reggie looked at me through narrowed eyes. "Why are you here?"

I glanced down at my sign. "I'm looking for a pollution solution! And my friend Kegan here—"

"Hey, I know you." Reggie offered Kegan his hand. "Seen you at a couple round table discussions. Deforestation, right? And watershed preservation. You presented a paper on overpopulation, too. I remember that. You're good people."

Kegan blushed. Before the lovefest could get out of hand, I stepped between them. "That's sort of what we'd like to talk to you about."

"Watershed preservation? Or overpopulation?"

"Well, not exactly. Environmental causes, though. And a group called Mother Earth's Warriors."

Reggie crossed his arms over his broad chest. He was wearing a gray sweatshirt that was already soaked. He didn't seem to mind. "I've heard of them."

"No doubt." This was from Kegan who, for reasons I couldn't explain, didn't seem to remember that back in the car, we'd talked about taking it slow and trying to lull Reggie into taking us into his confidence. I tried to deflect what I knew was coming, but Kegan was too quick for me. Before I could say a word, he raised his chin and glared at Reggie. "Do you know about the death of Joseph Grant, too?"

Reggie snorted. "That guy was a whack job. Died in one of his own fires, and I say good riddance. That's the kind of nutcase who gives people like us a bad name."

"Maybe he's not the only nutcase around here."

Reggie's chin came up, and the camaraderie that had brightened his eyes only moments before was replaced with suspicion. "Who you calling a nutcase?"

"Boys!" I hadn't been counting on things getting so far out of hand so quickly. I wedged myself between Reggie and Kegan. "That's not at all what Kegan is saying," I explained, sending a death ray look to Kegan as I did so he'd shut up and let me take over. "It's just that we're making some inquiries into the death of a guy by the name of Brad Peterson. Brad was a journalist out in Colorado at one time. We know he had a connection to Mother Earth's Warriors."

"So?" As questions went, Reggie's was legitimate enough. I might have pointed this out, if Kegan didn't step up to the plate.

"So we think that maybe Joseph Grant isn't dead. He was a tall guy with blond hair. And he might have known Brad Peterson was on his trail. If you know anything—"

"I don't."

"He doesn't." I didn't like this new, aggressive Kegan. I put a hand on his chest to keep him at bay. "What Kegan meant to say," I told Reggie, "is that there might be a connection, and with your contacts in the environmental community, we thought you might be able to help."

"Unless Brad knew the truth about you, and that's why you had to kill him to shut him up. What did you do with the proof? The stuff Brad sent to Gillian Gleeson. Did you find it when you went there to kill her, Reggie? Or should I call you Joseph?"

"Kegan!" I groaned my frustration. Not only had he embarrassed us, but he'd blown our investigation. I knew this for certain when Reggie turned on his heels and stalked away. "What on earth is wrong with you?" My voice was a little sharp. OK, it was a lot sharp. I couldn't help it. Watching Reggie disappear into the crowd, my temper soared, and my hopes of ever finding a solution that would prove Eve's innocence dissolved in the mud and rainwater that surrounded us. "That's not how you interrogate a suspect!"

Kegan's expression, so hard and unyielding while he grilled Reggie, faded into chagrin. "I'm sorry, Annie. I don't know what got into me. I've been watching detective movies to get ready for our investigation, and I guess . . . Oh my gosh, I really got carried away."

"So did our best chance of ever talking to Reggie." My shoulders slumped, and when I realized I still had my protest sign over my shoulder, I plunked the stick handle down into the soft grass. "We blew it."

"*I* blew it." I didn't think anyone could be more disconsolate than me, but of course, Kegan took my criticism to heart. "I'm sorry. I wasn't thinking. I thought . . ." He puffed out a breath of annoyance right before he craned his neck. "Maybe we can still find him," he said. "Come on."

Before I knew it, he had ahold of my arm. He dragged me through the crowd, and we searched near the tents where folks sold newspapers and magazines that supported environmental causes. We looked around over near the portable bathrooms (not too close!) and toward the back of the stage where, by this time, Benjamin Rhodes was talking about those black carbon particles and the folks in the crowd were applauding his every word and calling out their support.

There was no sign of Reggie anywhere.

"Dang!" Disgusted, I took refuge beneath the spreading branches of a tree that was just leafy enough to keep the worst of the rain away. I propped my chin in one hand and grumbled. It wasn't until I was all set to suggest that we try over on the other side of the park where the crowd was thinner that I realized that somewhere between the portable johns and the media tents, I'd lost Kegan.

"Dang!" I said again because, let's face it, it really was the only appropriate response. Now I had two missing environmentalists on my hands and no hope of finding either one of them if I stood there and tried to stay dry.

Which didn't stop me from grumbling some more. Right before I stepped back out into the rain.

I wound my way through the maze of heavy black cables behind the stage, and when I didn't see either Kegan or Reggie, I headed toward the far side of the park.

The way I remember it (and I think it's pretty safe to say I remember it pretty well since one, my memory is excellent, and two, nearly being killed has a way of sticking in your mind), I was almost there when the first shot plunked into the wet ground not ten feet from where I stood.

WHO COULD BLAME ME FOR STANDING THERE stunned and frozen with terror? Nobody who's ever been shot at, that's for sure. Lucky for me, my surprise didn't last more than a second or two. After that, I took off running.

Where was I going?

I didn't have a clue.

What would I do when I got there?

I only wish I knew.

Right about then, the only thing that mattered was that I

took one chance of looking over my shoulder, and in that one fraction of one second, I swore I saw the glimmer of rain-slicked, golden hair. Reggie Goldman was somewhere toward the back of the crowd, and no doubt, he was all set to take aim again. If I didn't get out of the line of his sight—and fast—what he'd started out on the George Washington Parkway was going to finish right there across the street from the White House. I could practically see the headlines now: "Arlington Woman Killed in Protest."

More's the pity, since I wasn't even sure what I was protesting.

My steps fueled by my fear, I raced across the park, heading as far from the protest as I could—until I realized my thinking was all wrong. I didn't need to get away from the crowd, I needed to get lost in it. With that in mind, I swung around a huge old oak, prepared to dart around the other side and head back into the heart of the crowd. I would have made it, too, if my sneakers didn't slide on the soggy ground. My left ankle turned; my feet went out from under me. I hit the ground face-first, and muck and mud aside, it was the best thing that could have happened to me. When the next shot hit, it slammed into the trunk of the tree, exactly where I would have been standing if I hadn't slipped.

Yeah, I thought about staying right where I was, rolling into a ball, and whimpering. But that wasn't going to help. With all the noise the protesters were making as they cheered Benjamin Rhodes, nobody could hear the shots. And with all the people milling around, no one was going to notice one lone woman running through the rain like a fool.

If anybody was going to save me, it was going to have to be me.

I hopped to my feet and took off again, this time toward the fringes of the crowd. As soon as it closed ranks behind me, I breathed a little easier. But only for a moment. I was short enough that I couldn't see far past the people in front of me. If I happened to take a wrong turn and bumped right into Reggie, he could finish me off at close range without anyone being the wiser.

I moved carefully. Earlier, I'd seen a couple of cops over near the stage. If I could make it that far . . .

I sidestepped my way around protesters waving signs and singing. I ducked around a guy dressed as a black carbon particle (don't ask me how I knew, just take it on faith that a few garbage bags and a lot of duct tape can work wonders). I dodged my way between a photographer taking pictures of the crowd and a guy keeping nice and dry under a golf umbrella who was catching a lot of flack from the people around him because they couldn't see the stage. I darted to my right, feinted to my left . . .

And slammed right into a tall man.

My heart clutched. Until I realized this guy was too thin to be Reggie. In fact, it was Kegan, and at the same time I let go a breath of relief, I punched him on the arm. "Don't do that to me!"

"Do?" He squinted and brushed a raindrop from the tip of his nose. "I lost you in the crowd. I've been looking for you. What's up?"

"He's trying to kill me, that's what's up."

Kegan didn't ask how I knew. He took hold of my arm and together, we headed over to talk to the cops.

BY THAT EVENING, I'D BEEN OVER MY STORY ABOUT the man with the gun with the cops at the park, who'd fanned out to investigate and came back empty-handed and looking at me as if I was the crackpot. I'd called Tyler not twice but three times, prepared to tell him I had a hot lead and he had a new suspect. Each time I called, though, I got his voice mail, and honestly, I didn't feel like leaving a message about how a guy who might be a guy who was supposed to be dead might not be because he'd just tried to kill me. I'd called Jim, too, to beg off going into the restaurant that night and yes, I did leave out the part about the guy who was supposed to be dead, but might not be and blah, blah, blah. It was Saturday night, and Bellywasher's was sure to be slammed. The last thing Jim had time to worry about was me.

Honestly, right about then, I didn't have the energy to care about much else. I was as wrung out as the clothes that were hung on the shower curtain rod and still dripping into my bathtub. I double-checked to make sure my door was locked, pulled on the warmest pair of pajamas I could find along with my fuzzy slippers and a robe, and made myself a cup of peppermint tea. I was halfway through drinking it as I sat in the comfiest chair in the living room when I fell asleep. The tea was already cold when the phone rang and woke me up.

"Bad news, Annie."

It was a voice I recognized, but it sounded so clogged and stuffy, I couldn't quite place it. I blinked away my sleepiness and tried to say something intelligible. It came out sounding more like, "Huh?"

"Bad news."

Finally, I recognized the voice as belonging to Kegan. That coupled with what he said made me shoot up straight in my chair, my heart suddenly beating double time, just like it had as Reggie Goldman hunted me down in Lafayette Park. "What's wrong?" I asked Kegan.

"It's because of the protest this morning, I'm afraid. I mean, I'm sorry for the trouble and all but—"

"But what's wrong?"

"It's not like I want you to worry or anything, Annie, it's just that I know if I don't come through like I said I would, you'll be disappointed, and I'd never want to disappoint you, but I know you must be tired and—"

"Kegan!" I gave him the verbal equivalent of a slap across the face. "What's wrong?"

"I've got a cold."

"Oh."

I guess the single word didn't disguise the fact that this was anticlimactic. Kegan sniffed. "I hate to make you come out in the middle of the night, Annie—"

"Oh?"

"But I've got my Smokin' Good Chicken Dip all ready, and I know there's no way I'm going to be able to drag my-self out of bed tomorrow. Not when I'm feeling this bad now. I thought if you could come over and get it, you could take it over to the shower for me."

"Oh." I wasn't exactly disappointed. More like so bone tired I was going to fall over, and I knew there was no way on earth I wanted to go out.

Until I thought of hurting Kegan's feelings.

And not making Fi's shower as nice as it could possibly be.

I told Kegan I'd be right over and dragged myself out of my chair and into my bedroom. Even in my exhausted state, I knew I couldn't leave the house in my pajamas and fuzzy slippers.

Nineteen

✖

IT WAS IMPOSSIBLE TO BE MAD AT KEGAN. EVEN when he dragged me out in the middle of a rainy night. He sounded terrible on the phone, all sniffly and stuffy, and the last thing he needed was to be out of bed. That in itself would have been enough to convince me to go over to his place to pick up the dip, but I also knew that if I didn't, Kegan would feel as if he hadn't contributed to Fi's baby shower. I'd already rejected him. And slapped him down (figuratively speaking, of course) because of the blunder he'd made when we talked to Reggie Goldman. I didn't want him to think I was holding any of this against him, because really, I wasn't. It was only a matter of time until I got ahold of Tyler, and when I did, I knew Tyler would track down Reggie. I was actually feeling pretty positive about our investigation.

As for the bit about hurting Kegan . . .

I reminded myself that guilt would get me nowhere, and it would do nothing to repair the tear in Kegan's and my friendship. Helping out when the kid was feeling lousy was much more likely to work.

I arrived at Kegan's a little after nine to find him scuffing around the apartment in flannel lounge pants that looked as if they'd been slept in and a T-shirt with a picture of a baby seal on it. The seal, I think, must once have been white. Now, shirt and seal were the same dingy shade of gray.

Before I was even inside, he started to thank me for coming, but I didn't let him finish. The second I was through the door, I knew I had more to worry about than just a little residual emotional angst.

Remember that peppermint tea? The results were predicable.

"Bathroom?" I asked Kegan, and when he pointed the way, I hurried inside. I was done and already washing my hands when I saw that the medicine cabinet above the sink was open and half-emptied. No doubt, he'd been looking for cold medication. I could have kicked myself for not asking if I could pick something up for him on my way over.

"Kegan!" My hands still damp, I opened the door and called to him so I could make the offer. He didn't answer, so I finished drying my hands and hung the towel back on the rack where I'd found it. Naturally, my gaze drifted over the products piled on the countertop next to the sink.

Toothpaste.

Mouthwash.

Dental floss.

Looked like Kegan had oral hygiene pretty much covered.

Deodorant (all natural with no aluminum added, according to the label).

A razor and blades.

And—

"Hair color?" I had the box in my hands before I could stop myself and realized a moment later that for the first time since being hunted in Lafayette Park, I had a smile on my face. It looked as if for all his talk about nature and a chemical-free world, Kegan made exceptions. He was just as vain as the rest of us. And prematurely gray, to boot.

Still grinning and glad that I had this new bit of insight into Kegan's personality, I put the hair color back exactly where I'd found it and walked out of the bathroom. I glanced to my left down the short hallway that led into the living room, but Kegan wasn't where I'd left him.

"Kegan?" I called to him, but he still didn't answer. I looked to my right. The apartment wasn't big, and I found myself looking right into his bedroom. For the second time that night, I was surprised by what I saw.

"There you are!" Before I even had time to process this new information, Kegan was right behind me in the hallway, and I jumped at the sound of his voice. "I was in the kitchen," he said, stabbing his thumb over his shoulder to point the way. His nose was red, and he sniffled. "The dip is all set and ready to go."

"Right. Of course!" I followed him to the kitchen, got the casserole dish, and reminded him that if he wasn't feeling well, he'd better take good care of himself. At the last minute, I remembered the cold medication.

"Don't need it." There was a plastic bag of what looked like pot on the kitchen counter, and Kegan pointed to it. "Eucalyptus," he said, appeasing my law-abiding heart with that one word. "This tea has spearmint and chamomile in it, too. A friend of mine grows the herbs himself and mixes this stuff up. It can't cure a cold, but it sure helps me feel better, and it helps me sleep, too. You know what they say, Annie, when you have a cold, you need plenty of rest. I'll bring some tea to Bellywasher's next week one day. Just in case you picked up my germs. I just wish I could be there to help with the shower tomorrow, but Fi and the girls don't need this cold, that's for sure.

"Not a problem." I pulled the car keys out of my pocket and headed for the door. "Feel better."

"Thanks." He closed the door behind me, and out in the hallway, I wondered at the facets of a person's personality. It looked like there were surprises in every relationship, even one I thought was as simple as Kegan's and mine.

The hair color was one of them. And the other? What I'd caught a glimpse of in the bedroom: laundry, folded and stacked on Kegan's bed in orderly piles.

Who would have thought anybody who started out so neat could always end up so rumpled?

OUR STUDENTS DID AN AMAZING JOB OF PULLING everything together for Fi's baby shower. Overnight, Bellywasher's sprouted blue balloons that bobbed from the backs of chairs and the top of the sandalwood screen that separated the entrance from the main part of the restaurant. They even rose from the antlers of the deer head (fake, thank goodness!) that hung behind the bar. There were blue and white flower arrangements on every table and a huge It's a Boy! sign above the buffet table where Margaret, Agatha, and Jorge were putting the finishing touches just as I walked in.

"Good thing I have a lot of neighbors who are good sports." Jim gave me a quick kiss on the cheek as he zipped by with a tray of fresh fruit. "I didn't know who else to invite. Between them and our students who all brought little gifts . . ." He looked over to the pile of brightly wrapped presents on the bar. "Call me crazy, but I'm glad we're able to do this for Fi."

"You're crazy." As long as he was standing right there (and not spouting bad poetry for a change), I took advantage of the situation. I gave him a peck on the cheek, too, and told him, "I wouldn't have you any other way."

I'd rushed out that morning and picked up a little boy's outfit from a local specialty shop, and I added my gift to the pile before I went into the kitchen to hand Kegan's dip to Marc, who had volunteered to come in to help. With that taken care of and the food and drinks in the capable hands of our students, there was nothing for me to do but sit back and relax. It wasn't a position I was used to being in—not at

home, not at the bank, and certainly not at Bellywasher's—
and after I'd convinced myself to get over the strange, antsy
feeling that always enveloped me when I didn't have
enough to keep me busy, I decided to go with the flow and
try to enjoy it. After all I'd been through lately, I deserved a
little R & R, and with that in mind, I went out to the bar to
sample the mimosas I heard were on the party menu.

I was just in time to be intercepted by Jorge. "Games,"
he said.

"Games?" I waited for more.

For all his talk about opening a restaurant of his own,
Jorge was flustered by the rush of preparations. He straightened the flowers in the closest vase and shuffled from foot
to foot, anxious to get on to the hundred and one other little details that needed to be handled before our guests
arrived. "My wife," he said. "Last night she told me that
women always play games at showers. You know, things
like pin the diaper on the baby or having guests stuff balloons under their shirts and pretend to be pregnant. You
know, fun stuff like that. Who knew? Guys don't go to
showers. I had no idea."

"You want to play games? Sure. I don't think Jim would
mind."

"I knew you'd be a good sport about it." Jorge smiled
with relief. "We'll need five or six, I think. You know, to fill
the time."

"Need?" He'd already turned around to take care of a
last-minute check on the table settings, so when I called
out my question, Jorge stopped.

"Yeah, need," he said over his shoulder. "We forgot all
the about planning games. We're putting you in charge."

With all the work our students had already done, how
could I complain?

Of course, that didn't mean I even knew where to begin.
I had just decided on a computer search when Jim came
sprinting toward me. "Fi loves chocolate, and I've got all

that fresh fruit cut up and ready to serve. I just had a brain-storm. Have you seen the chocolate fountain?"

Since I didn't know we owned a chocolate fountain, I wasn't much help. "Have you tried the supply closet?"

He winced. I wished him well and kissed him for luck. Any foray into the supply room deserved a hearty send-off. As much as I would have liked to be a team player and help him look, I had baby games to worry about.

To that end, I hustled toward my office. I was nearly there when Fi came into the restaurant. In a new pantsuit in shades of turquoise, she looked positively radiant, and for a change, she wasn't crying. At least not until she took a look around and was overcome with emotion. "It's lovely! Thank you, Annie." She pulled me into a hug.

"I can't take credit. This was our students' doing. And Jim's."

"Aye." Fi's eyes filled with tears. "He's a wonder of a cousin, isn't he? The best man there is on the planet."

"Oh, I don't know about that."

This was not something I necessarily believed, because of course Jim was A number one in my book. But when I looked past Fi and saw Richard near the front door looking a little unsure about how he was supposed to handle his role in the festivities, I knew I had to smooth his way. "I think you've got a good guy of your own," I told Fi.

When she turned toward her husband, Fi's smile faded.

"Hey, lover." Big points for Richard, he'd stopped at a florist shop, and he presented Fi with an elaborate and gorgeous corsage of white roses and blue-tipped mini carnations. "I thought you might need some help opening gifts."

Her chin went rigid. "I don't need help," she said, and something told me this wasn't the first time he'd heard these words from her. "I am capable of doing things for myself."

Richard dared a step nearer to the love of his life. "I know that. I just thought it would be fun. And besides, you might need a little help when it comes to figuring out the toys. You're not used to cars and trucks and dinosaurs."

"No. I'm not." Fi sniffed the roses, and a tiny smile tugged at the corners of her mouth. "You can stay, of course," she told Richard. "The girls are dying to see you."

As if she'd been waiting for the cue, Eve and Doc walked into the restaurant, the girls behind them in an orderly line. When they saw their dad, they tumbled into his arms.

Richard kissed them and told each girl how beautiful she looked (the day's matching outfits included denim miniskirts, pink tops, and sparkling hair barrettes that were exact duplicates of the one on Doc's head). After she was sure each of them was satisfied by Richard's attention, Eve clapped her hands.

The girls fell into line.

Richard's eyebrows did a slow slide up his forehead. "Are these my girls?" He looked over the line of smiling children. "I think the girls I know have been abducted by aliens and replaced with clones."

"Don't be silly, Daddy." The comment came from Rosemary, who at six had already lost a couple teeth and had a distinct lisp because of it. "Girls don't have to be noisy to . . . to . . ." Unsure of what came next, she looked at Eve, who pointed at Emma to continue.

Emma stepped forward. "Girls don't have to be noisy to assert themselves," she said. "We can prove we're smart in other ways."

"And we never have to fall prey to Weasels," Doris added.

A smile split Richard's expression. "Well, I don't know about this whole weasel thing. But I'll say one thing for sure, you've done wonders with them while you've been here in Virginia, Fi. If you can do this with the girls, I can only imagine what you'll accomplish if I let you loose on the house. I mean, after our boy here is born and you're ready for it, of course."

Fresh tears cascaded down Fi's cheeks. "Are you saying—"

Richard wrapped his arms around her and gave her a kiss. "I'm saying the floors are all yours if you want them to wash."

And Fi didn't have to answer. We all knew her answer when she kissed him back.

I joined in the applause, but only for a moment. Our guests were due in just a few minutes. And I had games to plan.

In no time flat, I was at my computer and making a list.

I decided to forgo Pin the Diaper on the Baby and the stuffed-shirt event in favor of games that weren't as corny and had the added advantage of not requiring as much room. To that end, I found one game in which our guests had ten seconds to write five things in selected categories (like baby food, or baby clothes) and another in which they had to come up with baby boy names for each letter of the alphabet. I was on the site that suggested the name game when I found another game we could play, and since Richard and Fi still needed to chose a name, it was perfect.

"What Does Baby's Name Mean?" I read out loud while I jotted down the words on the screen. This game was pretty self-explanatory, each player would have a list of names and have to guess their meanings. I numbered a paper from one to ten and filled in the names, starting with Richard and Jim. After that I added Damien and Marc, Jacques (Monsieur Lavoie was sure to be pleased), Kegan, and Larry, Hank, and Charlie in honor of our three best customers. I needed one more and threw in Reggie just for good measure.

Then I got to work checking meanings. It took a while, and none of them was obvious. I decided right then and there that this made the game perfect. Most of our guests didn't know each other, and if we paired them up for the game, it would keep them plenty busy, and we'd avoid long, uneasy silences.

"Richard means *strong power*," I mumbled to myself,

filling in the master list I'd use to check our guests' answers. "Jim is *supplanter*. Whatever that means. Marc means *from the god Mars*, and Damien . . ." I clicked around the baby name Web site I'd found. "That one means *to tame*. Kegan . . ." I did a little more searching and came up with the meaning: *ball of fire*.

OK, it wasn't fair, and I knew he'd be offended if he ever knew I did it, but I had to chuckle. Let's face it, Kegan was a lot of things, but one of them wasn't a ball of fire!

THE SHOWER WENT OFF WITHOUT A HITCH. FI GOT some great gifts, Jim was sweet enough to include presents for the girls so they didn't feel left out (little white aprons, chefs' toques, and kids' cookbooks) and our guests had a wonderful time. Big points for our students: if we were grading their food and presentation, they would have gotten an A+.

Things were finally winding down, but of course, that didn't mean the day's work was over for Jim or any of the other Bellywasher's staff. The dinner crowd would be arriving soon, and everyone was helping get ready for it. Richard had just taken out the last load of gifts to his van, and he stopped to thank me. "I've convinced Fi to leave first thing tomorrow morning," he said. "Can't thank you enough for all you've done for her."

"Thank Jim. And Eve." Richard had left behind a set of embroidered bibs, and I handed them to him. "They did more than I did."

"Maybe so, but from what I hear, you're the one who keeps everything—and everyone—around here sane and moving in the right direction." He laughed. "We could have used you in the navy. And hey, we could use you tonight, if you and Jim aren't too tired. We've got a lot of packing to do, and I'll bet you're the type who makes the most of every inch of space. I know the girls would love to see you one last time, too."

"And I'd love to see them." Now that the girls had turned from hell-raisers into paragons thanks to Eve's magic, this was actually true, and no one was more surprised than me to admit it. I assured Richard I'd be there to help, said good-bye to Fi and the girls, and sat down for a well-deserved rest.

Too bad I couldn't.

Rest, that is.

Something Richard had said niggled at my brain, and try as I might, I didn't know why. With Eve busy setting tables for dinner and Jim, Marc, and Damien scrambling around the kitchen, I talked out my problem with Monsieur Lavoie, who was sitting at the table next to mine and just finishing the last of the mimosas.

"Why would Richard talking about packing the van mean anything to me?" I asked him, even though I wasn't really expecting an answer.

"Ah, cherie. Perhaps he has given you an idea, yes? About moving along? Perhaps this suggests to you that you and Jim, you are ready to—how do you say it—take things to the next level?"

How we'd segued from Richard and vans to Jim and me and the perfect happily ever after, I didn't know. I wasn't sure I wanted to. Monsieur's weird advice aside, I thought through the problem again. "What do you do in a van?" I brainstormed out loud "You drive. Richard and Fi drive. From here to Florida. But not until they pack. And packing is what they want me to help them do. Because, of course, I'm an excellent packer. If I was going on a trip, I'd have everything folded and stacked so nicely—"

I sat up as if I'd been zapped by lightning, and Monsieur leaned forward, concerned. "Cherie? You are all right?"

"I'm an idiot, that's what I am!" I leaped out of my chair and raced into the office for my phone, and when I dialed and Tyler's voice mail came on—again—I grumbled a word I hardly ever used. Right before I told him where I was going and why.

"He's leaving town, Tyler," I said. "And we've got to stop him before he does. He's going to disappear off the face of the earth again. And then we'll never prove that Eve is innocent!"

Twenty

✖

BY THE TIME I GOT TO KEGAN'S APARTMENT I HAD convinced myself that I was crazy. Folded laundry doesn't mean a thing. Or at least it shouldn't. But when I added the folded laundry to the hair color and the fact that Kegan knew that the fumes from that aerosol can were going to ignite at cooking class that night . . .

My heart told me it wasn't possible that Kegan was the murderer I'd been looking for.

But it was looking more probable by the moment.

I parked in the lot outside his building and did a quick assessment of the cars there. Kegan's was parked near the door, and I breathed a sigh of relief. I could watch and I could wait. I could try Tyler again, and this time if he didn't answer, I could talk to one of the other cops and explain that I'd spotted a wanted fugitive.

This was the right course of action. It was safe and it was sane, and let's face it, if I am anything, I am safe and I am sane.

Of course, my safe and sane thinking didn't take glitches into account.

Glitch number one: Kegan came out of his apartment

with an armful of books. He tossed them into the trunk of his car. He took a gas can out of the car.

My blood ran cold.

When I dialed my phone, my hands were shaking.

"Tyler?" I was so relieved it was him and not his recorded voice, I could have cried. If I had the time. "Kegan isn't Kegan. He's Joseph Grant. The arsonist. He's leaving town. Right this very minute. And I think he's going to burn down his building before he does."

As I may have mentioned before, I am not a fan of Tyler the person. He is cold and arrogant, and once upon a time, he broke Eve's heart. For this, I can never forgive him. But Tyler the cop is another animal altogether.

"I'll be right there," he told me after he'd gotten the particulars of Kegan's address and apartment number. "So will the fire department. You stay put."

Of course I would. It was the safe and sane thing to do.

Except for Glitch number two.

Not far from where I was parked, a young mother got out of her car with a baby in her arms. She started toward the building.

Safe and sane went out the window at the same time I hopped out my car door. I stationed myself directly in front of her before she could set foot inside the building.

"Go," I said, and yes, she did look at me like I was some kind of crazy person. "The cops are on their way," I added because let's face it, this carried a little more weight than me standing there yammering. "There's a dangerous person in the building. You and the baby, get in your car and drive away. Fast."

She didn't argue. And me? As long as I was there, I figured I might as well make good use of my time.

I raced into the building and pounded on every door I passed.

"There's a fire! You have to get out. Fire! Call everyone in the building! You have to get out."

Doors opened, people streamed into the hallway and

headed outside. Theoretically, I was inducing a panic, and I could get in big-time trouble. It was a small price to pay for keeping the tenants of Kegan's building alive.

The last door in the hallway was his, and I'm lucky it wasn't locked, because I hit it full blast and stumbled into his living room just in time to see Kegan pouring gasoline on his dining room table.

"You'll never get away with it, Kegan. The cops are on their way." I was short of breath, and the fumes of the gasoline choked me. I fought for air. "Maybe I should just call you Joseph Grant, huh? That is who you are, isn't it? Joseph Grant, the arsonist. The murderer. I can't believe—"

"Give me a break! Nobody's as naive as you! It's not possible. It's not real." I hardly recognized Kegan, his face was so twisted with anger. He didn't look surprised to see me, and he didn't look especially concerned, either. As cool as can be, he consulted a book that was open on the table.

"*Home on the Range*." I choked as I read the title aloud. "I thought—"

"What? That I was looking to re-create life in the Old West? I guess in a way, I am, if it means ridding the world of the people who are trying to destroy it and returning Mother Earth to the way she's supposed to be. But sorry, Annie, this book isn't all about re-creating things; it's all about burning down buildings. I haven't done this in a while; I'm a little rusty." He finished what he was doing and tossed the can aside. "You couldn't keep your nose out of it, could you?"

"But you wanted to help with the investigation and—"

"Your little investigation was a perfect way for me to find out what you were doing and what you knew. Convenient, huh? You got me into Brad's town house so that I could erase his computer files. And in case you haven't figured it out yet, Gillian never would have ended up dead if you hadn't talked to her and I hadn't heard about that package from Brad. I was watching her house, you see. I knew the package arrived early that Monday and I knew I had to find out what was inside. When she wouldn't cooperate . . ."

He didn't elaborate. I was glad. My stomach went cold. My brain teetered on the edge of panic. It took more self-control than I knew I had to keep words coming out of my mouth. "Then there *was* something in that package!"

"There was nothing in it!" There was another gas can on the floor, and Kegan grabbed it. Yes, I should have taken this as a clue that things were not going to go well, but honestly, I couldn't help myself. This was Kegan. And he was my friend. Or at least I thought he was.

My eyes filled with tears. Maybe that was from the gas fumes.

Noticing my reaction, Kegan's top lip curled. "Brad recognized me in class. It's this damn blushing. Never have been able to control it. Don't you remember? That second week of class. We were leaving the restaurant—"

"And I thought I heard a cat!" In my current, befuddled state, it took a moment for me to put the pieces together. "But it wasn't a cat. It was Brad telling you he knew about Mother Earth's Warriors—MEW."

"Damn, if he would have just kept his mouth shut! But Brad was Brad. You know, a real pain in the ass. He tried to blackmail me. No way I was going to let him get away with it."

"So Brad had to die." I gulped down the sour taste in my mouth.

"And I do appreciate you giving me all those articles." He pointed to the file folder on the table. It was soaked with gasoline. "I planned to conveniently lose them, but this makes more of a statement, don't you think? If you had just kept out of it, Annie. Instead, I had to—"

"Take a couple shots at me at that protest rally! I thought it was Reggie."

"Reggie was a convenient scapegoat. Things would have been just fine if you would have left it that way."

"But I didn't. I couldn't. Not with Eve's life on the line.

I still can't stop, Kegan. You know that. Just like you know that if we didn't find the proof Brad claimed to have, it's still out there somewhere."

"Exactly why I've got to make sure there's no trace of me left once I get out of town." Just for good measure, Kegan sprinkled a few more drops of gasoline on the table. "No fingerprints. No nothing. That's the really good thing about fire, it has a way of taking care of things like evidence."

I gulped, and though I knew it was probably not the right thing to say to an arsonist with a gasoline can in one hand, the pulsing sound of fire sirens in the distance gave me courage. "That's why all those years ago, you faked Joseph Grant's death."

"Another sucker helped me out. A homeless guy who thought I was being charitable when I offered him a place to sleep for the night. You think he would have noticed that we were about the same height and weight, about the same age and build. Bones are bones, Annie. And it's hard to tell who they belong to when they're charred enough."

"You can't mean that." I took a step closer. "You can't be a stone-cold killer. We were friends, Kegan."

"Oh, please!"

"And Grandpa Holtz?"

"Got you on that one, didn't I? As soon as I realized you were one of those chicks who can't keep her nose out of other people's business, I knew I had to win you over. So I played the dead grandpa card. Works every time. Don't look so upset." He rolled his eyes. "You wanted to prove Eve was innocent, didn't you? There you go. You did it. Too bad you're not going to be alive to tell the cops when they get here."

I didn't see it coming, and even if I had, I never would have been able to move fast enough. Kegan reared back and pitched the open can of gasoline at me. Gas rained down on me, soaking my hair and my clothes. Instinctively, I closed my eyes and turned away so that I was facing the door, and by the time I did that, Kegan was already there.

"Thanks for all your help, Annie." He had a lighter in

his hands, and he held it up for me to see. "I'm going to be heading out now. My guess is that when they find you in the rubble, they'll figure you were just trying to get even. You know, for all that unrequited love."

"You mean even that wasn't true?" Yes, I had more important things to worry about, but talk about a blow to the ego! "You came on to me—"

"Just so you'd feel sorry for me. You were getting too close, asking too many questions. Now the cops will think you were depressed because I left town and left you all alone. Why do you think I made sure I called Jim so many times when we were out together? He'll tell them the truth. That he was worried and jealous. That you wanted me more than you wanted him."

"That's crazy!"

"Not so crazy. As a matter of fact, it's brilliant."

"Too bad it's not going to work."

These brave words didn't come from me, because by that time, I was shaking in my shoes. Thank goodness, help had arrived. Tyler and the SWAT team were right outside the door. Tyler had his gun out, and he held Kegan in his sights while another officer ripped the cigarette lighter out of his hands.

"You OK, Annie?" he called to me.

I wasn't. I was soaked with gasoline and scared to death. I needed a bath. And a hug. And—

"Annie!"

I saw a blur and heard my name. The fumes must have gone right to my brain, because I swore it was spoken with a Scottish accent.

The next second, Jim's arms were around me.

"Water." He said this at the same time he scooped me into his arms and carried me to the bathroom. He turned on the shower and plunked me down in it. "We need to get that gasoline off you. Hold still!"

This wasn't fair, since I wasn't squirming. I was too surprised to move.

He grabbed the handheld shower and poured water over my head and across my shoulders and down the length of my body.

"What on earth!" I sputtered. "How did you—"

"Putting the chocolate fountain away. I found an envelope. In the storage room. Brad must have hidden it in there."

"He stopped at the restaurant the Saturday before he died." This had not seemed significant when I first heard about it. Now, if I wasn't too stunned to move, I would have slapped my forehead. "And the envelope?"

"Had copies of old newspaper articles. And Brad's notes proving that Kegan was really this Joseph Grant character. And one of the forks from the restaurant. Carefully wrapped."

I squinted at Jim. It was the only way I could see him through the cascade of water.

"Can't say for sure." He worked the water through my hair. "But I think maybe Brad picked it up at class after Kegan had used it. Fingerprints, do you think? Or maybe DNA. It was the last thing he needed to prove that Kegan wasn't who he said he was. He was really Joseph Grant."

"I think you are brilliant!"

"And I think you take far too many chances." He kissed me. Hard. "I'm sorry I'm not the kind of man you want," he said when he was done.

And I looked at him like he was crazy, because of course he was. "That's why you were spouting that really bad poetry? You thought—"

Jim turned nearly as red as Kegan. "Lavoie is French. I figured he must know how to woo a woman. I thought if I could be more romantic, you'd stop hanging around with Kegan and—"

"You're the most romantic man I know." It was my turn to kiss him. "And the most generous and the most wonderful. I was investigating with Kegan. Nothing else. At least I thought I was investigating."

"Which means you never liked him."

"Which you wouldn't even ask unless you were jealous."

"A little."

I smiled. No easy task, since I felt as if I was standing under Niagara Falls.

Jim smiled back. Right before he climbed into the bathtub and wrapped his arms around me.

When the firefighters found us there, we were still liplocked.

RECICPES

✖

**Kegan's Smokin' Good
Chicken Dip**

Brad's Favorite Onion Soup

Jim's Dilly of a Chili

**As Corny as Monsieur Lavoie's
Advice on Love
Grilled Corn on the Cob**

**Annie's Hot
(But Not Too Crispy)
Chicken Wings**

Eve's Divine Mac 'n' Three Cheese

**Damien's (Organic!)
Horseradish Slaw**

Marc's Zesty Burgers

**Hot off the Grill Ice Cream Sundae
for Emma, Lucy, Doris, Gloria,
Wendy, Rosemary, Alice,
and Little Ricky**

The Bellywasher's Mojito

Kegan's Smokin' Good Chicken Dip

Serves 6 to 8

4 chicken breasts, boiled, chilled, and shredded
1 12-ounce bottle hot sauce
16 ounces ranch dressing
1½ cups chopped celery
2 8-ounce blocks, cream cheese

Heat oven to 350° F. In a large bowl, mix shredded chicken with hot sauce. Coat well. In skillet over low heat, combine the rest of the ingredients. When cream cheese is melted, add the mixture to the chicken. Stir to combine. Transfer the chicken mixture to a 9"×13" pan and bake, uncovered, for 45 minutes. Serve with tortilla chips.

Brad's Favorite Onion Soup

Serves 4 to 6

1½ tablespoons unsalted butter
2 pounds yellow onions, thinly sliced
1 large clove garlic, finely chopped
¼ cup apple brandy or sherry
1 bay leaf
4 sprigs fresh thyme

32 ounces low-sodium beef broth
1 small baguette
½ cup grated Gruyère cheese
½ teaspoon salt
¼ teaspoon black pepper
2 tablespoons chopped fresh parsley

Heat the broiler. Melt the butter in a large pot over medium heat. Add the onions and cook, stirring occasionally, until soft and caramelized, about 20 minutes. Add the garlic and cook, stirring for 1 minute. Add the apple brandy and cook until it reaches a syrupy consistency, about 8 minutes. Add the bay leaf, thyme, and beef broth and bring to a boil. Reduce heat and simmer 30 minutes. Meanwhile, cut the baguette in half lenthwise. Place the bread on a baking sheet, sprinkle with the cheese, and broil until melted and lightly golden brown. Transfer to a cutting board and cut crosswise into pieces. Remove the soup from heat, discard the bay leaf and thyme, and season with the salt and pepper. Ladle into individual bowls, sprinkle with the parsley, and serve with the bread.

Jim's Dilly of a Chili
Serves 6

1 large onion
1 leek
3 tablespoons olive oil
3 pounds ground beef
1 pound ground hot pork sausage
1 large green pepper, chopped

1 large red pepper, chopped
1 can whole tomatoes with juice
2 cans diced/chunk tomatoes
2 or 3 packets of chili seasoning mix
1 can black beans, drained and rinsed
1 can red kidney beans, drained and rinsed
1 can white northern beans, drained and rinsed
3–5 sour dill pickles, chopped

In large skillet, saute onion and leek in olive oil until soft. Add beef and pork. Brown, and drain excess grease. Transfer meat to large stock pot. Add peppers and tomatoes. Cook for 2 hours on low heat, stirring occasionally. Add chili seasoning to meat mixture. Cook 15 minutes. Add beans, cook an additional 15 minutes. Add dill pickles. Cook until pickles heat through, approximately 5 minutes.

Serve with shredded cheese and a dollop of sour cream.

As Corny as Monsieur Lavoie's Advice on Love Grilled Corn on the Cob

Soak corn in husks in cold water for at least 4 hours. Grill until husks are charred. Peel, butter, add some salt, and enjoy!

Annie's Hot (But Not Too Crispy) Chicken Wings

1 stick (½ cup) butter
2 teaspoons chopped garlic
1 teaspoon cayenne pepper
1½ cups cayenne pepper hot sauce (or any hot sauce of your choice)

1 teaspoon chili powder
½ teaspoon Cajun seasoning
1 teaspoon hot salt
2 ounces bourbon
3 pounds chicken wings

Note: adjust spicy ingredients up or down according to your taste

Heat oven to 350° F. In sauce pan, melt the butter and saute the garlic. Add remaining ingredients, except chicken, and cook until bubbly. Turn down heat and simmer for 5 minutes. Toss wings in sauce and bake for 45–60 minutes.

Eve's Divine Mac 'n' Three Cheese

Serves 6 to 8

1 pound elbow macaroni
1 cup dry bread crumbs
¼ cup grated Parmesan
¼ cup fresh flat-leaf parsley, finely chopped (optional)

¼ cup olive oil
2 teaspoons kosher salt
¼ teaspoon black pepper
5 tablespoons unsalted butter, plus more for the baking dish

1 medium onion, finely chopped
½ cup all-purpose flour
6 cups whole milk
2 cups grated sharp Cheddar
1½ cups grated Gruyere

Heat oven to 400° F. Butter a casserole or 9"×13" baking dish. Cook the macaroni 2 minutes less than the package directions so it is still a bit firm. Drain and rinse under cold water. Meanwhile, in a small bowl, combine the bread crumbs, Parmesan, parsley, oil, ½ teaspoon of the salt, and the pepper; set aside. Melt the butter in a saucepan over medium heat. Add the onion and cook, stirring, for 4 minutes. Sprinkle the flour over mixture. Cook, stirring constantly for 3 minutes (the mixture will begin to clump). While stirring, slowly add the milk. Cook, stirring occasionally, until slightly thickened, about 7 minutes. Add the Cheddar, Gruyere, and the remaining salt and cook, stirring, until thick and creamy, about 5 minutes more. Stir in the drained macaroni. Transfer to the baking dish and top with the bread crumb mixture. Bake until golden and bubbling around the edges, 25 to 30 minutes.

Damien's (Organic!) Horseradish Slaw

Serves 4

2 tablespoons organic sour cream
1 tablespoon organic plain yogurt
1 tablespoon prepared horseradish
2½ teaspoons cider vinegar
½ teaspoon salt

½ teaspoon black pepper
1 small head organic napa cabbage, shredded (about 5 cups)
1 organic granny smith apple, cut into matchstick sized strips
1 bunch organic scallions, thinly sliced

In a large bowl, whisk together the sour cream, yogurt, horseradish, vinegar, salt, and pepper. Add the cabbage, apples, and scallions, and toss to combine.

Marc's Zesty Burgers

Serves 4

2 tablespoons fresh lemon juice
1 teaspoon low-sodium soy sauce
¾ teaspoon honey
1 large shallot, finely chopped
½ teaspoon dried oregano
¼ teaspoon cayenne pepper

3 tablespoons extra-virgin olive oil
1 pound ground beef
4 hamburger buns, warmed
1 cup arugula
1 beefsteak tomato, sliced

In a medium bowl, whisk together the lemon juice, soy sauce, honey, shallot, oregano, and cayenne. Slowly add the oil in a thin stream, whisking constantly until emulsified. Spoon out and reserve 2 tablespoons of the sauce. Add the ground beef to the bowl and mix to combine. Use your hands to form 4 patties. Heat the skillet to medium-high and cook the burgers to desired doneness, 3 to 4 minutes per side for medium. Transfer the burgers to the buns, drizzle with the reserved sauce, and top with arugula and tomato. Serve with chips if desired.

Hot off the Grill Ice Cream Sundae for Emma, Lucy, Doris, Gloria, Wendy, Rosemary, Alice, and Little Ricky

1 pound ripe peaches
3 tablespoons lemon juice
1½ cups honey
¼ teaspoon ginger (or cinnamon)
¼ teaspoon allspice

Drop peaches in boiling water for 1–2 minutes. Drain and peel. Chop peaches. In a large bowl, combine peaches with lemon juice, honey, and spices. Place the mixture in double layer of foil and grill for approximately 20–25 minutes. Serve over ice cream.

The Bellywasher's Mojito

Serves 1

3 fresh mint sprigs
2 teaspoons sugar
3 tablespoons fresh lime juice
Ice
1½ ounces light rum
Club soda
Limes (for garnish)

In a tall glass, crush 2 sprigs of the mint with a fork. Add the sugar and lime juice. Stir thoroughly. Top with ice. Add the rum and mix. Top off with chilled club soda. Add a lime slice and the remaining mint, and serve.

GET CLUED IN

Ever wonder how to find out about all the latest Berkley Prime Crime and Signet mysteries?

berkleysignetmysteries.com

- *See what's new*
- *Find author appearances*
- *Win fantastic prizes*
- *Get reading recommendations*
- *Sign up for the mystery newsletter*
- *Chat with authors and other fans*
- *Read interviews with authors you love*

MYSTERY SOLVED.